Jimmy Coates can only
trust one man to keep
the country from falling
into chaos. But that man
has disappeared and
everything and everyone
is at stake...

Also by Joe Craig

TEAM UP WITH

JIMMY COATES!

WWW.JIMMYCOATES.COM

WWW.JOECRAIG.CO.UK

JOE CRAIG

JIMMY COATES
BLACKOUT

HarperCollins *Children's Books*

First published in Great Britain by
HarperCollins *Children's Books* 2013
HarperCollins *Children's Books* is a
division of HarperCollins *Publishers* Ltd
77-85 Fulham Palace Road,
Hammersmith, London, W6 8JB

www.harpercollins.co.uk

1

Copyright © Joseph Craig 2013

ISBN 978 0 00 752432 7

Joseph Craig asserts the moral right to be
identified as the author of the work.

Printed and bound in Great Britain by
Clays Ltd, St Ives plc

MIX

For Mary-Ann

THE BODIES

Buried four kilometres below ground and embedded in a concrete crust fifty metres thick, one of the British Government's seven supercomputers was about to be breached. It was housed beneath Menwith Hill Royal Air Force Station in North Yorkshire, but nobody on the base could have any idea the attack was underway. The battle was lost as soon as it began, when a new string of computer code flickered into life.

Instantly, it began worming through the system, a mere twinkle in a constellation of electrical impulses. Imperceptible. Insignificant too, if it hadn't been for the fact that at the exact same moment, hundreds of kilometres to the north and eleven kilometres above the earth, an Aurora Blackbird SR-91 plane pierced British airspace.

The two events were timed to perfection. The worm wriggled through the computer network exactly as it had been designed to do, creating a tiny corridor in the British satellite surveillance system – a sliver of shadow, which the Aurora Blackbird ran through like a fencer's blade. The precisely pinpointed surveillance blackout rendered the plane effectively invisible. It was high enough and fast enough to be missed by conventional, ground-based radar defence systems; its black neoprene-titanium panels didn't glint in the night, and even the fuel was caesium-based so that the exhaust fumes would be transparent.

In no time, the plane passed over the islands to the north of Scotland and reached the mainland. It was still travelling at 1,900 kilometres an hour when the doors in its undercarriage slid open. Two black body bags dropped from the plane's belly. Then it immediately wheeled away to leave British airspace as discreetly as it had entered.

The packages hurtled down through the atmosphere. They had reached terminal velocity even before they plunged through the clouds. They twisted as they fell, the wind pummelling the linoleum-coated material to reveal the contours of the bodies inside.

After a few seconds, two black parachutes unfurled automatically and the descent slowed. The body bags drifted and eventually bumped on to the heather, sixteen kilometres from the nearest road. That's where they lay for almost two hours, ten metres apart, motionless but for the buffeting of the wind.

Then, at the same moment, both bags twitched. They rolled over until their zips faced upwards. On any normal body bag the zips would have been accessible only from the outside. But these were different.

Simultaneously, the two bags peeled open and out climbed two people. They staggered to their feet – a man and a woman, both tall and dressed in black jumpsuits. They peered through the darkness to each other, not making a sound. They stretched and rubbed their heads, but both moved freely enough. The man blinked rapidly and shook his brain back to full consciousness, tangles of straggly black hair blustering around his head. The woman did the same a moment later, then they both gathered in the parachutes, piling up the black silk on top of the protective body bags.

The man produced a matchbox and two boiled eggs from his pocket. In seconds the parachutes and body bags were lighting up the hillside. They waited together in silence, controlling the fire with a ring of damp heather while they carefully shelled and consumed the eggs. Soon they were able to stamp out the embers, leaving no trace of the equipment that had enabled them to survive their epic fall unharmed.

Still without a word, the woman pulled out a compass and they marched south.

01 NOTHING APPLIES

Two security guards strolled back to their booth, sharing a joke.

"All clear," said one into his walkie-talkie, still chuckling.

"Thanks, beta station," came crackling back. "Next patrol at 0400."

"Just enough time for a brew," muttered the other guard in a soft Irish accent.

They clicked off their torches and hurried into the booth, eager to get out of the wind. The two men could have been built from the same Lego set: a square block from the shoulders all the way down to the ground. They wore blue uniforms with peaked caps, which revealed only the greying edges of their hair.

The booth was only just big enough for them to sit side by side, but they settled in and inspected the line of CCTV screens in front of them. From here they could watch the whole perimeter of the building they'd just been patrolling:

a small glass office block set within its own walls on London's South Bank. From here a man called Christopher Viggo had been running his election campaign – the only legitimate opposition to the British Government – and it would have been impossible for anybody to approach the main gate from the street without being in clear view of the booth window.

"What's that?" muttered the Irish guard. He reached forward and tapped his finger on one of the screens. "Which camera is that?" The image was grainy, enhanced by the camera's infrared night mode, but there was one spot of brightness showing two broad silhouettes in a hut.

"That's us," replied the other guard.

"I know that, you idiot, but what's *that*?" He jabbed his finger on the screen again. "This booth doesn't have a dome on the roof." They both leaned forward to examine the screen more closely.

"Is someone crouching up there?"

The end of his question was cut off by an ear-splitting crack. Suddenly they were showered in splinters and a black figure crashed through the roof. It landed on top of the older guard, instantly twisting to send the man's cap spinning across the booth. The peak of it struck the other guard precisely between the eyes. His whole body went limp and he slumped in his chair.

The first guard was pulled to the floor and rolled over

until he was underneath his assailant, the centre of his chest pinned to the ground by the attacker's knee. Only now did the guard see a face.

"Jimmy!" he gasped. "You're—"

"I'm not here," Jimmy cut in with a whisper. He forced his hand over the guard's mouth and fixed him with a calm stare. The green in his eyes glinted like alligators in a swamp. "I'm inside, asleep." He jerked his head back towards the building. The top floor had been converted into basic living quarters where he'd been staying, with his mum, his sister Georgie, and his best friend, Felix. Viggo himself lived there too, but the lights in the offices below indicated he and some of his staff were still working.

"Nobody knows I've slipped out," Jimmy whispered, "and it's going to stay that way. Got that?"

The guard nodded, his cheeks turning white under the force of Jimmy's grip.

"I'm going to release you now," explained Jimmy softly. "When I do, you make no sound unless I tell you to, OK?" The guard nodded frantically again. "You fix this roof with the board I've left behind the booth. In four minutes you revive your mate and explain everything, then when the time comes, you both go on your patrol as normal." Jimmy's tone was flat, but there was a burning urgency behind the words. "And I need to know that you two will let me back in later tonight. Got that?"

Jimmy slowly eased his grip and uncovered the man's mouth.

"Yes, Jimmy," wheezed the guard. Jimmy's knee was constricting his lungs. "But shouldn't I let Mr Viggo know?"

Jimmy narrowed his eyes and dug his knee in harder.

"If I wanted Chris to know," he hissed, "I'd have spelled it out in his alphabet soup."

"I have instructions. Rules I have to follow. Otherwise Mr Viggo will—"

"The rules don't apply." Jimmy forced out his words between gritted teeth. "Nothing applies. Got that?"

Jimmy heard the harshness in his own voice and reluctantly let off some of the pressure with his knee. These men were on his side, he reminded himself. They were there to protect him. They didn't deserve any serious pain.

"And please don't tell Chris about this," he added.

"Please?" spluttered the guard. "Are you asking me or telling me?"

"Whatever," said Jimmy, with a small smile. "Just keep it to yourselves or everybody will know how sloppy you two have been. What if this had been a real attack? What if someone had tried to kill Chris again?"

A darkness shivered across Jimmy's face. His words had brought back vivid memories. The first time the Government had sent anybody to kill Christopher Viggo, they'd sent Jimmy himself. That seemed so long ago now – when Jimmy had only just discovered the truth about himself: that he was genetically designed by the Government to be an assassin.

Back then, the Government hadn't allowed any opposition to exist at all and Viggo's protests had made him a target. Since Jimmy had changed sides, he and Viggo had forced the Government to change their position.

"Who's going to attack?" protested the guard. "Viggo's legitimate now. There's an election starting in a few hours. A real election, Jimmy! The first one for years. If there was still a threat, do you think Viggo would have been out speaking in public like he has for the last six months? Or living and working in a grand place like this and not hiding in some sewer?"

Jimmy was hardly listening to the man. He picked himself up and dusted the splinters from his tracksuit trousers and hoodie. His extraordinary abilities were still well hidden in the wiry frame of a twelve-year-old boy.

"If Chris is so legitimate now," Jimmy mumbled, "why does he have ex-military security guards? What's he afraid of?" His eyes flicked across the bank of CCTV screens as if the dark patches of blue hid the answer to a puzzle. "What's out there?"

"It's just shadows, Jimmy," said the guard. "It's more

dangerous for you than for Mr Viggo. You're still on the NJ7 hit list. You're lucky they haven't found out you're here."

Jimmy let out a low growl of disgust at the mention of NJ7. It was Britain's new breed of Secret Service agency. They were the best in the world: the most efficient and the most vicious. It was also the organisation that Viggo had once worked for himself, before he decided the Government was becoming too extreme. Jimmy glanced at both the guards. They'd been NJ7 agents too, but now they shared Viggo's views.

"You haven't exactly stayed sharp, have you?" said Jimmy, noticing three empty packets of pork scratchings on the floor. The conscious guard opened his mouth, but had nothing to say. He looked so embarrassed that Jimmy had to shake his head and look away.

"Just let me back in later," Jimmy sighed. "And don't let the others find out I've been gone, OK?"

"OK, Jimmy," said the guard, sheepishly. "But where are you going?"

He got no reply. Jimmy was already disappearing out of the door, into the darkness.

Eva Doren frantically pecked at the keyboard. She checked over her shoulder every few seconds now, terrified that someone would come in. The NJ7 technical computers had state-of-the-art encryption, and getting round it was taking longer than she wanted. She was no hacker, but she'd picked up a lot about NJ7 security in the months that she'd been working there, and she had clearance for most of the generic access codes.

She wiped the sweat from her face and hammered another set of figures into the machine. It failed again, and the error message seemed to flash up even brighter than before, along with a chilling image: a vertical green stripe – the emblem of NJ7.

Every time she saw that green stripe she felt another twist of horror. To her it represented the lies and the threat of violence that lurked never far from the surface. It was a threat that the whole country had been living under, even if they didn't know it. Anybody could be taken away by NJ7 at any time and locked up, or worse, for doing anything that suggested criticism of the Government. Nobody felt the danger more keenly than Eva herself.

As far as anybody at NJ7 knew, she had betrayed Jimmy Coates and left her family to be taken on as an apprentice by NJ7's ruthless Director, Miss Bennett. Eva lived in constant fear that someone would suspect the truth: she was still loyal to Jimmy. Jimmy's sister, Georgie Coates, was her best friend and Eva was doing everything she could for them.

Come on, she pleaded with herself, blinking hard to force away the tiredness. She refused to give up. She carefully entered another code and this time…

Yes! She clenched her fist in triumph, then immediately straightened herself in the chair and pulled her shoulders back. *It was never in any doubt*, she thought to herself proudly. But as she clicked through the files on the computer, it became clear that every file was individually encrypted in a way that Eva didn't recognise. She pursed her lips in annoyance.

"Pointless!" she muttered under her breath. It seemed to Eva like a perfect waste of time that the tech department guarded their secrets so closely. But underneath the hurt pride, Eva knew that nobody in the history of NJ7 had been more careful than the man whose files she was after tonight: Dr Higgins.

Dr Higgins had left NJ7 months ago now, in suspicious circumstances, but his shadow still seemed to loom over every corridor. He was the old NJ7 scientist who had overseen the design and creation of the first organic assassins: Jimmy Coates and Mitchell Glenthorne. Eva was at his old desk now, on the computer where his old hard drive had been stored and flagged for analysis.

If only I had more time, she thought. *Why tonight?* At the same time she knew that the timing was perfect: the election the following day was a huge distraction. Eva had been deep undercover at NJ7 for months, but this was the first time she'd been able to move through the tunnels of NJ7 Headquarters without worrying about being watched. With so much activity going on, nobody had paid attention to where she'd been going or what she was up to.

For a moment she pictured the streets of Central London, above. This late at night they'd be almost entirely deserted, yet the network of tunnels directly below was teeming with people. The quiet bustle of footsteps echoed off the bare walls and the rustling of papers mixed with whispered conversations. Swarms of black suits streamed through the concrete corridors, a tangle of green stripes. The NJ7 agents went about preparing for the coming election like ants building Hell.

If only Jimmy had told her which specific piece of information he wanted. She could have tried to find it some other way. But there hadn't been the chance for any discussion. Earlier that day, Eva had accompanied Miss Bennett as she oversaw the Prime Minister's press conference. Journalists' questions were always carefully selected months in advance, of course, but a few new ones were also allowed so that the PM could respond to the latest developments. As it was the day before the first general election for years, everybody wanted to ask fresh questions, so Eva had been helping to filter out anything that suggested anti-government feeling.

Each question was written on an official form, and Eva had no idea how Jimmy had managed to slip an extra one into her pile. She could still feel the chills she got when she reached the page. Even before she'd read it, she'd known who it was from because of the handwriting. When she'd looked up, she'd noticed the hunched back of a civil service cleaner lumbering away. Had that been Jimmy in disguise? Or was Eva's mind thinking up phantoms to explain what had happened?

All the note had said, in Jimmy's scratchy pencil lettering, was that they had to meet at a nearby car park late that night. Jimmy needed Eva to bring information from Dr Higgins' computer about the genetic design of the assassins: Jimmy's DNA.

Suddenly a noise sent a shiver through Eva's body. Somebody was coming, and there was nowhere to hide. At NJ7 there were no doors to the rooms, just one huge network of tunnels with open areas for desks and office space. She slammed her palm on the desk in frustration, leaving a sticky handprint on the leather which she immediately wiped off with her sleeve. The footsteps in the corridor mixed with the pounding of her heart. She would have to come back another night, when she had gathered all the access codes she needed.

Quickly and efficiently, she shut down the computer,

wiped the keypad clean, and went to the filing cabinet. It was locked.

"How do they run this stupid department!?" she muttered under her breath. But she refused to let it ruffle her. On top of the filing cabinet was a yellow document box. On the spine was the number seven and another green stripe. Any information was better than nothing, Eva reasoned. The alternative was to meet Jimmy empty-handed, which was no alternative at all.

She opened the document box to find a stack of thinner, coloured folders, old computer printouts and some loose, handwritten notes. There was enough dust on the document box to suggest it hadn't been checked in a while, so Eva quickly extracted sheets from the most dog-eared and tattered files. If there was going to be anything here about the design of the assassin DNA, Eva thought, it would be on the oldest pages. Where the folders themselves were thin enough, she grabbed them whole.

She was careful to wipe her finger marks from the dust when she closed the document box, then slipped out of Dr Higgins' old office with a bundle of papers and folders under her arm. There were two NJ7 technicians hurrying towards her, involved in their own hushed conversation. Eva watched their faces as she passed them. Had they noticed where she'd been? All she saw were expressions of calm efficiency, but that still fuelled the anxiety in her gut.

With every step through the network of tunnels it took a huge effort to maintain an air of confidence. Only looking like she was on legitimate NJ7 business, sent by Miss Bennett, would keep her from being scrutinised. Even though she was only thirteen, the other NJ7 employees had grown used to her being around and had either accepted it, or were too scared of Miss Bennett to question Eva's presence.

The corridors of the NJ7 tech department were less familiar to Eva than the rest of the complex. The murky haze of energy-saving light bulbs cast orange shadows around the concrete. Eva longed for the brightness of the proper light bulbs in Miss Bennett's office. She had long since become used to the lack of sunlight.

Eva clasped the piles of papers and kept her head down, doing her best to walk at a steady, confident pace. Every time she turned a corner she was met by more tunnels stretching out for hundreds of metres, or larger rooms where teams of agents were working at banks of computers. In her head she ran over the errands she could say she was on if she was stopped.

Tell them you're taking a message from William Lee to Miss Bennett, she decided. The two most senior people in the Government were known to hate each other. William

Lee was the Government's Head of Special Security. Once he'd tried to take over Miss Bennett's position as Director of NJ7 – he'd even tried to become Prime Minister himself. Miss Bennett had put him in his place.

Eva could use the games they played against each other to her own advantage now. But what message was being sent? Of course: a top secret one. She wasn't allowed to reveal it to anybody. That's what she'd say if an agent questioned her.

The idea was still smouldering in Eva's mind when she turned another corner and found herself in a deserted lab full of computer screens and whirring technical equipment. At the other end of the lab she realised that it wasn't quite deserted. Sitting at a computer station, staring at her over his shoulder, was the one man on whom Eva's cover story wouldn't work: William Lee.

02 *THE LIVING BOY*

William Lee jumped up, leaving his chair swivelling dizzily behind him. Eva was frozen to the spot, staring up at the unnaturally tall Eurasian man.

"Eva," Lee growled, the tower of hair on top of his head swaying slightly as he spoke. "Shouldn't you be with Miss Bennett?"

"Yes," Eva replied hurriedly. "Of course. I'm on my way now."

There was a horrible silence. In Eva's mind it lasted an eternity. She watched Lee's eyes scan her up and down, lingering on the folders and loose pages under her left arm.

Since Miss Bennett had outwitted him, there had been something physically weaker about this man, as if he'd actually shrunk a couple of centimetres, but his mind was still sharp. Eva thought frantically of what she could possibly say to explain what she was doing, but at the same time she knew that too much explanation would sound suspicious. Why wasn't Lee asking her what she was doing? Eva was almost desperate to have the chance to come up with an excuse. The silence did her no good at all.

At last, Lee spoke again. But it wasn't what Eva was expecting.

"I was just having a look at the satellite surveillance," he muttered. "It's been playing up." He stared blankly into Eva's eyes. She just nodded. Why was *he* explaining himself to *her*? Had Miss Bennett really weakened his confidence that much?

"I'm seeing if I can fix it," Lee went on.

"Should I fetch a technician for you?" Eva blurted out, eager to get away as quickly as possible.

"No, no," insisted Lee. "It's just a minor glitch. I have it under control."

Eva nodded again, and deliberately held her breathing steady as she turned to leave. *Don't look back at him*, she told herself. *And don't rush away too fast.* The papers under her arm had taken on the weight of bricks.

At last she heard the squeak of Lee's chair and the tap of his computer keyboard. Finally Eva was striding away down the next corridor. *Relax*, she ordered herself. *He didn't suspect. He didn't ask.*

But then the squeak of the chair echoed down the

corridor. Could she really hear Lee's footsteps coming after her, or was she imagining it? The corridor stretched out in front of her, with a crossroads about twenty metres ahead. Maybe if she could reach that she could disappear and Lee would let her go – for now. But it was too far away. She'd never make it before Lee came round the corner.

Then she saw her chance. There was a slim gap in the side of the tunnel. It was less than half a metre wide, and completely dark. Eva thanked her luck – she'd found a remnant from when different service tunnels had been joined together to create the NJ7 labyrinth. She rushed towards it, and stepped into the shadows.

To her shock, her step faltered and she nearly fell. The opening in the concrete was in fact a staircase leading downwards. Eva could make out a sliver of light at the bottom. She gingerly stepped down towards it, her shoulders brushing against the cold concrete on both sides.

She paused halfway down to listen for Lee's footsteps. There was no noise coming from behind her. There was, however, the sound of quiet conversation coming from below. Eva crept further on, but lurked in the shadows. When her eyes adjusted to the bright light of the room in front of her, what she saw banished any worries about William Lee.

Half a dozen NJ7 technicians were hurrying around the room, passing each other papers and mumbling instructions to each other. Their white coats almost glowed under an intense green light. In the centre of the room, on a large metal slab, was the scarred and scorched body of what looked like an older teenage boy. His limbs were being held in place and gradually manipulated by metal clamps. Aimed directly into his eye was an intense green laser being fired from a large machine attached to a computer.

Eva couldn't look away from the boy – not because of the laser, or the obvious injuries from these strange operations, but because his chest was steadily rising and falling. This boy was alive.

Jimmy took a twisting route through London, constantly scanning his surroundings. His brain was building millions of fragments of information into an instinct he couldn't explain. Someone was out there. Someone was following him.

Get over it, he urged himself. If somebody from NJ7 was on to him they would have struck by now. *It's nothing*, he insisted in his head, pausing to check the reflection of the street in a darkened shop window. *Just paranoia*. He rubbed his eyes hard. Every bit of him ached in a way he had never felt before: like his limbs were being compressed from every direction and his head was trapped under a spinning washing machine. He searched inside himself for the power of his genetic programming. It was constantly swirling in him, ready to burst through his veins and take him over in an instant. Jimmy relied on it more and more. Without it, the agony was too much.

He drew on that inner strength, a centre of burning power that felt like it came from just behind his stomach. It flooded through him with a violent surge, swamping the pain. Jimmy couldn't help letting out a gasp of relief, but it was combined with a low growl of aggression: the two sides of him battling together to sustain the whole.

He sprinted off with renewed energy. There was a buzz in the air in London's streets and Jimmy imagined it seeping into his skin. There were hundreds more people out than usual, because of all the rallies in support of both sides – final preparations before the ballot the next day. He found his way to Trafalgar Square, where a pro-government rally was just coming to an end. He mingled with the crowds to further protect himself from anybody following.

How can all these people support the Government? Jimmy wondered, looking around at the placards and banners. He considered whether they'd been paid to come out tonight, or even forced by NJ7. At the southern end of the square there was a big screen flashing messages and government slogans into the night: *"Efficiency. Stability. Security."* Jimmy couldn't help letting out a huff. In front of the screen was a middle-aged woman ranting into a microphone about how the Government would keep taxes low and manage the country better than Viggo ever could, because he had no experience.

"...And why should you have the stress of making important government decisions?" she went on. "Government is for governments! Giving people a say in what happens to the country just creates muddled decisions and confusion!" There was a general murmur of approval. "Why should you have to worry?" Everybody cheered, but Jimmy huffed again, a little too loudly this time. A bald man with a thick puffer jacket and a government placard looked round and glared at him.

Jimmy hurried to the other end of the square where a large group of Viggo supporters had set up their own, slightly smaller screen and were chanting in support of freedom, democracy and everything Viggo stood for. Viggo's smile flashed up on the screen and Jimmy couldn't help smiling too. For a few seconds he slowed down to watch, proud of the part he'd played in making this possible.

"Join me and change the country!" declared Viggo from the screen. It was showing some of the best bits of his speeches from the last few months. "Believe in change! Believe in democracy! Believe in freedom!" Each sentence drew a cheer from the pro-Viggo half of the square. Even the sight of the man's face, blown up so large on the screen, seemed to have the crowd mesmerised. Jimmy delighted in the genuine enthusiasm around him. Whole families were there, including people of about Jimmy's age. For the first time, Jimmy really felt part of something special, something historic. *The country's going to change*, Jimmy thought. *It's going to be great.*

Then something cut through Jimmy's excitement. A shout was out of place. Jimmy looked round and saw the crowd from the Government rally was dispersing and some of the supporters had come over to the pro-Viggo end of the square. The bald man with the puffer jacket was waving his placard and booing. Jimmy was ready to ignore it all and run on, but a Viggo supporter in a high-visibility jacket tried to wave the bald man away. Whatever he said, it wasn't taken well.

The bald man's face reddened and creased into fury. Suddenly he shoved his placard into the other man's chest. The Viggo supporter staggered backwards for a second, then hurled out his fists one after the other, trying to fight back. Jimmy responded immediately. He wove through the crowd, snatching a 'Vote Viggo' cap from the head of a teenager on his way past. He kept his head low, then at the last second jumped up and brought the cap down over the face of the Viggo supporter. In the same movement, he dragged the man backwards and took his place.

The bald man swished his placard clean over Jimmy's head. Immediately Jimmy delivered a jab to the man's gut with the knuckles of his left hand, then landed his right fist in exactly the same spot with a powerful cross punch. The man's puffer jacket wasn't nearly enough to cushion the blows. His eyes widened and he flailed at Jimmy even as he gasped for breath. Finally Jimmy extended his right thigh and held it steady while the lower part of the limb flicked out. His toes hit the man's kneecap like a spike in a pinboard.

Jimmy felt a rush of calm aggression urging him to deliver one more blow – a fatal one. *No*, Jimmy ordered himself, locking his arms and legs. After half a second, he snatched the 'Vote Viggo' cap again and mashed it on to the bald man's head.

"What was that?" the man gasped, rolling on the floor and clutching his knee. Jimmy was already sprinting away, but he heard the answer flashing through his head: *that was a fouette*. How did he know that? That swift kick was a move he hadn't used before, but its devastating effect was obvious. Suddenly a new world was flooding through his mind: *La Savate combat technique.* His programming was still adapting, still growing.

At the edge of the square he glanced back and saw more men and women in high-visibility jackets making sure the brief eruption of violence was definitely over. Jimmy crouched in the darkness of a doorway. *La Savate combat technique*, he thought to himself, stretching his limbs. *I like it.*

Eva shivered and hugged her coat more tightly around her. It was difficult, though, with such a pile of papers hidden in her arms. *How much longer will I have to wait?* she wondered. She was on the ninth floor of a multi-storey car park on Great College Street in Westminster, Central London. She rocked from foot to foot and peered around her into the deep shadows.

It had taken longer than she would have liked, but she had eventually managed to slip away from the NJ7 labs unseen. Now moonlight streaked in between the pillars of the car park, casting a dim sheen over patches of empty concrete. The rest was blackness. Only the silhouettes of a couple of cars interrupted the empty expanse. *Probably stolen or abandoned*, she thought to herself.

Suddenly she felt hot breath on the back of her neck.

"Don't turn round," came Jimmy's voice in a whisper.

"How did you—?"

"Were you followed?"

Eva gave a small shake of her head.

"Are you sure?"

"Jimmy!" Eva said sternly, spinning round to face him. They were standing in near-total darkness, but Jimmy's eyes caught what little light there was.

"I wasn't followed," Eva insisted. "I know what I'm doing. I have to live a secret life every moment of the day and night. What do you think that's like?" They were so close that Eva could feel the warmth of her own breath bouncing off Jimmy's face. "I might not be genetically perfect but I've learned a couple of things, OK? So don't be so..." She didn't know how to finish her sentence. She could feel Jimmy's tension and saw his eyes constantly darting around the car park.

"OK," he sighed at last. "I'm sorry. You're right. I need to trust you. It's just... inside me..." He closed his eyes for a moment and felt his teeth grinding together. "It makes me so..." He shrugged off his thought and opened his eyes again. "Did you...?"

Eva pulled the piles of papers from under her coat and thrust them at Jimmy.

"What's all this?" he asked. "I needed the data from his hard drive. Dr Higgins wouldn't have printed out what I need. He couldn't have."

"I couldn't get into his computer," Eva explained. "But

I will. When I've had more time. I'll get the access codes and..."

Jimmy had already stepped away and was spreading the papers out on the bonnet of a Range Rover, rifling through the pages. His hands moved swiftly to pass each sheet in turn across the car's bonnet and his eyes scanned each page for less than half a second. He was hardly even aware that his pupils were flicking at a rapid and regular pace, or that every detail seemed to be lodging somewhere in his mind.

Within a minute he swept his hand across the bonnet, letting the papers fall to the floor.

"These are useless!" he sighed. "You were meant to..." He stopped himself, struggling to contain his frustration, not wanting to shout at his friend.

"I told you!" Eva protested, scrambling on her hands and knees to gather up the papers that had slid to the floor. "It's not easy! I can't just break in and make a run for it. And there are NJ7 technicians in every bit of that whole department round the clock." She paused. Her voice was trembling more and more. "Jimmy, I saw the most horrible thing." She couldn't carry on gathering the papers now that this memory had come back to her.

"You won't believe what they're doing down there," she whispered. "They've got a boy, a young man I mean, but he can't be much older than me. And he's still alive, but unconscious, and they're firing this laser into his eyes, as if they're trying to zap his brain or..." She tailed off, fighting back the fear in her chest.

"I'm sorry," said Jimmy softly, crouching down to put a hand on her shoulder. "I shouldn't have taken it out on you, it's just that..."

"Jimmy, tell me..." Eva took a slow breath and fixed her eyes on the boy in front of her. "Is that how they made... you?"

Jimmy looked away. It was the first time that night that Eva had seen his eyes remain still for more than a moment. Then he looked back at her and explained.

"I've seen that boy too," he said, standing up and regaining his composure. "It's Mitchell's brother. I saw him a long time ago, when I managed to break into NJ7 to try to find out where Felix's parents were being held. I remember Dr Higgins had Mitchell's brother lying on a metal table. His name was Lenny. Lenny Glenthorne. I remember it. They must still have him, and they're still experimenting on him. What are they doing to him?"

"Is he also... an assassin?"

"No," Jimmy said quickly. "He's not like Mitchell or me. I don't think he is, anyway. For Mitchell and me they did have a laser, I think, but before I was even born. The laser was to build the chemical combination of my DNA. I think the laser they're using on Lenny must be different.

Otherwise—" He stopped himself suddenly and every muscle tensed, like a startled animal.

"What?" Eva whispered, but Jimmy cut her off with a firm gesture. He slowly beckoned for her to follow him round the other side of the Range Rover, where they crouched, looking over the bonnet towards the pedestrian lift.

Eva couldn't believe how fast her heart was beating, and how thin the air felt. It was like she was being strangled.

Jimmy looked up at her, an urgent stare in his eyes. He made small, forceful gestures, pointing at her, then at his eyes, then in the direction of the lift, telling her to keep watching the lift doors. She nodded, but Jimmy knew she'd have no idea what she was meant to do if she saw anything. He dropped down to the wheel of the Range Rover and carefully removed the hubcap.

A few seconds later a crack of light appeared between the lift doors. Before they could open more than a centimetre, Jimmy was in action. A single flick of his wrist sent the hubcap spinning towards the lift with the impetus of a torpedo. As soon as it left Jimmy's hand, he grabbed Eva's shoulder and pulled her across the concrete to the other side of the car park, where the shadows were darkest and the down ramp offered an escape.

Jimmy moved so fast Eva was half running and half being dragged. But then came a noise that stopped them in their tracks. It wasn't the thud of the hubcap connecting with an NJ7 attacker. Instead came a clang as the disc slammed into the back wall of the lift. It was followed immediately by a short, nervous burst of laughter, then a boy's voice:

"That was so cool!"

03 THE CLASS OF SCIENTISTS

The voice echoed through the concrete structure, and sent a thrill through Jimmy's heart. He dropped Eva's collar, hardly noticing when she stumbled to the floor. Then came another shout, this time a girl:

"Jimmy, wait!"

It was the voice of his sister, Georgie. She was with his best friend, Felix, who for some reason had his hands pressed down on the top of his head. Together, they were strolling out of the lift, huge smiles on their faces.

"What are you...?" Jimmy's words were breathless and soon drowned out by Eva and Georgie running to each other and crushing each other in a hug. Jimmy was so stunned he didn't even take in the happy words they were exchanging. He quickly came to his senses again.

"You want to chat a bit louder?" he whispered. "I think there's a deaf wombat in Australia who didn't quite hear you. And how did you find me?"

"We nearly didn't," panted Felix. "You run too fast. We saw you come in here, but we didn't know what floor you were on. We've just had to check every level!"

Jimmy couldn't help smiling. He hadn't wanted anybody to know what he was doing, but at the same time he was impressed that Felix and Georgie had managed to follow him.

"You nearly took off the top of my head!" said Felix, his grin revealing the longest line of teeth Jimmy had ever seen, every one of them at a slightly different angle. Meanwhile, his hands were still clamped down on top of his crazy nest of black hair. Finally Jimmy realised what had happened.

He jogged to the lift, where the hubcap had lodged in the back wall, trapping a clump of frizzy black hair with it. "Er, yeah," Jimmy mumbled, realising he had aimed the missile at the level of an adult's chest, but that instead it had skimmed the top of Felix's head. "Sorry."

Felix shrugged. "I needed a haircut anyway."

"What's going on?" Georgie asked, in her most stern voice. "You can't just go sneaking off, you know."

"Looks like you've done the same," Jimmy replied. "Didn't Mum notice? Or Chris? And what about the security guards?"

"Everybody is so distracted with the election we could have driven a herd of geese through the building," Georgie explained. "And we saw what you did to the security guards so we just told them we were with you."

Jimmy shook his head in amazement.

"I thought you might have gone out to get some midnight snacks or something," said Felix. "I don't think I'd have come if I'd known you were meeting Eva. No offence, or anything, Eva, it's just, you know…" Eva glared at him, so he held up his hands and stretched his eyebrows so high they looked like they were going to merge with his hair. "What?" he squeaked.

"Why didn't you tell us you were meeting Eva?" asked Georgie.

"It's complicated," Jimmy replied, sheepishly.

"So explain it." Georgie wasn't going to be put off. Jimmy suddenly felt as powerless as any normal boy. There were no assassin skills designed to get round an older sister. Georgie stood there, arms folded, her head tilted to one side and her lips pursed.

"You're in so much trouble," Felix whispered. "All the way here she's been telling me what she's going to—"

"Shut up, Felix," snapped Georgie. "Let him explain."

Jimmy felt like the pressure of a waterfall was building up inside his head. His whole life was constructed out of secrets. The first secrets had been the ones his parents kept from him: that they were really NJ7 agents given the long-term mission of raising an experimental government assassin, designed genetically and grown organically.

As soon as he'd discovered the truth about himself, Jimmy's life had imploded. His father had betrayed him, choosing to stay loyal to NJ7 rather than join him and his mum on the side of Christopher Viggo. Then the man had revealed that he wasn't even Jimmy's real father. He had been richly rewarded for his loyalty to the Government: Ian Coates had risen to become Prime Minister of Britain.

All this flashed through Jimmy's head as he wondered whether to reveal his latest secret to his sister. It was possibly the most dangerous secret of them all, and one that he had guarded obsessively for the last six months. He could feel his fingers shaking, while his mouth and lips seemed to have frozen, refusing to form the words.

"Well?" said Georgie, but her expression was softening. She stepped up to her brother and placed her hands gently on his shoulders. Jimmy looked up into her face. It was a long time since he'd felt like a younger brother, but Georgie's searching brown eyes somehow made him feel glad he was.

Slowly, he raised his hands and turned them round to show his sister the backs of his fingers. In the strange half-light of the car park it took a few seconds for her to see what he was showing her. But then her expression changed.

"They're blue," she gasped. "What is this? What happened?"

"It's still happening," Jimmy said in a whisper, almost choking on the words. "I have radiation poisoning."

His own whisper echoed back to him and spun through his head. He looked at the confusion on the faces of Felix, Georgie and Eva and suddenly found himself unable to stop.

"It was in Western Sahara," he said quickly. "The French Secret Service tricked me. They sent me to a uranium mine. They told me it was safe, but they knew it wasn't and..." The words tumbled out of him, as if they'd been building up for months. At times he talked so fast he hardly made any sense, but eventually his story came out, along with all the information he'd gathered in the last few months.

"I read about what happens with radiation," he said, "but it just tells me what's *meant* to happen. And some of it isn't happening, or it's different because, you know, I'm..." He paused, breathless.

"It's OK, Jimmy," said Georgie. "Go on."

"The level of exposure I had should have... well, it should have killed me by now. I have some of the symptoms but not all, and not all the time. My muscles ache, but sometimes it might be to do with my programming and I know that sometimes I might just be feeling it because

I think I'm meant to. But I also have headaches – worse than I've ever had – and this..." He held up his fingers again, wiggling them. "...the blue spread at first and I thought my fingers were going numb, but then it stopped, or maybe it's just slowed down, I can't tell any more. But I don't know if this would happen in anybody else, or if it's just in me. I keep thinking I should be dead by now, but I'm not, and I don't know whether I feel weaker because of the poisoning or because my programming is changing, or taking me over and making the rest of me weak, or..."

At last he had to stop. His breath was short and he could feel the muscles in his face contorted in anguish. Felix, Georgie and Eva were staring at him. What were they thinking? Jimmy longed for them to still see him as normal. Now he felt so stupid. He should have known that eventually Georgie and Felix would find out everything.

"You need to see a doctor," said Felix with a shrug, as if Jimmy had merely sneezed or revealed that he had a nasty rash.

"Thanks, genius," said Jimmy. "I tried that already. The first doctor just checked that I'm not a danger to other people – which I'm not, by the way. Then NJ7 got to him. After that I tracked down a specialist, but NJ7 got to him first." Jimmy dropped his eyes to the floor. "It looks like my illness is more deadly for doctors than it is for me."

"You should have told *us*," Georgie said softly. "Why

didn't you? You idiot!" She couldn't help raising her voice now, and she clenched her fists in frustration. "Didn't you think we'd help?"

"What could you have done?" Jimmy asked. "What will you do now? Invent a cure?"

"You have to tell Mum," said Georgie. "Forget about the election. That's nothing compared to this. Tell Mum and Chris, and they'll help you..."

"Chris knows," Jimmy admitted. "He found out from the first doctor I went to see. Chris was tracking me and he found my test results. It was months ago now. I made him promise not to tell anybody, then all this election stuff happened and—"

"So Chris has known about this for months?" Georgie was furious now. "But you didn't think you should tell me? Or Mum?"

She stared at Jimmy, and all he could do was look anywhere but into her face. Then after a few seconds he heard his sister's breathing change. When he finally looked at her, he saw that now there were lines of tears on her cheeks catching the light.

"It's OK," Jimmy found himself saying, unsure whether he believed it himself. "I told you – the blueness has stopped spreading." He held up his fingers again, but the sight of them only seemed to make Georgie even more upset. "So it's probably not getting any worse."

"That's just weird," said Felix in a whisper, examining Jimmy's fingers.

"Didn't you notice it?" Eva asked, looking from Felix to Georgie and back. There was shock on all their faces. "I mean, you've been living with him for the last few months, haven't you?"

Felix stretched his eyes in wonder and Georgie bit her bottom lip.

"Sorry, Jimmy," Felix muttered. "I guess there's been a lot going on. I did see that your fingers were blue once, but I just thought, I don't know, you hadn't washed your hands, or something."

"It's not your fault," Jimmy reassured him. "I've been hiding everything. I didn't want to tell you. I..." His voice faded from his throat. He wasn't even sure why he'd been trying to keep his poisoning a secret. He told himself it was because he didn't want to distract everybody from trying to win the election, but deep down he knew that it was something more. Telling people about his secret would have made it seem more real. Not telling made it easier to deny the danger spreading within him with every beat of his heart. It made it easier not to take notice when his condition got worse.

"I'm going to be fine," Jimmy announced with force, pushing his fear away. "I just need to find out more about how my body works. That's why I asked Eva to—"

"You can't heal yourself, Jimmy," Georgie cut in. "No matter how much you find out about yourself, you're not going to be able to make yourself better."

"But I told you," Jimmy replied, anger rising in his chest, "even if I could find a doctor who knew how to cure radiation poisoning in a genetically modified freak, they'd be killed by NJ7 before I got close to them."

Georgie immediately stepped forward and wrapped her arms around her brother.

"You're not a freak," she whispered into his ear. "I won't let you say that."

Jimmy felt himself crumbling.

"What about one of *these* doctors?" It was Felix's voice, and it seemed to soothe the confusion in Jimmy's head. Felix was picking through the piles of papers that Eva had brought from Dr Higgins' office. He held up an old photograph.

The photo showed about a dozen people lined up in two rows, like a football team photo, except it was a mixture of men and women, who all looked at least fifty, and they were wearing white coats. They seemed to be standing in some kind of lab, and most of them were smiling awkwardly, as if they'd much rather be getting back to work.

"This lot look ugly enough to cure anything," Felix quipped.

"How does this help?" Jimmy grunted. He knew he should be used to Felix's humour. *Maybe that's his superpower*, Jimmy thought to himself.

"This *could* help," said Georgie. "Look." She pointed to a tall man in the back row. "Isn't that...?"

"You guys are so slow," Felix sighed. "It's Dr Higgins!" He shook the photo in exasperation. "This must be, like, some kind of NJ7 crazy scientist end-of-term photo."

"I don't think they have terms," said Georgie. "But whatever – I think you're right. He looks a bit younger, doesn't he? But it's definitely him."

"So these other people..." The pieces were falling into place in Jimmy's head.

"These must be some of the scientists who designed..." Eva paused, unsure how to put it. "...who worked on your genetics, Jimmy."

Jimmy grabbed the photo and ran his finger across the faces. Dr Higgins was the only one he recognised.

"Have you seen any of these people at NJ7?" he asked.

"I don't think so," replied Eva. "But there are hundreds of people working there. It'll take me some time to find out who they all are and what's happened to them since this photo was taken." An idea flashed across her face and she dropped her voice, almost talking to herself. "I can scan it in and run it through the facial recognition programme, then the NJ7 database..."

"Is Dr Higgins still in America?" Felix asked. "He'd probably help you."

"Maybe he would," said Jimmy, "but he could be anywhere in the world right now. Eva..." He thrust the photo into her hand. "...if you can find one of these other scientists, that's my best chance."

"As long as they're not still loyal to this Government," said Georgie. "Otherwise they'll turn you in and NJ7 will kill you."

"I have to risk it," Jimmy insisted. "I don't have a choice."

"OK," announced Eva, "I'll see what I can find out." She started gathering all her documents together again, keeping the photograph on the top of her pile. "I'll send you a message in the Sudoku."

"The who-do-what?" Jimmy asked.

"You know," said Felix. "The puzzle at the back of the paper."

"Since when do you read the paper?" Jimmy asked.

"Since your mum started trying to get me to do school work."

"Oh, right. Sorry about that."

"It's OK. I just do the puzzles and tell her its maths."

"Don't," Eva cut in. "Don't ever do the Sudoku."

"What?" Felix looked hurt. "Why?"

"Or the crossword." Eva looked genuinely scared at

the thought. "The Government controls all those puzzles. Every day the numbers and words are arranged by a government computer to make you feel calm and happy. It's like a drug. It's one of the ways they make sure people will do whatever they say."

Jimmy couldn't believe what he was hearing.

"You mean the puzzles in every newspaper are designed by the Government to make everybody more obedient?"

"Every newspaper except the *Daily Mail*," Eva explained. "They have too many puzzles and I think their readers are obedient anyway."

"All this time they've been brainwashing me!" gasped Felix. He gripped his skull in his hands and his mouth dropped wide open. "I knew it!"

"I think your brain would take a special kind of washing, Felix," said Georgie with a smile. Then she turned back to Eva and was serious again. "So if these puzzles are controlled by a government computer how are you going to use them to send us messages?"

"I have access to the computer programme," beamed Eva. "So get *The Times* and hold the Sudoku up against the crossword clues. Whatever words it highlights, search for them online and go to the first message board that comes up. I'll change which message board I'm on every day, and if I have an urgent message for you I'll just put it straight into the clue words."

"Thank you, Eva," said Jimmy, but he wasn't sure whether he sounded grateful enough. He knew Eva was risking her life for him. She just smiled and headed for the lifts until Felix stopped her.

"Eva, wait." His voice was suddenly low and his eyes downcast. "When you look through all the stuff on NJ7 computers and in their documents and everything..."

"What is it?" Eva asked, but Jimmy knew straight away what was on Felix's mind. He recognised the darkness in his friend's eyes that had never been there before a certain day several months ago – the last time anybody had seen his parents.

"Do you ever see anything about my mum and dad?" Felix's voice was level, but it was obvious how much effort it was taking. His parents had been seized in New York, and at first everybody had assumed it must have been NJ7 that had taken them. But Jimmy had found out the truth. The head of the CIA admitted that he'd taken them.

Jimmy would never forget how it had happened. He could still see the triumph in Colonel Keays' eyes, the wrinkles on his face all seeming to point to his devilish smile. The man had used his power as head of the CIA to send Jimmy on a fake mission to an oil rig. The result had been Colonel Keays gaining even more power. In fact he was now on the verge of becoming President of the USA.

"The CIA has definitely got them," Jimmy went on. "Not NJ7. Colonel Keays had no reason to lie about that. It's going to take time, but we *will* get them back."

"I just thought it was worth checking," mumbled Felix. "In case NJ7 knew something. That's all." He shrugged slowly and Jimmy felt a shot of intense sadness shoot through him. It was like an injection of pure darkness. *At least my programming still lets me feel sympathy*, Jimmy thought to himself.

"Sorry, Felix," whispered Eva. "If I find anything about your parents I'll definitely send you a message straight away. But I think Jimmy's right."

She hurried away towards the lift, the beat of her footsteps echoing through the car park.

"We should wait until she's gone," Jimmy whispered to Felix and Georgie. "Then we'll go down the other way together."

"Oh," Eva called out, swivelling round as she waited for the lift. "I saw William Lee. He said something about trying to fix the satellite surveillance system. It wasn't working properly or something."

"Across the whole of London?" Jimmy asked hopefully.

"That's what it sounded like," said Eva. "And it didn't seem like he was doing a good job of fixing it." The lift arrived and Eva stepped in. "So they might not have such good coverage of the streets as usual. I'll send you a message if that changes. Don't forget – the puzzles in the paper!"

"Thanks again, Eva," whispered Jimmy.

"Good luck." Eva's words were lost in the shadow of the lift doors.

04 FRENCH CHAMPAGNE

"We're going to have some explaining to do," said Felix with dread. Georgie and Jimmy nodded, silently, as the three of them looked up at Christopher Viggo's campaign headquarters.

There were more lights on inside than when they'd left. They could make out the silhouettes of Viggo's staff throughout the building. Most importantly the lights were on on the top floor, where Jimmy, Felix and Georgie were meant to be fast asleep.

"Looks like Mum's up," said Georgie. "Probably waiting for us."

"This is when being invisible would come in handy," said Jimmy.

"Yeah, right," Georgie replied. "So you could sneak in and leave us to get into trouble!"

"What happens to your clothes when you become invisible?" asked Felix, sounding genuinely confused. "You know, if that was actually something you could do."

"I don't know." Jimmy shrugged. "They go invisible too, I guess."

"That's ridiculous," said Georgie. "What would be the point of invisible clothes?"

"That's obvious," said Felix. "To stop other invisible people seeing you naked."

"OK," sighed Jimmy. "Do you want me to take you through all the reasons why that makes no sense at all?"

They grinned sheepishly at the guards, who opened the gate without question, even though they looked like they would happily have murdered all three of them. Inside, they hurried to the lifts. Members of Viggo's campaign staff were bustling about, taking calls and having heated discussions while two TV screens showed the rolling news station. Jimmy kept his head down and his hood up. Since the campaign started, he'd been nervous about NJ7 having a mole in Viggo's camp. There'd been no sign of it, but he still preferred to remain anonymous. If NJ7 found out he was there it would only lead to trouble for everybody.

Felix and Georgie didn't bother to hide. In fact, Felix beamed at everybody, especially the women. He was used to joking around with Viggo's staff whenever he got the chance.

"I told you we should have gone through the service

entrance," Jimmy muttered.

"What's the point?" Felix replied. "Your mum obviously knows we're not there."

"This lot don't talk to Mum anyway," added Georgie while they waited for a lift. "Chris has kept it all so... separate."

Jimmy knew Felix and Georgie were right, but he still felt awkward. He glanced at the faces of all the people working with Viggo to overthrow the Government. At the moment the Government usually ran the country without interference from ordinary people. There was normally no voting. The system was called 'Neo-democracy', which really meant no democracy at all. The Government had only agreed to hold this election because of the pressure from Jimmy and Viggo.

Jimmy looked again at the people busily going about their work. They believed strongly enough in democracy and freedom to risk their lives. They would all be marked out as enemies of the state if Viggo lost the election the next day. *But he won't lose,* Jimmy thought with a smile. *We'll overthrow NJ7 at last.*

As the lift took them up to the top floor, Jimmy felt his mind humming, but not with thoughts about the election.

"We'll get off at the floor below," he announced quietly. "Then take the stairs. We can be back in our rooms before Mum stops us."

"How does that help?" asked Felix, stifling a yawn. "She'll still go mental with us in the morning."

"No, she won't," said Jimmy. "The election starts in a few hours. She'll be too busy helping with that. Then by the time it's over and she gets the chance to talk to us about tonight, she'll be a lot calmer. And hopefully she'll be so happy because Chris will have won..."

They did as he said, stepping into the darkness of the corridors on the floor below the apartment. They crept up the stairs with Jimmy leading the way.

"This is genius, Jimmy," whispered Felix. "Maybe we can pretend we never even left."

Jimmy held up a hand to tell him to be quiet and peered round the corner at the top of the stairs. The corridor was dark, but he could see the light from the door of the living room, where he reasoned his mum would be waiting, listening for the lift. He was about to signal for his friends to creep back to their rooms, but the sound of voices stopped him.

He moved quickly and silently into the corridor, the carpet cushioning his steps. But instead of turning left towards where he was meant to be asleep, he dashed to the right and pushed his back up against the wall outside the living room. The door was slightly ajar, and from his position Jimmy had a perfect view through the crack at the hinges.

"What are we doing?" Felix whispered, his hot breath exploding into Jimmy's ear.

Jimmy whipped round and planted a hand over his friend's mouth. He held it there until he felt Felix's body relax and signalled that he was listening. In turn, Felix turned to Georgie behind him and pressed a finger to his lips. Georgie rolled her eyes and mouthed a sarcastic, 'Oh really!?'

Jimmy's eyes adjusted quickly to the bright light coming through the crack in the door. He could see the back of his mum's head. She was sitting on the sofa in her dressing gown. But she wasn't alone. To Jimmy's surprise, Christopher Viggo was in the corner of the room, gripping the neck of an open champagne bottle in his fist.

"I told you," said Jimmy's mum, the frustration in her voice obvious, "you don't need to wait with me."

"I saw the light was on and I was worried," Viggo replied. "That's all." His voice was deep, but slightly hoarse.

"You've been making too many speeches," replied Helen Coates. She shifted uncomfortably on the sofa, and Jimmy could see her head subtly following the movement of the champagne bottle. "You should rest your voice."

"Don't worry. It's nearly over." Viggo ran a hand across his stubbled chin and pushed some stray strands of hair behind his ear. "Or it's just beginning, depending on how you look at it." There was a glint in his eye, a brown twinkle in the soft lighting. He stood fully upright, a tall man dominating the small space. The lack of any furniture apart from the sofa made him seem even more imposing. His lips were set in a flat smile.

"You need some sleep," said Helen, pulling her dressing gown around her against the cool of the air-conditioning. "No point working through the night when you need to look fresh for tomorrow."

"You need sleep too," he said softly. "Is Saffron in bed?" His eyes flicked across the room, sending a shiver through Jimmy, but he was confident he couldn't be seen.

Jimmy quickly glanced up the corridor towards the room that Viggo shared with Saffron Walden, his girlfriend. The door was closed, with no light coming through the cracks.

"What are they saying?" Felix whispered suddenly. "I can't hear them."

Jimmy reluctantly shuffled over slightly to give his friend a view through the door crack. Meanwhile, Georgie was less and less interested.

"This is stupid," she whispered. "I'm going to bed. Tell me what happened in the morning."

Just as she turned towards her bedroom, Jimmy reached out and caught her arm, then pulled her towards him until his mouth was right by her ear.

"Thanks for coming after me," he said softly.

Georgie simply nodded and threw a smile back up the

corridor as she walked away. The voice of Jimmy's mother pulled him back to the crack in the living-room door.

"Either get back to work or go to bed," Helen said to Viggo. "The kids will be here soon."

"How do you know?" Viggo was confused. "Where have they been? It's the small hours of the morning!"

"Do you care?" Helen snapped, suddenly fixing Viggo with a stare. All Viggo could do was hold up his hands in defence, letting the champagne bottle swing from his fingertips. "I checked with the guards," Helen went on. "The three of them left a couple of hours ago. There was nobody with them. Now put that bottle down. You look ridiculous."

"Celebrate with me," Viggo said, almost pleading.

"You haven't won the election yet."

"But I will." He smiled and every tooth seemed to gleam as brightly as his eyes.

"So what is there to celebrate tonight?" Helen stood up slowly and stepped towards Viggo. "The fact that we hardly speak to each other any more?"

"Stop this." Viggo changed his tone, sounding more gentle than triumphant. He put the bottle on the floor and took Jimmy's mother by her wrists. "We're making history. I'm going to change the way this country is run. I know you want the same thing! So all this…" He hesitated and brought Helen's hands together in his. "…it's all going to be worth it."

Helen Coates turned away and for the first time Jimmy could see the emotion weighing heavy on her face. Her short brown hair cast a net of shadows that seemed to accentuate the worry lines round her eyes.

"It seems like you're worth quite a lot," she whispered. "To somebody."

"What do you mean?" Viggo asked, letting her go and stepping back.

"This building," Helen explained. "All the staff downstairs. Your whole campaign. How much has it all cost? Even that." She flicked a hand at the champagne bottle as if she wanted it to topple over. "How did you get hold of real French champagne? That's almost impossible the way things are. Who's providing all of this? Where's the money coming from, Chris?"

Viggo turned his back on her and stared out of the window.

"It doesn't matter how many times you ask me," he grumbled, "I'm keeping my promise. I'll tell you – of course I will. But not until I've won the election."

"Why?" Helen raised her voice. "You're driving everybody crazy! You have to trust us!"

"I do trust you." Viggo's voice was so low Jimmy could barely make out the words. "But it's..."

"What? What is it? Dangerous?" Helen sighed and

ran her hands through her hair. "Are you ashamed of it? Money that you're ashamed of isn't worth having, Chris."

"Even if it means I can make the changes we've all hoped for? If I don't win this election tomorrow, NJ7 will be more powerful than ever. The Government will never let anybody vote again. They'll lock up or kill anybody that speaks out against them and the whole of Britain will be like one giant prison! Tomorrow is everything, Helen." He clenched his fists and narrowed his eyes, desperate to get his message across. "We might never have a second chance to bring down this Government peacefully. And if that takes money then I don't care where the money comes from, I'm going to use it."

Jimmy pressed his face closer against the crack in the door. Felix was crouching below him doing the same. In the last few months they'd talked many times about where all the money had come from to fund Viggo's campaign. Jimmy had even tried to ask Viggo about it, but Viggo always seemed distracted at just the wrong moment. Jimmy and Viggo had hardly had a proper conversation for months. It didn't sound like his mum was having any more luck.

"I didn't come up here to argue," Viggo said gently. He started towards the door, so Jimmy jumped to one side, dragging Felix with him.

"We're finished now, Jimmy," Helen called out. "You

can come in. You too, Felix."

Jimmy and Felix looked at each other, the deep shadows not enough to hide the shock on their faces. That moment, Viggo charged out into the corridor. He turned towards the lifts without even glancing at Jimmy and Felix.

"She's waiting for you," he grunted, before disappearing into the lift.

Jimmy and Felix edged into the living room.

"How did you...?" Jimmy gasped.

"Don't be surprised," his mother replied. "I was trained by NJ7 once too. And even though you were *so* quiet out there..."

Jimmy dropped his head, embarrassed at the obvious sarcasm in his mum's voice.

"Sorry, Mum, we..." Jimmy's voice trailed off.

"We'll talk about it in the morning," said his mum.

Jimmy felt so stupid, and wished his programming could give him some way of dealing with the situation. His hands automatically went deep into his pockets. So far, his fingers were the most obvious sign of his poisoning, and he'd grown used to hiding them. This time, however, he was more aware of them than usual. His friends had found out his secret and there was a part of him that felt relieved. Was this the moment to explain everything to his mum? He wasn't sure how he could do it. He wasn't even sure of the facts himself – at times he felt fine, but at times he was convinced he was getting worse and it terrified him.

"Everything OK?" It was Saffron Walden. She'd appeared at the door, wrapped in a full-length black dressing gown. Jimmy turned to look at her, amazed that she could seem so poised and so beautiful when she'd obviously just been woken up in the middle of the night.

"Just Chris being weird again," said Felix quickly.

"And these two running off to who-knows-where," Helen added.

Saffron nodded slowly.

"Chris being weird isn't news to me," she said softly. Her voice seemed as smooth as her skin, and had some of the same darkness.

"Do you think we should, erm, keep him under surveillance?" said Felix quickly.

Jimmy smiled. He was always impressed by Felix's ability to distract attention from anything that could get him into trouble – and as long as they were talking about Viggo, they couldn't talk about Jimmy, Felix and Georgie sneaking off together.

"I know he has a lot on his mind," Jimmy joined in, "but he's kept so many secrets from us. He hardly talks to us any more."

Saffron and Helen looked at each other, but Jimmy

couldn't read their expressions.

"It's the money that worries me," admitted Saffron. "You might be right, Felix. We might need to keep an eye on him – for his own safety. I don't know how well we can trust his campaign staff or even his security guards. Everybody was hired in such a hurry."

"We've come this far without any problems," said Helen, now eyeing up Jimmy and Felix, as if to tell them *she* hadn't forgotten they were in trouble. But so far, Jimmy thought, Felix's distraction technique was working. They hadn't been sent straight to bed yet.

"But with the election so close..." said Saffron softly. "This is when it counts. If he loses—"

"He won't lose," Felix cut in. "How can he? Everybody knows this Government is evil. They tried to go to war with France, and they haven't let anybody vote about anything until now."

"But if he does lose," Saffron went on, "I doubt many of his so-called supporters will stick by him. And if he wins it could be worse. We'll find out how many of them have been using him for their own power."

There was genuine concern on her face. It was obvious to Jimmy that she still cared deeply about Viggo, despite his erratic behaviour since his campaign had become official. The man had worked against the Government in secret for so long, thought Jimmy. Maybe he just wasn't used to being allowed to do it in public. Maybe sometimes secrets could protect you.

Jimmy felt his fingers tingling. He knew it wasn't his programming, or even the radiation poisoning. It was his mind churning, unsure whether to show his mum. While he was deep in his thoughts, Saffron said goodnight and went back to bed. Now Jimmy looked at Felix. To Jimmy's relief, his friend saw the uncertainty on his face and immediately understood what to do.

"OK, bye then," said Felix brightly. "I need my beauty sleep, you know." He tilted his head and patted his hair, as if he was some kind of supermodel, then hurried out of the room. Jimmy couldn't help smiling, despite the dread in his heart.

"You too, Jimmy," said his mum.

Jimmy didn't move, but he couldn't say anything either. It was several seconds before he forced his arm muscles to pull his hands from his pockets.

"What's this?" asked his mum, taking his hands and turning them over to examine them.

"Mum," choked Jimmy, "I have to explain where I went tonight, and why and..." He paused, staring at the floor, knowing that if he looked at his mother's face he might not be able to stop himself crying. "...and I have to tell you what's happening to me."

05 OPERATION BLACKOUT

The White House seemed to glow in the late-afternoon sun. The perfectly neat lines of its construction were broken by the flashes of red and blue coming from the dozens of Stars and Stripes flags that flapped wildly. In the centre of it all was Colonel Keays.

His medals glinted off his navy uniform. He was a stocky man of about sixty, but today, with his chin high and triumph in his eyes, he looked a little younger. The seal of the President of the United States was emblazoned on the lectern in front of him. It may as well have been on the man's chest.

"...I am greatly humbled by the honour the people of this great nation have thrust upon me," he was saying. His words boomed over the public address system. The gathered crowd listened obediently, smiles fixed. The whole occasion was perfectly stage-managed. Even the few thin hairs left on top of Colonel Keays' head were greased flat so they wouldn't misbehave.

"...and I promise to you all that the country will be made even greater by my efforts, within our own boundaries and beyond. For example, while our cousins in the United Kingdom struggle through their own election, I pledge to help them in their first steps towards real democracy, whatever the outcome of their vote."

He puffed up his chest and stretched his shoulders, appearing even more broad than usual. Behind him, the marching band was given their cue. They lifted their instruments, light shimmering across the crowd as the sun reflected off the brass.

"I have already extended the hand of friendship to the British," Keays went on, "and will continue to do so in countries around the world. We must never waver in our determination to extend our influence across the globe. This is the greatest nation on Earth." There was a small 'hurrah' from the crowd. "And I pledge to you now that as President I see our future as the greatest nation the human race has ever seen." Another cheer, slightly louder, just as well orchestrated. "God bless America!"

Finally the crowd was allowed to give full-bodied applause. The carefully positioned Secret Service staff made sure it lasted just the right amount of time, never dropping below a spirited level, but remaining civilised.

The brass band struck up a lilting chorus of 'Hail to

the Chief' and dozens of government staff lined up for Keays to grip each hand in turn and grin into the nearby TV cameras.

At the end of the line, the cameras were escorted away and a team of aides bustled around Keays.

"Congratulations, Colonel," whispered one, as they marched into the shadows, away from the crowds.

"I'm no longer a colonel," Keays barked immediately. "I'm now Commander-in-Chief. You'll address me as 'Mr President'."

"Yes, Mr President." The aide was so embarrassed he almost bowed.

"Any news from Britain?"

"Not yet, Mr President. Still a few hours to go. But Operation Blackout is in play."

President Keays let out a stabbing laugh that echoed off the colonnades, then he led his staff quickly away through the doors of the White House.

Eva felt her eye muscles twitching. She'd gone through the whole night without sleep, but so had most of the staff of NJ7, she realised. She guessed that outside the labyrinth of NJ7 HQ the sun was probably rising, but down here in the tunnels there was no difference between night and day.

She stared at her notebook, watching her pencil move across the page automatically, barely able to focus on what Miss Bennett was saying. Instead, all Eva could see were the faces from an old photograph. Not only was she exhausted, but every time Miss Bennett looked at her she imagined the woman could see straight through to her back pocket, to the scanned copy of a tattered snapshot of a dozen old scientists.

Three of them already had bold black crosses over their faces. Those three could be no help to Jimmy now. The records of their deaths had been relatively simple to find, though Eva had been shocked to discover how easy it had been for NJ7 to assassinate their own staff. Now she had to fight to force the image from her mind.

"Eva, are you bored?" Miss Bennett's voice was cool and steady. She slipped so effortlessly from dictating notes to barbed comments that Eva almost scribbled down 'are you bored' before she realised what Miss Bennett meant.

"Bored? No, of course not," said Eva in a hurry. "Sorry." She looked up from her notebook to see a compact smile on Miss Bennett's lips – a bright red flash across the middle of her pale face, like a 'no entry' sign in negative. The Director of NJ7 was leaning against her desk, her long legs crossed casually in front of her. Her brown hair was, as always, immaculate, and with a glossy sheen that made it look almost unreal. She was dressed in a sharp black business suit, with a black shirt. How did she look so smart, Eva wondered, when she's also been up for almost 36 hours without sleeping?

"Good. Then we're done for now," said Miss Bennett, gliding across her office to make her way out. "No need to read anything back to me. You can deal with it all in the car on the way to the airport."

"Airport?" Eva could feel the tiredness enveloping her mind.

"Are you under the impression that the final word of anything I say needs translating into gibberish?"

Eva froze in Miss Bennett's glare.

"Er, no, Miss Bennett."

"Then let's get on with the day, shall we?"

Eva hurried after her boss, mentally kicking herself – until now she'd completely forgotten that the first item on her schedule for that day was accompanying Miss Bennett to Heathrow. She longed to run as far away from NJ7 as possible. Every hour now felt like the prelude to her execution.

"This is going to be very delicate," Miss Bennett explained as they walked briskly through the NJ7 complex. "The United Nations inspection team hasn't been making enough noise."

"Isn't that a good thing?" Eva asked, terrified that her tiredness and her fear would make her give something away. "Doesn't it mean that they haven't found anything illegal or unfair about the election campaign so far?"

"Of course, but what's the point in me inviting the UN to send a team if they don't make a big fuss about how fair we're being? And are you going to ask stupid questions all day?"

"I will if you will," quipped Eva before she could control her mouth. Miss Bennett glanced back, as shocked as Eva herself. Then, to Eva's huge relief, Miss Bennett raised an eyebrow and smiled. She was impressed.

"So now..." Eva went on, eager to show that she wasn't completely off the ball. She quickly flicked through her notebook, consulting her notes. "...now you've asked the head of the inspection team to come and oversee everything, and the Prime Minister is meeting him off the plane to introduce him to the press..." She flicked through another few pages, expertly keeping up with Miss Bennett's rapid march while also reading her own ordered scribblings.

They hurried through a small metal door and the surroundings changed. The bare concrete was gone. Suddenly there was plush red carpet. The walls were covered in ornate golden wallpaper and there was natural daylight. But Eva was used to this. She didn't even break stride. They'd passed through the secret entrance from NJ7 HQ into the back of Number 10 Downing Street.

"Everybody in the country..." Miss Bennett said,

smoothly taking a cup of coffee from a waiting aide. "…everybody in the whole world, in fact – they'll all know that today's election is utterly fair. So when we win, our enemies will have no possible comeback."

They swept through the building, their path lined with civil servants and government officials. Each of them handed Miss Bennett something she needed, or took something she was finished with. Eva noticed several of them couldn't help bowing their heads.

"Once this election is over, it's over," announced Miss Bennett. "The last vestige of old-fashioned democracy dies today."

Eva was taken aback by the certainty in Miss Bennett's tone. Finally the front door was held open for them. The brightness of the morning made Eva blink hard, but within seconds another aide held open the back door of a waiting car and they slipped into the black leather interior.

"I've been waiting here for ten minutes." Ian Coates was already in the back seat, but the Jaguar was easily roomy enough to accommodate the three of them.

"I hope you've used the time to memorise the speech I wrote for you," replied Miss Bennett, giving the driver a nod.

"Watch how you talk to me, Miss Bennett," spluttered Ian Coates, "I'm still Prime Minister. Technically, I still run the country."

"Yes," Miss Bennett purred, "but who's running *you*?"

The Prime Minister had no response. Eva had seen these tiny battles a hundred times in the last few months, but the result was always the same. Ian Coates might have been Prime Minister, but he was nothing more than Miss Bennett's puppet.

"Straighten your tie," Miss Bennett ordered, as if she was talking to a teenager. Ian Coates did as he was told. "And when you get out of the car, remember to smile a little."

Coates nervously stretched his lips into a hideous grin.

"Less than that," Miss Bennett sighed, without even looking at him. "You're British, remember."

"So nobody knows how he can afford to rent this building?" asked Felix, twisting on the sofa until his knees hooked over the side.

"Get off me," Jimmy insisted, shoving Felix's head away from his leg.

"Get a room, lovebirds," joked Georgie. "And keep quiet." She pointed at the TV screen to indicate she was trying to listen. The sofa was the only place to sit to watch the TV, so the three of them were closely bunched up together. "Chris is meant to be making a speech. If we're not allowed to be there ourselves then we can at least watch it on TV."

Felix and Jimmy were silent for a few seconds before Felix deliberately nudged Jimmy's thigh with the top of his head.

"That's it!" Jimmy exclaimed with a laugh. He jumped up and landed with a bump right on Felix's face. Felix made a big show of wriggling and twisting to escape.

"Aargh!" he cried when he'd finally pulled himself free. He clawed at his own face and staggered round the room. "It's toxic, super-powered, genetically modified gas... Nooo!"

They all laughed, and Jimmy said, "I bet that's the first thing you'd put into someone's programming if you were designing them."

"No," Felix replied. "The first thing would be... never having to go to sleep!"

"Never sleeping?" Jimmy chuckled. "You'd be even more hyper than you are now!"

Soon they were distracted by images at the top of a news bulletin on TV. There were shots of a plane landing at Heathrow, then a tall, wiry man in a light-grey suit climbed down to the runway to shake hands with the Prime Minister.

Nobody said a word, but Jimmy could feel the joy draining from the room. He stared at the pictures of Ian Coates, the man he had thought of as his father for the first eleven and a half years of his life. On the screen, he was gripping the visitor's hand and twisting his face into a horrible, false smile. For a second Jimmy remembered laughing with him, messing around with him – loving him.

He forced away the emotion. Instead, he shifted his attention to his sister next to him. The man on screen really was *her* father, as far as they knew. Jimmy knew her feelings were as painful and complicated as his own, and he wanted to say something. He opened his mouth, but nothing came to his lips and his tongue felt dry.

The TV report cut away from the Prime Minister and went back to the wiry man, showing snippets of his speech. The caption on the screen read 'Dr Newton Longville – UN Election Inspector'. Beneath it was a scrolling message that announced, 'Chief UN Inspector welcomed by PM to monitor today's election.'

"My team will make sure there is no intimidation at the polls," declared Dr Longville in a melodious American accent. In close-up he was much older than Jimmy had first thought. His nose was bony and crooked. "The ballot will be carried out under strict observation," he went on, "using state-of-the-art technology known as HERMES – the Higher Echelon Remote Monitoring Election System."

"HERMES?" said Felix. "Sounds like some kind of disease."

The UN man's grey eyes stared into the TV camera, not blinking. "The design, manufacture and testing of every component has been overseen by UN engineers in controlled conditions. I'm certain that every voter will enjoy using the secure touch-screen kiosks that are currently being installed at polling stations around the country. The votes will be sent digitally, but securely, to the central hub in a secure location near Milton Keynes, where they will be counted by the HERMES mainframe computer."

"He looks like some kind of robot," said Georgie.

"Do you think he's telling the truth?" Jimmy asked, leaning towards the TV as if lies would give off a scent. Inside, his programming was rumbling, suppressing another wave of pain, but at the same time making him throb with suspicion. "Do you think NJ7 will control his team? Or him? Have they already rigged the vote?"

Before anybody could answer, the news cut to the next item – and there was Christopher Viggo. His head was held high and his presence seemed to fill the screen.

"Look!" Felix exclaimed, pointing at the very edge of the picture. "It's your mum!" Helen Coates and Saffron Walden were standing among Viggo's supporters, listening to his speech.

"I've travelled thousands of kilometres around Britain," the man said. "I've heard millions of voices: in person, in letters and in messages on the internet. Every one of those voices – your voices – is telling me that change must come."

"He shouldn't admit that he hears voices," Felix cut in.

"Shh," said Georgie. "I want to hear this!"

"Those voices," Viggo went on, "tell me that you no longer want to listen to your doubts and fears, but to your greatest hopes and aspirations!"

He was building to a climax, and so was the response from the crowd, but the report cut back to the studio, where three women were droning on.

"What about the rest of his speech?!" Georgie complained. "How is that fair? He can't win an election if they won't even show his speeches on the news."

"They showed a bit of it," Jimmy replied. "That's better than it used to be. And at least they admitted that he made a speech – they even called him 'the opposition leader' instead of 'enemy of the state' or 'traitor'."

Georgie grabbed the remote control from Jimmy's knee and switched off the TV in frustration.

"We didn't see anything," she said.

"He was wearing a new tie," mumbled Felix.

"You say the most random things sometimes," said Georgie with an exasperated sigh.

"It's not random," Felix replied. "I was just thinking..."

"What?"

"Somebody must have paid for that tie." He pushed himself off the floor. "And we still don't know who."

06 *YOU'RE NEVER ALONE*

There was no great fanfare to the start of the election. Felix realised that he'd been wrong to expect it. He'd never witnessed an election before. The last election in Britain had come before he was born. But he knew there'd been a time not too long ago when elections were routine events. *They must have had them all the time*, he thought to himself. *What a hassle.*

He turned up the collar of his duffel coat and hunched his shoulders against the wind.

"Vote Viggo," he said automatically, thrusting a leaflet into a woman's hands as she walked past, into the school hall behind them. Felix imagined school halls all over the country similarly transformed into polling stations.

"Efficiency. Stability. Security!" Felix read aloud from one of the government posters in a mock-serious voice. He went on, waggling a finger in the air, "Insanity. Stupidity. Toxicity, and a nice cuppa tea!"

"Shh!" said Georgie, with a smile.

Felix let his thoughts stray to whether the hall of his own school was also being used for the election, then he wondered whether he'd ever be going back there. He would never have admitted it out loud, but he missed some things about school life – the security, the friends, the football... his parents telling him to do his homework.

Viggo and Saffron had left Felix and Georgie to handle this location on their own, while Viggo travelled round to as many other places as he could to gather last-minute support. *Every vote counts*, he'd said over and over to them.

Felix peeked round the doorway into the hall. A couple of armed policemen stood chatting to a young woman with identity tags who was obviously in charge of running this polling station.

"Hey, you can't go in there!" Georgie whispered.

Felix waved away her concern. "I'm just looking."

Past the policemen was a registration table, piled high with papers, and beyond that Felix could see the school gym. Lined up in rows up and down the length of the hall were dozens of voting machines. Each one was a touch-screen kiosk that looked to Felix like it could have dispensed train tickets or lottery tickets.

Strange way to choose a government, he thought, imagining how great it would be if instead of having to pick one of the choices the machine gave you, you could go on the internet and select anybody in the world to be Prime Minister.

Felix watched the woman he'd given the leaflet to. At the moment she was the only voter in the hall. She bent forward so close to the screen on her kiosk that her forehead almost pressed against the name at the top of the machine. Every kiosk bore slanted silver letters saying HERMES.

After a few seconds, the woman tapped her finger against the screen, gave a firm nod, as if the machine could see her, and marched back out of the hall. Felix kept his eyes on her, searching for some clue about who she'd voted for. The woman's face was completely blank until she passed Felix, when she briefly glanced at him and gave a quick smile. Felix drew in a sharp breath. *Did that mean...?*

"Hey, Felix!" Georgie whispered. Felix turned to see a gaggle of people arriving. Georgie moved towards them and forced leaflets into their hands. "Vote Viggo!" she said. "End the oppression of Neo-democracy! Vote for freedom! Put control of the country back in the hands of the people!"

From then on, they were busy all day as a constant stream of people arrived to register their votes. Some of the voters smiled at Georgie and Felix, some ignored them completely, while a few tried to shoo them away.

"Vote Viggo!" Felix recited to the ones Georgie had missed.

"Be more cheerful," Georgie whispered. "Every vote counts!"

"How many times do I have to hear...?" Felix stopped complaining, ready to give the most cheerful greeting of all time to his next 'customer'. "Good morrow, fine gentleman!" he exclaimed in his brightest, squeakiest voice. "Top of the morning to you!"

"Felix!" Georgie gasped. "What are you doing?"

Felix waved a leaflet above his head, dancing an odd jig that involved twirling his wrists and clicking his heels.

"Happy voting!" he declared to the bemused man hurrying past him. "Place your finger in a voting nature on the button for *Signor* Viggo, the finest gentleman in the whole of old Eng-er-land!"

The man hunched his shoulders and scurried to the registration table, while Felix and Georgie burst out laughing.

"You can't do that!" Georgie protested, her giggles telling a different story.

"Votes might win an election," Felix said grandly, "but make people laugh and you rule the world."

Georgie shook her head in despair.

"If you had me at every polling station all over the

country," said Felix, "we'd win this, no problem."

"Or we'd all get put in a loony bin."

"That, my friend," Felix replied, grandly, "is entirely possible."

Jimmy stalked in front of the giant window on the top floor of Viggo's headquarters, glimpsing London through the gaps in the blind. The vertical slats were beginning to feel like iron bars. He'd watched the lights come on as the afternoon faded into evening, and now the darkness seemed stronger than the illumination, as if it was creeping across the whole city, smothering the place completely.

Two copies of *The Times* lay on the sofa behind him, folded open to the puzzles. There was no message yet from Eva. It was too soon, and he knew that, but he'd still used the puzzles to find the message board and checked for messages every hour. It was as if his body relished the new element to his routine.

A message would come eventually. Jimmy had confidence in Eva. The only question was whether it would come too late. Despite his desperate attempts to find a doctor, and his near-obsession with learning about the effects of radiation, he had to admit he had no idea what it was doing to him.

All he had to go on was what he could see and what he could feel. His head was pounding and his muscles felt weaker than he'd ever known them to be. He flexed his fingers instinctively but closed his eyes, forcing himself not to examine them again. The blue stain made him feel like he'd dipped his hands in pure terror and couldn't wash it away.

Now it was all he could see, as if the radiation gripped his brain and shifted every image into the shape of death. There was no comfort in the blackness. Yet Jimmy had been alone with the shadows all day, and now late into the night. He was the only one who was still being actively pursued by NJ7. Even standing this close to the window was a risk – if the Government had the building under observation, which was almost certain, Jimmy knew that advanced imaging techniques might pick out his silhouette and enable them to identify him.

I'll be ready for them, he heard himself thinking. A rush of adrenalin fizzed through his body. But was it adrenalin, or his programming eager for action? Jimmy pictured millions of tiny tigers charging through his blood, with his body as nothing but a giant cage.

A flash made Jimmy open his eyes. Something had reflected off the window of a passing vehicle, and even with his eyes closed his retina was so sensitive he'd been aware of the change. At the very edge of the room, his back to the wall, Jimmy peeked out of the window, down to the street.

Lights. At the front of the building, right by the main gate, was a TV news van. Whatever they were filming was obscured by the trees and the top of the security fence.

Jimmy turned to look at the TV. He'd had it on constantly in the background with the sound muted. Even though he knew that every channel was controlled by the Government, he'd wanted to keep up with the events of the night. Now he realised he'd been so distracted by his thoughts that he hadn't noticed how quickly the results were coming in from the polls across the country.

Now Christopher Viggo was on the screen with a clutch of microphones thrust towards his face. Jimmy quickly realised the scene was taking place outside the building he was in, the campaign headquarters. Jimmy rushed to turn the sound on. Had Viggo won the election already? Surely it was still too early for a result.

On TV, Viggo was talking rapidly about the election campaign and the state of the country, but Jimmy didn't understand the context. He wished he could go downstairs to see what was happening in the flesh. If this was Viggo's acceptance speech, Jimmy wanted to be there with him. If Viggo was Prime Minister already then maybe Jimmy could go outside freely. He could live without the unseen eyes of the Secret Service scouring the streets to find him and eliminate him. Jimmy felt relief rising up inside him, but forced himself to hold it in check. *Not yet*, he told himself. *Find out for sure.*

Then Viggo's words started to sink in:

"...with thankfully little disruption, and what looks at the moment to have been a cleanly fought ballot..."

Jimmy noticed now that the man's voice seemed unusually hollow – not the slow, resonant tone he had always used for his speeches before. He was also glancing down at a sheet of notes, which wasn't like him, and his eyes darted around anxiously.

He's tired, thought Jimmy. But he quickly realised it was something more.

"Thanks to the amazing technology," Viggo went on, "the running total of votes has been made available to us much sooner than expected." Was his hand trembling? Jimmy couldn't tell. There were dozens of camera flashes exploding on the man now.

"Of course, there is a great deal of formal procedure still to unfold, with the numbers being checked and tallied... but nevertheless, the time has come when I am forced to admit that it is no longer possible for me to win this election."

There was a rising chatter of questions from a clutch of journalists off-screen. Viggo ignored them and carried on, leaning into the microphones.

"I had hoped that today would mark the beginning of a new era. A new hope for Britain, for democracy... for change." There was a catch in his voice as he said it. "You, the people of Britain, have decided that the time is not yet right to embrace that change. So I concede defeat. But I will be back another day."

With that, Viggo's face seemed to relax for a second, before he turned away from the camera and hurried through the gate into the grounds of his headquarters.

Jimmy found himself at the window again, watching the tiny figure of Viggo below, rushing back towards the building. Had it really just happened? Had Viggo just lost the election?

"No," he gasped aloud. How was it possible? How could it have happened so quickly? Even if the votes could be counted straight away, how could the public have turned against Viggo? How could people have voted for Ian Coates? For this Government?

"They don't know..." Jimmy said softly, unable to keep his thoughts inside. "They don't know about NJ7." His chest was churning with the shock. For a moment he was sure he was going to throw up. He felt an uncomfortable tingle in his nostrils. *Another nose bleed*, he thought, squeezing the bridge of his nose to cut it off. Then, with what felt like the force of a hurricane, Jimmy's programming swept through him. He leapt off the sofa and turned off the TV, then he dashed across the room and hit the lights.

His head throbbing, Jimmy ran to the side of the window again and peered between the slats of the blind. *It's happening*, he could hear in his head. While half of him still refused to believe that Viggo might have lost the election, the rest of him was already dealing with the consequences. If the election was over, and if the Government had won, NJ7 could attack at any moment. Jimmy could almost hear the whiz of the bullets. In his mind, he saw the glass shattering. His head was already plotting his strategy – evasion, survival. How could he escape the building?

"Stop!" Jimmy shouted. His voice reverberated round the room. This was madness. There was nothing to suggest that the Government was about to attack. But Jimmy's mind swirled with doubt. He couldn't work out whether this was his paranoia or a legitimate reaction to a genuine risk. Had he unknowingly seen something out of the window that suggested an imminent attack?

Jimmy held his head and scrunched his fingers into his skull, as if he was digging for the answer. Then he had to find a tissue from his pocket and wipe the blood that was trickling from his nose.

Suddenly there were noises. The corridor. Voices. Footsteps. Jimmy felt his muscles awash with power. The door burst open and the light flicked on.

"Jimmy?" It was his mother. "You OK? Why are you in the dark?"

Jimmy held himself still. It took all his effort. He diverted the tissue in his hand to wipe the sweat from his face and scrunched it up to hide the spots of blood. But before he could say anything, Viggo burst in, past Jimmy's mother.

"NO!" he roared, not even glancing at Jimmy. He charged at the sofa and kicked it a dozen times.

"Chris, calm down!" yelled Helen Coates. From behind her came Saffron Walden, making soothing noises. She tried to take Viggo by the shoulders, but he turned away and landed a sharp kick in the centre of the TV screen. The glass cracked and the whole set toppled over.

Jimmy heard a gasp and noticed that Felix and Georgie were lurking in the corridor, unable to stop themselves watching, but sensibly staying out of the way.

"Chris, stop this!" Helen shouted. Viggo stopped trying to destroy things, but Jimmy thought it was only because he'd run out of furniture to kick. "What did you expect?" Helen asked. "That you were invincible?"

Viggo turned away, resting with his hands against the window, breathing heavily.

"You've done a great thing," said Saffron softly. "You should be proud. You established an opposition... you forced them to have an election in the first place... you—"

"I lost!" Viggo exploded with rage again. Jimmy had never seen him like this. All the man's power and charisma had fractured into a burning fury.

"So you'll keep fighting," Helen suggested. "You have to. We'll find a way – somehow. We'll prove that the ballot was rigged."

Everybody turned to look at her.

"Oh, come on," said Helen. "You all know it must have been."

"Those machines…" said Saffron, nodding. "It's obvious. NJ7 must have got to them, or to the central computer…"

"They didn't," Viggo groaned, hardly audible. "Don't you think I expected that? Don't you think I had staff working to stop it happening? To gather proof if it *was* happening?"

"Your staff?" Helen asked, with acid in her voice. "Where are your loyal staff now? If they were so good at their job, and so loyal… where are they now?" There was no reply. Helen marched to the window and pulled back the blind. "Look!" she ordered.

Gradually, figures appeared in the grounds of the building. They were scurrying away, towards the gate. Viggo's campaign staff were abandoning him.

"It's a stampede!" said Helen, as they watched the trail of figures swell into a crowd, then a rush for the gate. Soon they would all be gone. "The building's empty,

Chris," Helen continued. "They couldn't have got out of here faster! Apart from us, there's nobody here!"

"That's not quite true." The voice came from the shadows of the corridor behind Georgie and Felix. They both let out a startled gasp. It was a woman's voice, delicate but insistent. "You're not alone, Mr Viggo."

07 *DO YOU HAVE IT?*

"Who are you? How did you get in?" Saffron Walden fired out her questions. At the same time she jumped to one side so she was blocking the new woman's view of Viggo. Jimmy knew instinctively she was in the firing line.

Saffron pulled her mobile phone from her pocket and hit two keys.

"Stop," said Viggo softly.

"I'm calling security," Saffron replied, pressing her phone to her ear.

"It's too late," said Viggo, guiding Saffron aside. "She's already here. That means security is already compromised."

Finally the woman stepped through the doorway, into the light. Jimmy was surprised to see that she wasn't much taller than himself. Her small, round face was framed by hair so black it seemed to swallow all the light in the room, while her skin was a deep olive brown. It was a contrast to the bright white of her wool coat, which entirely enveloped her.

"He's right, Miss Walden," the woman announced, cocking her head to one side. "Security is… compromised." There was a twinkle in her eye that sent a shiver through Jimmy. It immediately reminded him of Miss Bennett, another woman full of smiling cruelty. But there were differences – this woman's voice was much harsher and couldn't hide her anger, or she chose not to. It was in the downward curve of her mouth and the tense lines round her eyes.

"What do you want?" asked Viggo. Something in his tone made Jimmy study his expression. Viggo was afraid, but trying to hide it.

"Do you have it?" The woman asked the question with a quiet intensity. She was staring directly up into Viggo's face, ignoring everybody else in the room, but the assassin in Jimmy noticed that she had positioned herself so that nobody could get behind her or leave the room without her being in the way.

"What?" A look of shock crossed Viggo's face.

The woman snorted. "Do you have it?"

"Let's talk alone," Viggo said, almost pleading.

"We don't need to talk, Mr Viggo. I just need to know the answer: do you have it?"

Jimmy watched Viggo's eyes flick across the faces of

everybody else. Why was this woman dangerous? She certainly seemed hostile, but Jimmy had confidence in his skills. He could already feel that buzz in his blood, his second soul putting every fibre on alert. *The side of her skull*, it seemed to whisper to him. *Two fingers. One jab.* He could see the exact spot, just above her ear. It may as well have had a target painted on it. *Take her down, but keep her conscious.*

His programming was straining for action. Every second of delay was a second in which the potential danger increased. Still, Jimmy fought to hold himself steady. *Wait*, he begged himself. He was gripped by curiosity – about Viggo. In the seconds since this woman arrived, Viggo had revealed more about himself than he had in the last six months. Jimmy was desperate to find out more.

"You know I don't have it," said Viggo, between gritted teeth.

He's trying to seem strong, Jimmy thought, but even from a couple of metres away he could pick out the rapid movement of Viggo's pupils and the man's shallow, irregular breathing.

"What's going on?" asked Jimmy's mother, directing the question towards Viggo, but keeping her eyes on the new woman. "Who is this?"

The woman snorted again, but this time it sounded

more agitated. She was getting angrier.

"You have a problem, don't you?" she said. Only now did Jimmy detect a slight accent in her English. Jimmy's mind reverberated with an instant playback of every vowel sound that had left the woman's mouth since she'd arrived. Was it Irish, or a hint of something Mediterranean?

"Who is this?" Saffron echoed Helen, more insistent. "Chris?"

Viggo ignored her and stepped closer to the woman, as if he hoped to speak without anybody else hearing.

"I said I'd give it to you when I won..." Viggo argued. His voice trailed away.

"And do you have it?" asked the woman.

"I... I didn't win," Viggo stammered.

"You lost." The woman smiled for the first time, but her eyes remained stern and her head was still cocked to one side. Jimmy felt a heat rising up in his chest. The urge towards violence was unbearable now. He couldn't contain it. It was infecting every thought.

"Chris!" Helen shouted. "Who is this? What's happening?" Now she grabbed Viggo by the collar, pushed him back and took his place directly in front of the new woman. "Who are you?"

"I work for a large company," came the reply, straight away. "Your friend Mr Viggo spent a lot of our money in his election campaign and made certain promises about how that debt would be repaid. I have come to see that those promises are fulfilled."

"I promised it to you when I won!" Viggo shouted. Jimmy was amazed to see such a strong man shrinking smaller and smaller. His face was crumpled in anguish and he was supporting himself on the back of the sofa. "I said I could never give it to you unless I won. That's what I promised!"

"As of now," the woman sneered in response, "your promises have changed."

"You can't do that!" came a voice from the corner of the room. It was Felix. "Whoever you are. You can't change someone's promise after they've…" He swallowed the end of his protest as the woman slowly spun to face him. "… you just can't," he mumbled, shrinking back to his corner.

"Idiot!" Helen whispered to Viggo. "Is this why you wouldn't tell us where your money came from? You've been borrowing from crooks?"

"We're not crooks," said the woman. "We're called the Capita."

The truth bit into Jimmy's senses. He'd never forget the Capita. It was a huge organisation that had started by covering all of Europe, and had now spread out into every corner of the world. As far as Jimmy understood it, the Capita was a modern, streamlined version of old criminal networks like the mafia. They'd joined together and become more efficient, more ruthless... more businesslike.

"The Capita are worse than crooks," he announced quietly. The woman turned to him. He ignored her face and noticed only the speed and balance with which she moved. This woman was strong.

"Hello, Mr Coates," she announced. "I've heard everything about you."

And I know more about the Capita than you'd like, Jimmy thought to himself. His previous encounter with the Capita had started off as cooperation. They'd helped him escape the French Secret Service in West Africa and brought him through Europe, all the time keeping him safe from the French and the British. Jimmy remembered how impressed he'd been by their operations, but also the frightening way in which they secured and used their power. To the Capita, torture, deceit and murder were just business expenses. The organisation was made up of lifelong criminals, retired Secret Service agents and ex-soldiers from around the world who were all united in their love of money. Unfortunately, Jimmy had also found out how easy it was to be betrayed when money was the basis of an agreement with the Capita.

"We'll get you your money," said Jimmy firmly. "Just tell us how much it is and give us time."

To his shock, the woman let out another snort.

"Thank you for the offer," she said. "But if we only wanted money, this is the last person we'd lend it to." She flicked a hand in the direction of Viggo. "Don't pretend you don't know what we want." She shuffled forward until she was eye to eye with Jimmy. He could smell the soapy flavour of her make-up. "I think you know what we want," she whispered.

Jimmy shuddered. He couldn't stop himself glancing over at Viggo, whose face looked desperate.

"Do you have it?" the woman barked, swivelling abruptly and looming towards Viggo. Jimmy's head was spinning. What did she mean? What would the Capita have been after that Christopher Viggo could have promised them?

Viggo shook his head meekly.

"Fine," said the woman. Suddenly she dipped a hand into the pocket of her coat. *A knife.* Jimmy's thoughts formed even before he knew what was happening and his reactions exploded. He dived towards her. The moment her hand emerged from her pocket, Jimmy was there to slam her wrist back against the wall, pinning the woman in place. But there was no blade. Instead, her fingers squeezed the button on a remote-control clicker.

Jimmy's head was rocked by a high-pitched squeal. He lost his grip on the woman and pressed his hands to his ears, but the noise was still unbearable. Around him, the others were dropping to the carpet, hands clasped around their heads. Then the glass of the window shattered. The frequency of the sound had been carefully calibrated. Finally the lights blew out.

That's when Jimmy's instincts shifted from attack to survival. He knew this was only the first wave of an imminent attack and with the window blown apart they were all exposed. Jimmy forced himself to withstand the pain of the noise and rolled for his friends. He pulled Felix and Georgie behind the sofa in one heave. Then he pushed the sofa towards the wall to create a more secure shelter. It took less than a second.

Finally the squeal stopped. In the darkness, Jimmy felt that intense tingle just behind his retinas. It was as if his whole head was humming. His natural night-vision kicked in and the room was cast in a rough blue haze, his eyes enhancing the available light. Shadows moved through shadows, every wall and every bit of floor shifted with the tiny fluctuations in the light level. This was one of Jimmy's body's amazing assassin skills, and it had saved his life many times.

Now one thing shone out – the Capita woman's white coat. She was locked in a brutish fight with Viggo. He'd managed to knock the clicker from her hand, and now Helen and Saffron both leapt to help him at the same time. The Capita woman ducked and kicked, and in the darkness her movements were fast enough to avoid every attempted strike. *I'll sort this out*, thought Jimmy. He took his first step towards the fight, but three vertical black lines dropped outside the hole where the window had been.

"Ropes!" Jimmy shouted. Nobody could hear him above the echo of the screech in their ears, the tinkling glass, and somebody screaming. *Was that Georgie*, Jimmy wondered, *or Felix? At least I know they're alive.*

As Jimmy scrambled towards the ropes, three masked soldiers with torches shining from their heads swung into the room. The swish of the nylon ropes sliced through Jimmy's heart.

"Watch out!" he shouted. He was in position to block the first soldier. He dug his heels into the carpet and slammed his elbow into the man's midriff. The grunt still in his ears, Jimmy moved on to the second intruder. He tripped him with a low, sweeping kick just as he landed – another *La Savate* combat move. But in the corner of his eye Jimmy could see what the Capita woman was doing. She wasn't trying to win her fight. She was simply inching towards the window, bringing her closer to her reinforcements – along with her unsuspecting opponents.

"Look out!" Jimmy roared, hurling himself across the room. The third soldier had already caught Viggo's shin. Jimmy cried out again and reached for his friend, but the soldier swooped away through the smashed glass. Viggo lurched through the darkness with him, out into the night, straining to fight back.

Jimmy was about to leap after them, but the first two soldiers were on their feet again, and they were shifting machine guns from their backs to their hands.

"Get down!" Jimmy roared, dropping to the carpet.

The two attackers spun for half a second, spraying machine-gun fire round the room. Jimmy heard the pounding of the bullets on the walls. A shower of concrete fragments exploded around him, but he couldn't stop moving. He rolled towards the soldiers. They were backing up to the window, about to escape the same way as their partner.

Jimmy felt his whole body pumping, every muscle responding in perfect synchrony. He rolled across the floor towards one of the ropes, just snatching a glimpse of one of the machine guns as the tip dipped, aiming for his head. Before the soldier could fire, Jimmy snatched the rope and flicked it up to catch the tip of the gun. Immediately he whipped his wrist over. The machine gun jerked out of the soldier's hands, but Jimmy wasn't finished. He kept rolling, all the time whipping the rope like he was conducting an orchestra.

In less than a second, the soldier's legs were tightly trussed up. He flailed his arms, trying to keep his balance, but with a final tug, Jimmy tripped him and jerked him towards the centre of the room for Saffron and Helen to finish tying him up.

The other soldier was about to disappear from view, but Jimmy never stopped moving. He flung himself out of the window and caught the man's rope. For a second he swung into the night, then straight away he was back, crashing into the room.

He landed on his feet and kept running, pulling the rope after him. He forced his whole body onwards, using his impetus to drag the soldier back through the window. Jimmy charged across the room, heaving on the rope. To pull the soldier far enough across the floor, Jimmy sprinted forward and took two steps up the wall in an athletic back flip. He landed with a crunch, his knee striking the soldier's chest.

"Where is she?" Jimmy shouted, spinning to survey the room. Felix and Georgie were frozen, crouched against the wall, staring into the blackness. Saffron and Helen were in the middle of the room, acting quickly to make sure both the soldiers were secure. But the small woman with the white coat was gone.

08 THEY KNOW, THEY DON'T KNOW

Jimmy was breathing hard, but he was acting automatically, the assassin in him refreshing his strategy every second. While the others crowded round the two captured attackers, Jimmy rushed back to the window. On the carpet were two small cylinders of yellow sponge – the Capita woman's earplugs. Jimmy kicked them out of the window in annoyance.

"Where did she…?" he began, but he knew there was no point.

"Sorry, Jimmy," said Saffron. "I tried to bring her down, but she was sturdy. She made it to one of the ropes." Then the purpose of the attack finally sunk in. "They've got Chris…" she gasped.

Jimmy leaned out of the jagged hole, searching the shadows below. Was Viggo still in the grounds of the building? How many other Capita fighters were waiting beneath them?

Helen pulled the torches from the soldiers' heads and set them up on the floor to illuminate the room. Jimmy turned to look at the walls. The bullet marks formed a line around the room, but it was high up. Surely if the men had wanted everybody dead they could have easily spread the gunfire. It was obvious to Jimmy that they were trained fighters. In a small room like this, with only a flimsy sofa for cover, there was no way anybody would have survived by accident.

"You left us alive," Jimmy declared. "Why? Why do you need us alive?" He strode towards the two men. They were balanced on their knees, with their arms held tightly at their sides by their own rope.

"It's OK, Jimmy," said Saffron firmly. "Let's find out what's going on." Immediately she turned and slapped one of the soldiers across the face.

Jimmy was startled by the anger in Saffron's voice. He knew Viggo had trained her over several years, and he'd even seen her impressive combat skills in action. But still he couldn't imagine Saffron using any kind of brutality to extract information from her enemies – she was the most gentle person Jimmy had ever met.

She moved round behind the two attackers and gripped the rims of their helmets, ready to rip them off. But Jimmy felt something whiz past his ear. Then came two soft thuds, one after the other. A metal rod about ten centimetres long pierced the centre of each man's flak jacket and lodged in their chests. Both men went limp and slumped forward. A pool of blood oozed into the carpet beneath them.

Jimmy's veins froze. At first nobody reacted. It was too shocking to scream. Georgie and Felix lurched backwards.

"Oh god!" Georgie gasped, her voice trembling. "What have they...?"

Jimmy spun round to see where the shots had come from. *Crossbow darts*, he heard in his head. Inside, he felt nothing. His emotions were squeezed in a tiny ball in his chest, held in place by a far more powerful physical reaction. He heard Felix puking in the corner. *Should I throw up as well?* he wondered. But the question was crushed by a new calculation – were he and his friends still in the shooter's sights? What were the sightlines? How many of them could make it to the corridor before another arrow reached them?

"Sorry..." moaned Felix, still retching. "I..."

Suddenly there was a piercing ring. It made everybody jump.

"What's that?" Felix yelled, even though it was obviously a mobile phone. "I mean, *where* is it..."

Jimmy felt his heart pounding. Somewhere in his mind he could feel an exploding horror, but it was instantly quelled by a cool wave. He watched his limbs moving as if they weren't his own, businesslike, unaffected by the murders that had just taken place less than a metre away from him. In fact, he found himself moving towards one of the men. He reached down and pulled the ringing mobile phone from under the flak jacket on one of the bodies.

Warm blood smeared the screen, but it didn't stop Jimmy answering the call.

"You should have let them go," said the person on the phone, at last. It was the woman's voice, breathy but full of confidence.

"You didn't..." Jimmy could hardly speak. He held the phone away from him for a second, clenching his face to fight back tears. "What are you doing?"

"Collecting a debt," came the reply. "Mr Viggo is going to tell us what we need to know."

"What are you talking about?!" Jimmy protested, shocked by the strength in his own voice.

"Mr Viggo should have told you while he had the chance."

"That's not funny."

"I'm not a comedian." The woman sighed. "In twenty-four hours you can have him back. Possibly alive, if he cooperates. Meanwhile, I'm giving you the chance to help him. I assume you don't have the money, but bring us the H Code."

"The what?" Jimmy exclaimed.

"The H Code. Viggo's hidden it somewhere or knows how to get it."

"How much money do you need? And what's the H Code? I've never heard of it!" Jimmy looked back to the others, but their faces were blank. "What does Chris have that you want?" He shouted the question, half into the phone and half to Saffron and his mother. Were they hiding the truth from him? Had they shared in some of Viggo's secrets? They looked just as stunned by what was happening.

"The H Code!" insisted the Capita woman. "Either Chris will tell us where it is, or you will bring it to us. If you want Chris back, you'll meet us twenty-four hours from now. Bring the H Code. Goodbye."

"Wait!" Jimmy was too late. She had disconnected. "We don't even know where to…" Jimmy frantically tried to retrieve the number from the phone – or any information at all – but there was nothing. He dropped the handset to the floor. "She's playing games!" he yelled. "She says they've taken Chris hostage until they can get what they want."

He glared at the others, anger flaring up in his belly. His mother and Saffron had slowly started dragging the bodies away, while Georgie couldn't take her eyes off the blood on the carpet. Felix was crouched in one corner, shaking his head in disbelief.

"Can't you say something!?" Jimmy shouted at them.

"Hold on, Jimmy," It was his mother. "We need a second. We're only human."

For a moment, Jimmy saw his friends with disgust. *I'm stronger*, he heard in his head. *More than human.*

"No!" he shouted out loud, forcing those thoughts away with an eruption of sheer will. Finally he pulled in a deep breath and explained, quietly, "She said to get Chris back we have to take her the H Code twenty-four hours from now."

"What's the H Code?" Saffron asked. "And where do we take it?"

Before Jimmy could even shrug, the answer came. It arrived on the end of a crossbow dart that pinged into the back wall and lodged there. Fixed to the stem was a postcard bearing an address and a single word: LOCO.

"They don't know!" wailed Christopher Viggo. "Leave them alone! They don't know!"

His arms and legs were tied to a chair and his head was covered with a black cloth bag, secured tightly at the neck. There was something warm trickling down his front, which he assumed was his own blood, but he hardly had any sensation left in his face. Somehow the pain remained, though. It seemed that the Capita were experts in their field. They'd even managed to carefully preserve his ability to speak – which was, after all, the whole point of the exercise.

"If they don't know," came a hot whisper in his ear, "that would be very convenient for you, wouldn't it?" It was the only voice he'd heard for several hours. The voice of the woman who had come to collect the Capita's debt. "Because if you're the only one who knows, that means we have to keep you alive. And yet if you're telling the truth, and your friends really don't know where to find what you owe us, then we should kill them, shouldn't we? So which is it?"

"They know," Viggo declared boldly. "Of course they know. Everybody knows."

"Stop playing games, Mr Viggo. You owe us the H Code."

"They know. They don't know. They know. They don't know." Viggo reeled off the words until they had no more meaning. The Capita may have been experts, but this wasn't the first time he had been interrogated, and he had been trained by the very best. Being an ex-NJ7 agent had some advantages at least. "They know. They don't know. They know. They don't know."

His head was growing heavier by the second. His limbs felt far away, as if they weren't attached to him any more.

He knew that was just the cocktail of drugs they'd injected into his spine. *Stay focused*, he ordered himself. "They know. They don't know." He chanted it under his breath, distracting himself by trying to deduce exactly which chemicals were in his system and when his next dose would be coming. "They know... they don't know... they know... they don't know..."

Viggo stopped when he heard the faint whir of a tiny electric motor. Were they about to subject him to a new procedure? No, it didn't sound powerful enough for that. Then came the thin voice of an old man with a strong Italian accent.

"Isn't there a more efficient way of doing this, Miranda?"

'LOCO.' Jimmy turned the postcard over in his fingers while the word revolved in his head. The lettering was ornate and gothic. Above it was a simple black and white drawing of two snakes twisted round each other up and down a microphone stand. On the back of the card was an address in North London: 5–17 Highgate Road. It wasn't an area Jimmy knew, but this was obviously a flier for one of the illegal music nights that happened all over the city.

Public performances were closely monitored by the Government, so clubs were forced to move from night to night, with bands, promoters and even the audience at risk of being arrested if they were caught. Jimmy had never really thought about it before, but it seemed likely that most of these events were run by the Capita. From what he had heard, they operated in every sphere of illegal activity in Europe.

"You should all go to bed," said Jimmy's mother, pulling him out of his thoughts.

"How am I meant to sleep?" Georgie asked. "I'm not even going back up there."

They had abandoned the apartment at the top of the building and come down to the offices in the basement. Saffron and Helen had been switching between planning their response to the Capita and looking after Felix, Georgie and Jimmy.

"Aren't you even shocked?" Georgie asked. "Did you see what they...?" She didn't finish. Her mother looked gently at her.

"I know, Georgie," she explained. "Come here." Helen pulled her daughter into a hug. "It's going to be OK. We've been through some horrible things. Things I never thought I'd see again." Her tone was soft and measured. "But don't forget I was trained for all of this once. You don't have to go back up there, but we do need to stay calm and get some rest until we can work out what we're going to do."

Jimmy looked at his mother and his sister. They had both shown themselves to be more capable than he could ever have imagined – and without the benefit of the programming in Jimmy's blood. Watching them handle this crisis made him feel proud, but it also reinforced how different they were from him now. In Jimmy, any shock or disgust at the assault on the top floor had been crushed by that swirling power inside him.

"I'm not sleeping tonight," announced Felix. Jimmy could tell he was trying to sound a lot more cheerful than he felt. His voice was trembling. "I'm going to come up with a plan. Jimmy, get me a pad of paper, some pens, paperclips, lots of elastic bands and something to eat."

"Elastic bands?" Jimmy asked.

"Never mind." The energy drained from Felix's face. "Maybe just something to eat. Except I still feel sick."

"I could never eat after…" Georgie's face was twisted in horror. "…after what we saw."

"Actually," said Saffron gently. "I think Felix is right for once. We're all in shock. Eating something will help." She quickly searched the drawers of one of the desks and gestured to the others to do the same. Within minutes, they were sitting round the largest desk with a pile of crisp packets and sweets in the centre.

"We should search the desks and computers for

information as well," said Jimmy's mum. "There has to be something in this building about Chris's arrangement with the Capita. Something about the H Code. What about in his office?"

"I'll see what I can find," said Saffron, "but he was so secretive. He refused to have his own computer in case it was hacked, and I wouldn't be surprised if he hid anything about the Capita from his advisors. After all, he hid it from me."

She turned away and started work on one of the computers, but Jimmy caught a glimpse of the heavy sadness in her eyes. She and Viggo were meant to love each other. How much of that was left after all these months of secrets and deception?

"What if it wasn't the capital?" Felix asked.

"*Capita*," Jimmy corrected him. "It means 'the head', or something..." He trailed off, lost in the memory of his encounter with the Capita's boss. Darkness had obscured the man's face, but he remembered the hoarse Italian whisper and the hiss of the man's wheelchair. His immense power had come at the expense of the use of his body. From what Jimmy had seen, the Capita boss was a head kept alive on an almost-dead body. His men even referred to him as 'The Head'.

"Whatever," Felix went on. "It might not be these 'head people'. I mean, the woman might have been lying. She could even have been from NJ7!"

"She wasn't NJ7," Jimmy said urgently. The voice was thrust from his gut before he even realised he was talking.

"I agree with Jimmy," Saffron added over her shoulder, still tapping at one of the computers. "NJ7 would have killed Chris straight away. Now the election is over, Chris will be a marked man again. But the Capita have good reason to keep him alive."

"They might even have taken him partly to protect him from NJ7," Helen added, thinking aloud. "The Government has been trying to show everybody how fair and honest they are, but now they've won it'll be time to punish their enemies. That includes Chris and anybody who supported Chris during his campaign."

Jimmy looked round at the rows and rows of empty desks. The place had obviously been abandoned in a hurry. Several chairs had been knocked over. Jimmy knew that not one person would dare turn up for work in the morning – even if it was just to collect some of the personal belongings that were strewn across the desks and the carpet.

"The Capita wants this 'H Code' from him," Jimmy muttered, "and we have twenty-four hours to deliver it to them if we want Chris back alive."

There was a deadly silence and Saffron stopped typing.

Jimmy immediately regretted what he'd said. The feeling side of him seemed cut off from the world while his calculating assassin side tried to work out what their next step should be.

"Why don't we just pay them back the money?" Felix suggested. Jimmy was grateful to his friend for breaking the silence, but not impressed by the idea.

"Yeah, nice one, Felix," he said. "Let's all chip in and see how much we've got."

"Don't you know what you could do?" Felix asked, scrunching his wild hair in his fingers. "You're sitting there with these amazing... skills, and you don't even know what to do with them. You have superpowers! Rob a bank!"

Jimmy's mum stood up straight away.

"Felix!" she cried with a laugh. "Are you serious?

"Why not?" said Felix.

"Are you a criminal all of a sudden?"

"If I need to be," Felix insisted. "If we can save Chris by paying the Capita lots of money, then we should just, you know, rob a bank or something. It's not as if we'd get caught, is it? You and Saffron could probably do it with your training, even if you didn't have Jimmy to help."

Helen waited until Felix had finished, then lowered her face and spoke softly.

"I didn't think I would have to say this, but..." She

let out a deep sigh. "...while your parents aren't here, I'm the one who's meant to be looking after you, right?"

Felix's expression changed immediately. Jimmy knew his friend thought about his parents every day. They all did. Jimmy was angry with his mum for mentioning them like this. It seemed like a cruel way to win an argument with Felix. But then he knew she was right.

"What would your mum and dad say?" Helen asked. Felix didn't need to answer. He simply shrugged, slouched in his chair and reached for a packet of crisps.

"Anyway, robbing a bank wouldn't be enough," Saffron cut in, swivelling from the computer to look at the others. "Do you know of any bank with twenty million pounds in the vault?"

"Twenty million pounds?" Jimmy gasped.

"From the look of Chris's campaign accounts," Saffron explained, "that's a rough estimate of what he's spent."

"And it's all the Capita's money?" Helen was aghast.

"For all we know it could be," said Saffron. "Everything's been pretty well disguised in these accounts. It looks like it comes from lots of unrelated donors, but..."

"...but that's just the way the Capita would operate." Jimmy finished Saffron's sentence for her. "I can't believe Chris was so stupid."

"He's not stupid," Georgie protested. "He's brave.

He needed money to try to get rid of this Government and this was probably the only way he was going to get enough."

All the information buzzed round Jimmy's head. He couldn't make sense of it.

"Twenty million pounds?" he said under his breath, half to himself. "What could be worth that much to the Capita?" Nobody had an answer. "Is there any more information on the computer network?"

"There's plenty," Saffron replied. "And we can see it all if we like. Chris may have been secretive, but he's never had a password I couldn't guess."

Jimmy jumped up with excitement. "So what does it say about—?"

"Nothing." Saffron interrupted. "I've already run every kind of search I can think of. There's no mention anywhere on the network of any code or anything to do with the letter H. No H Code. Nothing on the internet either. Well, nothing that looks relevant. But you know how useless the internet is while it's so heavily censored."

"So what can we do?" asked Georgie. Jimmy was impressed that she and Felix were regaining their composure so quickly. The image of the two dead attackers being dragged across the floor was only now starting to play on his mind. His programming was relaxing, allowing his human fears to seep through.

"What if we could get enough money?" Felix asked suddenly.

"We're not robbing a bank!" Helen laughed.

"No, you don't understand. We wouldn't need to rob a bank if we had all the Government's money. They've got billions."

"So now you want to rob the Treasury? Felix, the Government doesn't just keep all its money piled up in a vault waiting for you to go and steal it..."

"But if we *were* the Government..."

"Chris isn't Prime Minister," Georgie cut in. "Didn't you notice? He lost the election."

"But did he?" Felix scooped up the last crumbs from the bottom of his crisp packet and licked them off his fingers. "Do you really think he lost? I thought we all agreed that the Government must have rigged the election."

"That's still no good to the Capita," said Jimmy. "So it's no good for us."

"No, I think Felix has a point," said Saffron, rising slowly to pace round the table. "What if we could actually overturn the result of the election? Or at least show that the result is void and force another one? That would at least give Chris another chance to give the Capita what they want, or do... well, whatever he needs to do."

"Exactly!" Felix's face suddenly lit up with delight. Jimmy had almost forgotten how easily his friend came up with crazy schemes. But it looked like this one was being taken seriously. "The Capita only took him because he lost and can't give them this code thing," Felix went on. "Or pay them their money back. But if there's still a chance he could win an election, they might keep helping him until he won. Then he can give them whatever they want."

They all looked at each other. Jimmy could sense everybody trying to work out the flaw in Felix's logic, but there wasn't one.

"I think he's right," said Jimmy at last. "Question is: how do we overturn an election?"

"Hold on," said his mum. "Let's think about this..."

"That UN Inspector man," Georgie exclaimed. "We have to tell him."

"Tell him?" Helen frowned. "He's had an inspection team in the country for months watching everything that's been going on and they've found nothing wrong. You think if we just turn up and tell him the result was rigged he'll listen to us?"

"We don't tell him." It was Jimmy this time, his mind racing on. "He needs evidence. So let's find some." Jimmy could feel an exhilarating rush in his veins. A plan was growing in his imagination faster than he could get the words out.

"What do you mean?" Georgie asked him. Everybody leaned in closer, and he could see from their faces they were already thinking along the same lines.

"The UN team can't have watched everything," he explained.

"That's right," Saffron chipped in. "They will only have seen what Miss Bennett wanted them to see. It was a show. To demonstrate to the world how 'fair' the election was."

"So all we have to do," said Jimmy with a deep breath, "is find out how NJ7 rigged the election, get hold of the evidence and find the UN Inspector so we can show it to him."

"And we'll have to make sure the Capita know what we're doing," added Georgie.

They all looked to Jimmy's mum, as if asking her permission. She puffed out her cheeks, widened her eyes, then finally announced, "Looks like it's going to be a very busy day."

09 *MALTESE ILLUSION*

The journey from the Scottish Highlands to London had been long and uncomfortable. For two passengers on the 4.30 arriving into Kings Cross it had also been silent. Neither the man nor the woman had spoken a word. Now, they stepped off the train, blending into the small crowd with ease, having discarded their jumpsuits in the rubbish bins. Underneath they looked like any other weary businesspeople, with long, grey woollen coats. The only difference was that neither of them carried a briefcase or baggage of any kind. And they were the only two passengers shelling boiled eggs as they walked up the platform.

The smell of the eggs wafted away in the cold wind, but that was the only trace they left. They were careful to hold on to every fragment of shell, gathering it all together in their pockets while they bit into the white flesh of the eggs.

The man's straggly black hair was pulled back into a rough ponytail now, revealing a single silver stud in his left ear. His hands moved in smooth but direct bursts. There was no unnecessary action. Everything was done to maximise efficiency, but in his eyes was a vague hint of puzzlement, as if he didn't know he was watching his own limbs.

The woman next to him wore the same expression, as if neither of them could keep any thoughts in their head beyond the fact that they were shelling and eating eggs. By the time they reached the end of the platform, they had finished their first and simultaneously they each pulled out another one from a hidden pocket inside their coats.

The other passengers filtered away along the concourse, but these two stood still and faced each other. As one, they cracked into their eggs with a firm squeeze of their fists and started pulling away shards of the shell.

This time, the flesh inside wasn't white. The man's hard-boiled egg had been stained black, the woman's was a deep red. They glanced at each other, but neither of them seemed surprised. If anything, they both stood a little straighter, as if they had suddenly remembered something they had to do.

Within a few seconds they had both devoured their eggs. Then the man reached up to his left ear, to the silver stud. The woman pushed her hair back, revealing that she was wearing an identical earring. At the same moment, they squeezed their earrings between thumb and forefinger. Then, still without a word, they turned away from each other and marched in opposite directions. If all went well, they would see each other again very soon. Once two men were dead.

The drone of the vacuum cleaner drilled into Ian Coates' head.

"Why do they have to clean now?" he groaned. "It's the middle of the night!" He increased the setting on the running machine and pumped his legs harder.

"It's actually morning, sir," said William Lee softly. "People will be arriving to start work any minute."

The Prime Minister wiped the sweat from his face and glanced around him, as if searching for the daylight that he knew wouldn't be there. They were down in one of the offices of NJ7, underneath Number 10 Downing Street. It was nothing but a concrete bunker dressed up with a bit of office furniture. An empty bottle of champagne was perched at the edge of the desk. Ian Coates had been the one to ask for a running machine to be installed.

"And they have to clean up NJ7 some time," Lee added.

Coates merely grunted in response and kept running, but then a piercing voice startled them both.

"People will not be *arriving* for work." It was Miss Bennett, leaning against the wall in the open doorway. "Because nobody went home."

"What do you mean?" At the sight of Miss Bennett, Ian Coates smacked a button on the machine and slowed to a halt. He wiped his face again, as if he could wipe away his tiredness, suddenly conscious of the contrast between his own appearance and Miss Bennett's. Her hair was glossy and neat, her skin glowing. Coates was bedraggled and pale, having managed to disguise the effects of the champagne by working up a sweat on the running machine. Meanwhile, Miss Bennett, even after such a long night, looked as if she had arrived fresh from a spa break. *She doesn't need sleep*, Coates thought to himself. *Just power.*

"I mean exactly what I said, Ian," Miss Bennett explained. "I always do. Nobody went home from the party. You remember the party, don't you? The one celebrating your election victory? The one you didn't show your face at?"

Coates hated the sarcastic tone in Miss Bennett's voice.

"It was *your* victory, not mine," he muttered.

"But there were still hundreds of civil servants and politicians too afraid to go home until they congratulated you in person."

Coates shrugged and climbed down from the treadmill to towel himself off.

"We should all have gone home," said William Lee, picking up his suit jacket from the back of his chair.

"I am home!" roared the Prime Minister, taking the other two by surprise. "This is it!" He suddenly swung his arms through the air, knocking the champagne bottle to the floor, where it bounced and clanged, but didn't break. "I'm the Prime Minister! Everybody knows I live at Number 10 Downing Street. What they don't see is that the Director of NJ7..." He paused to give Miss Bennett a theatrical bow. "...runs my life from the cellar."

"Sit down before you embarrass yourself," said Miss Bennett. "I'm no good at sympathy." As she glided into the room, William Lee tried to scurry past her to leave, but she placed a firm hand on his shoulder. With that single touch, and a stare, she forced him back to his seat. "Your story breaks my heart, Prime Minister," she went on, "but you know it's a lie. If you weren't happy with the fact that NJ7 runs the country in your name, keeping you in power, you could have the whole place underwater in two minutes."

Coates waved her comment away with disgust.

"Why don't you?" she went on, mocking. "Turn the right lever and in 120 seconds all of these corridors would be flooded with Thames water. But you won't. Instead you sulk down here, worried about what the world thinks of you. Well, I can tell you what the world thinks of you. The world thinks you run Britain. Is that such a bad thing? Do you have such a terrible life?"

Coates couldn't look at her. He knew she was right. Yet he also knew she couldn't possibly understand the fears and horror in his head. As far as he knew, she'd never had a family of her own.

"Why can't I go?" asked Lee suddenly, breaking through the fog of Coates' thoughts.

"Our satellite surveillance system still isn't working properly." Miss Bennett spun on her high heels to face Lee. He was by far the physically larger of the two, but he shrunk into his chair as Miss Bennett loomed over him.

"I know," he said, a slight tremor in his voice. "I've been trying to fix it. The tech team identified a time lag on the feed, and occasional blackouts."

"The occasional blackouts are becoming more regular. If you're trying to fix it, you're making it worse." Miss Bennett leaned down until she could whisper into Lee's ear, a strand of her hair falling to irritate the man's cheek. "Maybe you should try to make the problem worse and then you'd fix it?"

A glint of hatred flared up in Lee's eye, but he gritted his teeth and forced out, "Yes, Miss Bennett."

"Our surveillance isn't working properly?" Coates gasped, just catching up with the conversation. "That's a disaster. Are we under attack?"

"No, no," said Lee quickly. "It's just a glitch. I'll fix it."

"You'd better." Coates was regaining his confidence, or perhaps the effects of a night's alcohol really were wearing off. "Without surveillance, how are we going to run the country?"

"It's all so inefficient!" added Miss Bennett. "I have assassins posted all over the place, waiting to know the whereabouts of their targets."

"Their targets?" asked Lee.

"Just get those satellites back online," Miss Bennett hissed. "We've been through one ridiculous election and, thank god, we won it. But none of us wants another one. As soon as we're back to full surveillance capacity, my agents will track down every living soul that supported our enemies. We'll eliminate every opposition candidate in a single hour."

"What about Viggo?" asked Coates, with a grimace.

"He's finished," replied Miss Bennett. "He lost. He'll never be a threat to Neo-democracy again." She ran a finger over the desktop and checked it for dust. "So we'll kill him anyway."

*

It took Jimmy only a few minutes to post a message for Eva online. He double-checked the puzzles in the back of the newspaper, placing the Sudoku squares over the crossword puzzle clues and holding them up to the light.

Only two words were clearly outlined by empty boxes: 'Maltese' and 'illusion'. Jimmy searched for them online, just as he had done every hour since that day's papers had come out, and found the same message board.

He just hoped Eva wouldn't have already moved on somewhere else – the next day's papers must have been rolling off the presses and on to the street already.

"We should leave it in code," Felix suggested, and the others had murmured their agreement.

"No time," Jimmy insisted, already typing a message. The blue tips of his fingers flashed across the keyboard. "Eva's system is safe enough. It has to be. We can't make it harder for her with a code when we need her answer right now. Anyway, I'm not going to sign the message or anything like that, and we can delete it as soon as she's read it."

They decided together to ask Eva three things. First, they needed to know the location of the central computer that had supposedly counted the votes and given out the result. Second, they needed to know where the Head UN Inspector was going to be for the rest of the day. Finally, but most important, they asked whether Eva could find evidence somewhere in NJ7 HQ or government files that the election had been rigged and get it to them.

"She must be able to uncover something," Georgie thought aloud as Jimmy typed. "I mean, she's working directly for Miss Bennett."

"That doesn't mean she can find solid evidence," Saffron pointed out. "We know how crafty Miss Bennett can be."

Crafty? Jimmy thought. *What about cruel, violent, power-hungry and evil?* He kept his head down and refocused on the computer screen.

"And even if she can find it," Helen pointed out, "it might take her longer than it would take us. She has to be discreet. Once we know where the central vote-counting system is housed, we can go straight in there and get what we want."

Jimmy was excited to hear his mum talking with such determination, even though they all knew it wouldn't be that easy.

"OK," he announced, and clicked 'post message'. "Now we wait."

"No," Saffron declared. "We get moving."

"What?"

"She's right," Helen agreed. "We know the votes were sent to a facility somewhere near Milton Keynes. The UN Inspector announced that on TV. So let's set off in that direction and check for messages on the way." She went to a laptop on one of the desks, ripped out the leads and tucked it under her arm. "Let's go. But you two stay here." She pointed firmly at Georgie and Felix.

"What?" Felix moaned.

"Mum," Georgie protested. "That's not fair. How many times do we have to show you how useful we can be?"

Helen was about to explain, but Saffron took her arm.

"I think you should stay here with them," she said, gently. The two women looked at each other for a few seconds, but Jimmy couldn't work out what they were thinking. "Three of us are trained," Saffron explained, glancing at Jimmy. He realised how strange it must be for her to describe him as 'trained' when all the skills he'd developed had come to him naturally. His 'training' took place while he slept, with electrical impulses hurtling through his muscles.

"So we're the three who should go," said Helen. "I trust Georgie and Felix to look after themselves."

"But we need someone who's trained to be in London to track the movements of the UN Inspector. Otherwise once we've got the evidence, what good will it be?"

"She's right," Jimmy cut in. "Two teams. It's more efficient." He could feel the urge to command the others bubbling up inside him. *Take control*, it seemed to whisper. *Use them.* Jimmy forced the voice away.

"Should I go with Jimmy?" said Helen, "You track the UN Inspector with Georgie and Felix."

"I can't let you do that," said Saffron.

"Why not?"

"You're his mother."

There was a long silence, but Jimmy knew exactly what Saffron was going to say.

"Your first instinct will always be to keep Jimmy safe," she explained at last. Helen didn't protest. "On a mission like this," Saffron went on, "I'll obviously try to protect my partner, but I won't be afraid to let him take care of himself, either."

Jimmy's mum was about to say something, but stopped herself. It was obvious the agent in her could see that Saffron was right, despite her instincts as a mother.

"It's OK, Mum," said Jimmy. "Saffron will make sure I'm safe."

"But I won't jeopardise the mission by worrying about my partner," Saffron added. "And if necessary..."

"If necessary what?" Helen asked. Saffron hesitated, so Jimmy replied for her.

"If it's necessary for the mission," he said, "she'll abandon me and save herself."

Nobody had an answer to that.

10 FIND SOME SHADOWS

Jimmy noticed immediately that Saffron drove just like Viggo: fast, and never in a straight line for more than a minute at a time. They were even in the same car that Viggo always drove – the racing-green Bentley Arnage T that he'd taken in a hurry years before in his first escape from NJ7.

Jimmy and Saffron were hurtling through the morning traffic roughly northwest from London, towards Milton Keynes. There was something almost aggressive about the way Saffron gripped the wheel in her fists, while Jimmy looked on from the passenger seat, the laptop perched on his knee.

Before they were forty kilometres out of London, there was a reply from Eva on the message board.

"Got it," Jimmy announced. "Chisley Hall. Eva says that's where the HERMES central computer is." It took him less than a minute to find directions online and tell

Saffron where to go. As soon as they were confident they were heading the right way, Jimmy flicked back to Eva's message.

"She doesn't know anything about the election being rigged," he said through gritted teeth. "She's says she'll try and find something."

"That's just what we thought," said Saffron. "It'll take her time."

We don't have time, Jimmy wanted to say, but Saffron's voice was soft and soothing, and he could hear the strength beneath the surface. He knew there could be nobody more determined than her to expose the truth about the election. Not only could it free the country from this dictatorship, it would save her boyfriend's life.

"Does she have the UN Inspector's schedule?" Saffron asked.

"According to this he's at the Langley Georgian Hotel at Heathrow airport and he's flying out at 5.15 this afternoon."

"We have to catch up with him before then." With every thought, Saffron seemed to press harder on the accelerator. "Text all the information to your mum. She needs to hold him there until we can get to him."

Jimmy took Saffron's mobile phone from his pocket. It was a cheap prepay phone, but decent enough for them to have been using it to connect to the internet on their journey. They'd bought a matching pair before they set off, and Helen Coates had the other one. As far as the Secret Service was concerned, the numbers would be anonymous and as long as Jimmy didn't use any dangerous keywords, his text messages wouldn't be flagged up by government computers.

Jimmy sent the text then turned back to Eva's message.

"She's put up a link." He clicked it, and found himself on the website of a company called Janua Systems. At first he couldn't work out why Eva had wanted him to see it, but finally he realised. "This is perfect," he said.

"What?"

"Eva found the website of the company that the UN used to make the HERMES voting system."

"To make it?" Saffron asked. "What do you mean?"

"Design it... build it... whatever." Jimmy was frantically clicking through the pages. "It's all here. Eva – thank you!" He clenched his fists in triumph. A flood of gratitude washed through him. For a long time he'd been amazed by Eva's bravery. Now he saw how smart she was as well. It had never even crossed his mind that information about the design of HERMES would be online.

What's more, he'd assumed that if the UN had created a new voting system, it would have been built in Switzerland or Germany or somewhere else, and its secrets would have been locked overseas, or at best on a foreign website that the British Government would have blocked. But here it all was, and now Jimmy started to understand why: the Government promoted British industry and businesses as much as they could, and excluded anything foreign. So they must have forced the UN into some kind of compromise: if there was going to be a voting system used in Britain, the UN could oversee it or even design it, but the Government would have insisted that it was British-built.

"This is just what we need," Jimmy said with confidence, finding the pages about HERMES. The company was obviously proud enough of its achievement to publicise it on the website, and presumably the Government was keen to allow a British business the chance to show off.

"It says here," Jimmy explained, his eyes flashing across the laptop screen, rapidly pulling out all the information, "that people's votes are transmitted straight from the voting kiosks to the central computer, which keeps track of everything, counts the votes and stores everything securely. But then for added security and accuracy, the kiosks themselves are brought back to the central hub and the data is uploaded directly into the HERMES mainframe from the kiosk hard drives."

"So you mean it double-checks everything?"

"Something like that." Jimmy was aware of so much information flying through his head at once he could almost feel his brain vibrating.

"So that's all we need to do," Saffron announced. "We compare the two sets of data." She powered the car forward, twisting along the minor roads that shadowed the motorway. "You find one of the voting machines and pull the raw data. I'll go straight to the central computer and find the numbers for that particular machine."

"Genius," said Jimmy. "If anybody's rigged the system, the votes cast on the kiosk won't match the votes in the central computer for that kiosk."

Jimmy understood the plan, and was already trying to work out a way to get past security. He concentrated on every sliver of doubt that crept through him. He had to trust that they could get inside, then find the right machinery and operate the system.

Finally Saffron slowed the Bentley to a crawl, pulling up to the hedge by the side of the road.

"There it is," she said softly, nodding through the branches. Jimmy's doubts suddenly doubled. On the other side of a large field he could see the top of Chisley Hall, its flagpole poking up above a high perimeter wall of old red brick. Even at this distance and with the wall blocking the view, the place was obviously huge. It had originally been a stately home, but now it served as the perfect fortress. The wall was at least twelve metres high, and curls of barbed wire had been added along the top.

They circled the roads around the estate, but all they learned was that there was no opportunity for a covert approach – the perimeter wall was separated from the roads by open fields, apart from one corner that backed on to a patch of trees that was far too thin to provide any cover. Even the wrought iron gate at the main entrance was set back at the end of a fifty metre driveway, with a longer stretch on the other side of the wall before they would reach the house itself.

"There'll be cameras," Jimmy muttered, half to himself.

"Of course," replied Saffron. She was studying what they could see of the place as intently as Jimmy. "And guards and guns and dogs and..." She turned with a smile. "...all kinds of fun."

Jimmy smiled back, then glanced up at the sky. For the first time he could remember, there wasn't a cloud in it – a perfectly clear, crisp autumn morning.

"It's not exactly dark," he said, his programming rumbling around inside him, throwing out a million reasons why this whole mission was a bad idea.

"It'll be too late by tonight," said Saffron.

"Then I guess we'll have to find some shadows," Jimmy replied, nodding slowly. "Or make them."

Jimmy crouched in the bushes, his eyes scanning the

fields around Chisley Hall. He was wrapped in a big waterproof coat with the collar turned up against the wind. Saffron had gone to buy a few items. Jimmy had given her a list that included ten more prepay mobile phones with old handsets, a large saw, some elastic bands, some paperclips, three Cornettos and as many fireworks as she could find. It wouldn't be hard, Jimmy thought. Fireworks day was coming up in a few weeks and every corner shop was already well stocked up.

Saffron had quickly worked out some of what Jimmy had planned and left him to continue circling Chisley Hall on foot, staking it out. In fact, he'd done more than that. He'd jogged round the entire area, found the nearest houses and overturned the rubbish bins from alternate homes, spreading the contents haphazardly across the street. Then he'd found a public phone box and put in a call to the local council.

"There's been a fox attack on the area," he said quickly, his voice distorting itself naturally into the deep tones of a fully-grown man. "Or teenage vandals. You need to send a rubbish truck to clear this up immediately!"

"We don't do that, sir," came the response. "We—"

"Don't you know what facility is nearby?!" Jimmy raged. "Chisley Hall is a highly sensitive government building. All this rubbish is blocking the emergency access routes! It's a security risk!"

He slammed the phone down and ran, his head pounding and his muscles aching. Now he was hoping Saffron would get back with enough time before the rubbish truck turned up. That was just phase one of his plan, and there were several more elements to be put in place. At last he heard the reassuring growl of the Bentley's V8 engine.

"Any problems?" Jimmy asked when Saffron stepped out.

She shook her head and tossed him two black plastic sacks. "Everything you need," she said. "I got it all from different stores in different towns. Nothing suspicious."

"Good." Jimmy was already tearing into one bag like he was opening presents on his birthday. He ripped open the boxes of mobile phones, stuffing the packaging back into the plastic sack, and he lined up the handsets on the grass verge.

"Better get a move on," Saffron urged. "We're not exactly inconspicuous here. We shouldn't have come in the Bentley."

"It's OK," Jimmy reassured her, kneeling over the selection of fireworks. "I've got alternative transport on the way."

"I thought you might." Without consulting him, she was ready with the toolkit from the back of the car. Jimmy took it from her with a rush of excitement. He could feel his nerves tingling, but his programming was converting any gram of anxiety into power, strength and confidence.

He programmed the numbers of the ten new phones into the phone he already had, but found as he was doing it that the information was sticking in his memory anyway. The digits seemed to lodge in his head, each one backing on to the next so there were no gaps, no blanks. When he was finished, he slipped his phone back into one of the deep pockets of his coat and looked over the other handsets, lined up on their fronts next to the pile of fireworks and a box of elastic bands. *Time for phase two,* he thought.

It was fairly simple to remove the casing from the phones and twist the paperclips to make new connections to the phone batteries. Jimmy didn't really understand what his fingers were doing until after they had done it. His hands manipulated the screwdriver and the tiny phone parts without any hesitation. Then he stripped the cardboard from the casing on several rockets and reassembled them to make nine tubes, delicately pouring in the powders from all the fireworks. Jimmy could feel his heart beating faster. *How dangerous is this?* he asked himself. He would never have been so stupid as to play with fireworks normally. But the assassin in him was executing a plan with total focus and determination.

In his head he could hear a roll call of chemicals as

his assassin instinct picked up the scent of each one. It may as well have been an alien language to Jimmy, but somewhere inside him was an expert, revelling in the names of the explosive compounds: *barium chloride, sodium nitrate, lithium carbonate...*

In no time, Jimmy had nine highly explosive rockets. With amazing precision, he attached the fuses to the wiring of the mobile phones and held everything in place with the elastic bands. Now each device could be detonated remotely with a simple phone call.

"Looks like your ride is here," said Saffron, glancing up the road. A rubbish truck was trundling in their direction, then it turned off towards the residential area where Jimmy had caused such a mess.

Without another word, Jimmy and Saffron gathered their tools and new devices into one of the plastic sacks and jumped into the Bentley. They caught up with the rubbish truck just as it turned into the first road. Faced with a street covered in rubbish, it slowed to a crawl. Saffron drew up alongside it and as soon as the passenger door of the truck opened, Jimmy burst into action.

He jumped out of the Bentley while it was still moving and ran round to the truck. The rubbish man was just climbing out of the cabin when Jimmy launched himself at him. He leapt up, caught the top of the open door and swung his feet into the centre of the man's chest.

Together they clattered back into the passenger seat and knocked the driver sideways. Both rubbish men cried out, but Jimmy immediately crushed their shouts with simultaneous jabs in the throat with the base of his palms. Both men choked for air. Jimmy knew it was only temporary. He'd struck with the precision of a surgeon and knew that they would pass out in fifteen to twenty seconds, then come round in another minute. That was all the time he needed.

Saffron appeared at the driver's door and dragged the two rubbish men from the cab. She nodded to Jimmy, acknowledging his skill and efficiency. Jimmy was already jumping down to the street and running to the first house, while Saffron took the bin men to the Bentley and bound them in gaffer tape.

When Jimmy had faked the fox attack, he'd only overturned alternate bins. Now he headed for the ones he'd left standing. He dragged the first one out to the back of the truck. The stench was thick and fruity, but it didn't bother him. Without emotion he noticed the third member of the refuse team – a fatter man that Saffron had already dealt with. He was nestled among the rubbish inside the truck, unconscious, like a baby hippo sleeping in a polluted swamp.

"Don't forget this one," Jimmy said firmly. His heart was pumping but his breathing was steady, a plume of condensation flowering from his lips with every breath. In seconds, Saffron was back with the bag of explosive devices. She tied the last man up with his colleagues while Jimmy took the first device from the bag and plunged it deep into the full bin. Then he wedged the bin upright in the back of the truck.

He did the same with seven more full dustbins, until they were all stacked up on top of each other in the truck. Meanwhile Saffron left the Bentley round the back of a line of garages, then ran out with the handsaw and the Cornettos. Jimmy took the handsaw and two of the ice creams from her as she jumped into the cabin of the truck. The engine was still running.

"South corner, twenty minutes," she called out, taking the first huge lick of her Cornetto. Jimmy gave a firm wave with the saw, ripped the top off his own ice cream, and jogged away, back in the direction of Chisley Hall. Exactly nineteen minutes later, their attack began.

11 CHISLEY HALL

Jimmy sprinted round to the southern corner of Chisley Hall just in time to see Saffron roaring up the road in the rubbish truck from the other direction. She spotted him and smiled. Immediately Jimmy signalled not to slow down. She gave a nod, and Jimmy jumped on to the back of the truck as she passed. There was no need for any more communication between them. They both knew their jobs. Jimmy could see from the back of the truck that she'd played her part so far – only one rubbish bin was left. Saffron must have distributed the others round the perimeter wall of Chisley Hall, just as she was supposed to.

Jimmy tossed his handsaw among the rubbish and brushed the leaves from his huge coat with one hand, then wiped the ice cream from round his lips. His other arm was looped round one of the pistons of the truck's dumping mechanism. His mouth and nose were filled with the rich rubbish stench.

Had he done enough to make escape possible? He wished he had more time, but time was one thing they had very little of. *I did all I could*, he told himself. It would have to be enough. He would find out for sure later. For now, the main part of the operation was just beginning, and making his escape seemed a long way off.

The truck turned the corner into the top of Chisley Hall's driveway. Jimmy knew they were only about fifty metres from the gate now. He tried to steady his nerves. His programming was rushing through him, gathering pace along with the acceleration of the truck. He felt power surging into his muscles, swamping the fear and weakness in his heart. Then he picked out the first warning. A voice bellowing through a loudspeaker came to him on the wind that swirled round his head. The words were lost, but Jimmy knew it would be a message instructing the driver of the truck to stop and turn back.

They were charging closer and closer. Jimmy forced himself to resist peering round the side of the truck to see the main gate of Chisley Hall looming towards them. Then came the second warning, this one shorter than the first – more urgent. Jimmy braced himself, ready for action, each step of what he was about to try running through his imagination. *Stay calm*, he ordered himself. *Do this one step at a time.*

A rifle shot cracked through the air. *Just another warning*, Jimmy reassured himself, and he urged the truck onwards, faster and faster. Finally a volley of gunfire blistered across the country road. Jimmy winced, certain that Saffron would have ducked down beneath the dashboard, but terrified nonetheless.

The gunfire didn't let up. They knew this was an attack now but the truck was already too fast to be stopped. There was no going back. The battle was on. Jimmy pulled out his mobile phone, scrolled to the first number and poised his thumb over the call button.

CLANG!

The truck crashed through the gates like a charging rhino. The huge wrought-iron structure buckled and twisted, desperate to hold on to its hinges. Chunks of brickwork ripped out of the wall as the gates flew into the air. Jimmy knew he was through, into the grounds of Chisley Hall. He pressed his thumb down on the call button of his phone. At the same moment, he dived from the truck and rolled across the grass. For a split second he was exposed. The truck wasn't shielding him any more, and the gunfire was thundering down from all directions. But then:

BOOM!

Jimmy's phone call connected to the device in the back of the rubbish truck. The spark from the wiring in the phone ignited the fuse, which detonated the explosives. It was perfect. The blast was magnified by the extra pressure from the device being packed into the bottom of a full rubbish bin, and as if that wasn't enough, some of the material in the bin was flammable. Jimmy had counted on that. He felt the thrill of executing a good plan to maximum effect.

The truck bucked violently in a shower of bright flashes and flames. The back end leapt off the ground until Jimmy was sure the whole thing would tip over. Immediately his view was obscured by thick black smoke – and so was the view of every security guard trying to fight off the attackers. By the time the back of the truck slammed down on the ground, Jimmy was swamped in total blackness.

He pulled himself across the turf on his front, digging in with his elbows. After a few seconds he could make out Saffron doing the same thing a few metres ahead of him. Guards were descending on the burning truck, but visibility was so bad they were in chaos. Some were shouting orders, some were firing wildly into the metal, while a few were trying to take control and warn the others away – for all they knew there were more devices hidden on the truck timed to blow up.

Jimmy coughed and spluttered in the fumes, but kept moving forward. Then, beneath the shouts and gunfire,

Jimmy picked out two sharp grunts. Saffron had struck. One of the guards had stumbled too close to her and she'd pounced, bringing the man down with a single strike, but following up with a second to be certain he was out cold. Jimmy caught up with her just in time to see her dragging the guard's uniform off him. *Quickly*, Jimmy urged in his head. *As soon as the smoke clears we're exposed.*

Saffron pulled the uniform on over her clothes and jumped to her feet. Jimmy shadowed her, staying just close enough to stay in touch, but far enough back so that whoever she came in contact with wouldn't see him.

"Man down!" Saffron yelled, deliberately stumbling and coughing. She brandished the guard's walkie-talkie above her head and headed for a second security man. "They need two more to secure the control centre! We need to get there!"

"What?" The second guard was confused. At first he swung his handgun towards Saffron, but lowered it when he could make out the uniform through the smog.

"The control centre!" Saffron repeated. "You and me. Let's go."

"The attack is here!" the man shouted back. "The control centre is..." He pulled out his walkie-talkie to check. Before he could speak, Jimmy placed another call. The sound of the second explosion came from far away on the other side of the Chisley Hall grounds, but it was powerful enough to resound in Jimmy's ears.

The guard spun round in the direction of the second explosion.

"Come on!" he shouted, and set off towards the main house, beckoning for Saffron to follow. Jimmy tore after them, shrouded in smoke. After a few metres, however, the blackness cleared and Jimmy saw Chisley Hall itself. The glory of it made him catch his breath, despite the danger. The red brick seemed to glow, while flashes of autumn sunlight pierced the smoke and picked out the cream stone trimmings. The frontage was divided into three, with each section boasting three lines of three windows. The elegant balance of the proportions made Jimmy wish he knew something about architecture – not that he had any time to admire it.

There were guards everywhere now, swarming over the plush green lawns and through the ornamental gardens. Jimmy quickly set off another explosion using his phone. The security forces turned as one in the direction of the latest blast to see a black tower of flames and smoke rising at the edge of the estate, along with a few brightly coloured sparks. The distraction was enough to cover those few vital seconds when Jimmy was exposed. He and Saffron made it to the front door of the house on the heels of the security guard, who was unknowingly acting as their guide.

To Jimmy's delight, the inside of the house was in almost as much disorder as the outside. Security guards were charging in every direction, looking totally out of place next to the wood panelling and marble floor. Stuffed heads of dead animals lined the walls, peering down on the mess, disgruntled. After a couple of seconds, Jimmy realised he didn't even need to hide himself. The guards obviously hadn't been expecting an attack – not the day *after* the election.

Jimmy kept his head down and pushed through the rush of people. He caught two female guards glancing at him, but in his pocket, his thumb was poised on the buttons of his phone. Another explosion outside quickly drew attention away from him, and in seconds he and Saffron had been led out of the entrance hall, down a dark wooden staircase.

There were more guards running ahead of them now. Four more had been enlisted by the man at the front to help secure the control centre and Saffron blended in with them effortlessly. There was too much panic for anybody to notice that her ID didn't match her face – she was neither white nor male – and obviously nobody had found the unconscious guard outside yet.

Two floors below ground level Jimmy was beginning to marvel at the unseen enormousness of the place. The kitchens and old servants' quarters stretched out in corridors that reminded Jimmy of the NJ7 labyrinth under London. While the group of guards, including Saffron, ran up one long corridor, Jimmy hid behind a huge stuffed bear until he could follow without being seen. Then his body glided forward, every muscle shifting to keep him light on his feet, moving silently.

Down another flight of stairs came the cellars. At first, they were the original cellars of the stately home, but the next level down took on a very different appearance. Instead of well-worn flagstones, stuffed animals and a wooden staircase, the deepest level had a concrete floor and modern strip lights – again, just like NJ7 HQ. It had clearly been excavated and constructed much more recently than the rest of Chisley Hall, but it wasn't modern. From the yellowing paint on the walls, Jimmy suspected it dated from the Second World War.

Jimmy felt his body preparing to strike. That throbbing violence beneath his skin bubbled constantly, building until it even seemed to infuse the breath in his lungs. The guards filed through a large black door. As soon as it shut behind them, Jimmy burst into a sprint. He heard one brief shout, then a series of grunts that echoed off the walls. He charged through the door and crashed straight into the backs of two security guards. One went down straightaway. The other tried to swivel to defend himself, but Jimmy was too fast – and unexpectedly small. The guard's fist swished well over his head, while he jammed the base of both palms into the man's gut.

Saffron had already brought down the other three guards. She was calmly collecting their walkie-talkies and making sure they were unconscious. Jimmy did the same for his two, while all the time there were two more men sitting bolt upright on swivel chairs with their hands up. These two were obviously technical staff, not security guards. Their build was much more delicate. Both wore slightly crumpled suits with ties dangling loosely from their necks. Jimmy immediately noticed a food stain on the younger man's shirt.

"Whatever you want, we'll cooperate," said the older of the two men calmly. "We don't need to be heroes. But you can't change anything now. The election's over. The votes have been counted and the result—"

"We're counting them again," Saffron interrupted. "How do we get to the machines?"

"The machines?"

Saffron slapped him across the cheek. "I thought you were cooperating?" Jimmy was shocked by her sudden but serene aggression. "The voting kiosks. Where are they?"

The two technicians were sitting with the backs of their chairs pressed up against the work station – a desk covered in a bank of monitors and four keyboards, each one with a green stripe on it. Stacked up at either end were two piles of computer hard drives with multicoloured wires spilling out of them. The constant whirring blended with the frightened panting of the two computer operators.

Saffron sighed and raised her hand, ready to administer another slap.

"OK," said the older man quickly. "I told you, I'm cooperating!"

"So…?" Saffron's open hand was still hovering over her shoulder.

"The kiosks are being decommissioned."

"Sorry, I'm not fluent in geek," Saffron replied, not dropping her hand.

"Dismantled," the younger technician cut in. "He means they're being automatically and securely taken apart. Up there." He nodded towards the corner of the room, where six metal rungs attached to the wall led to a hatch in the ceiling. "To recycle or destroy the components without exposing the sensitive data."

"Without exposing the way people really voted, you mean." Saffron gave Jimmy a nod. He was already halfway up the ladder.

"You can't go up there!" the older technician shouted. Saffron slapped him, but Jimmy noticed it was softer this time. "It doesn't matter how many times you slap me," the man protested, rubbing his cheek and cowering slightly.

"I meant it's dangerous to go up there. It's a mechanical production line and it's running. It could rip you apart."

Jimmy hesitated at the top of the ladder, his fingers hovering on the brass latch. He hadn't failed to notice the bright-orange hazard sign staring him in the face.

The moment of silence was broken by the other technician. "We can turn it off," he said quietly. Without waiting for Saffron's permission, he turned to one of the computer keyboards and tapped a few keys.

"Now *that's* cooperating," Saffron beamed. "But it does make it harder for me to do this."

"What?" Before the word had fully escaped the technicians' mouths, Saffron's hands jerked out. With two deft flicks she chopped both men in the side of the head simultaneously. She caught them as they slumped forward and settled them in their chairs, unconscious.

"Get up there, Jimmy," Saffron ordered. "If we're lucky we've got about two minutes before anybody—" She turned to see an empty ladder and an open hatch. Jimmy was already gone.

12 DECOMMISSIONED

Jimmy clambered up on to a rickety metal platform a couple of metres square. It overlooked a dimly lit, cavernous hall six metres below that must have stretched out under the whole building. A line of voting kiosks wound its way round the hall like the Great Wall of China. They were clamped on to some kind of conveyor belt that at times disappeared into huge grey blocks of machinery. *All of this just so that people can vote*, Jimmy thought.

As the production line continued, the kiosks were more and more stripped down, like bodies with the flesh removed, revealing the skeletons underneath. In fact, there were only a few left intact. *Did any of them still have the data he needed?* Jimmy wondered.

He dashed across the platform, swung himself over the safety rail and climbed down the wall to the production floor. He ran to the start of the conveyor belt, where the last few kiosks were still complete, and he could be sure they hadn't lost their hard drives yet. He searched one for an identification or serial number. He felt like he was inspecting a soldier at the head of his regiment. The serial number was on the bottom corner of the machine and as soon as he found it, Jimmy pulled out his phone. Saffron answered straightaway.

"I wasn't sure we'd have phone reception down here," she said.

"Nor me," Jimmy replied. "But I'm glad we do." He was thinking of setting off another explosion in the grounds outside to try to buy them a little more time. "I need you to find the data for voting kiosk number MA-C*080-5."

"No problem."

Jimmy still had the screwdriver on him from when he'd built the explosive devices. He knelt down at the back of the machine and cradled his phone in the crook of his neck while he unscrewed the cover on the kiosk to expose the wiring. Meanwhile, he could hear the faint tapping of keys – Saffron was playing her part at the other end of the phone. But while Saffron could simply download the data on to a flash drive, Jimmy had no way of powering up the kiosk to try hacking the software. He'd come prepared to dismantle the guts of the machine and find its hard drive. That's where the raw data would be stored – the actual votes that people had made in the election. And that's what he would need the UN Inspector to compare to the data Saffron found. "How you doing?" Jimmy asked, teasing out the wires of the kiosk with his screwdriver.

"I'm nearly there," Saffron replied. "Just a few codes to get through…"

Jimmy felt a smile creep on to his face, despite the tension in his chest. His hands were steady and it felt like the screwdriver was simply an extension of his finger. He reached deep into the kiosk and pulled out the components one by one, aware that somewhere in his head he knew what each part was and that his instincts were using that knowledge to navigate towards the hard drive. He could almost hear a whisper, listing the components as he removed them: *motherboard, sound card, fan…*

Then suddenly that whisper was torn apart by a sound at the other end of the phone. It was a muffled thud. Jimmy's muscles froze. "Saffron?" he whispered, gripping the phone tightly in his fist. Then came more noises – a crash, then shouts. Was that Saffron's voice?

Jimmy jumped to his feet and dashed towards the platform. Had they found Saffron so quickly? Just then, two huge security guards climbed up out of the hatch and stood on the platform, peering out into the murky hall, their guns held out in front of them. Jimmy spun to run back the other way, but he was too late.

"There!" one of the guards shouted. It was drowned out by the crack of his gun. Jimmy dived for the cover of the kiosks. The bullets pinged off the metal in rapid succession. Jimmy instinctively curled himself up as small as possible behind one of the kiosks and covered his head with his hands, but his programming was burning in his veins. He could already hear the guards descending from the viewing platform to hunt him down. Then the echo of the shots faded, drowned out by a huge creak and a succession of clunks. The conveyor belt Jimmy was crouching on started moving.

Jimmy peered round the side of the kiosk and immediately regretted it. The blast of a guard's gun lit up the hall. Jimmy leapt backwards just in time. The bullet struck the kiosk close enough to his face for a spark to hit his cheek. Jimmy glanced down the production line, where, one by one, the kiosks filed into the gaping mouth of the first piece of machinery that would decommission them. A curtain of rubber strips meant Jimmy couldn't see what happened inside, but he could feel an intense heat and it was getting stronger as the conveyor belt took him closer to the machinery.

The kiosk he'd been dismantling was a few metres further down the line, in the direction of the decommissioning mechanism. *The hard drive*, Jimmy thought. Meanwhile, beneath the cacophony of the production line he could hear the guards descending on him from the other direction.

Another flash lit up the darkness and gunfire peppered the kiosks. The guards were shooting at any change in the shadows. Jimmy felt a throbbing urgency in his chest. He couldn't stay sheltered behind this kiosk for much longer, and the hard drives he needed so badly were seconds away from entering the decommissioning unit. He knew he had no choice.

Jimmy took a deep breath, set his muscles, then exploded into a sprint down the conveyor belt. Gunfire flashed around him, but Jimmy paused for a fraction of a second behind each kiosk, rolling and ducking to create a totally irregular path. There was no way the guards could hit their target. But perhaps they wouldn't need to. The last kiosks were entering the machine now. On either side, bright-orange hazard signs burned into Jimmy's consciousness as intensely as the flashes from the gunfire.

"Saffron!" he shouted into his phone, still clutched in his fist. "Saffron, what's happening?! Are you there?!" For a split second, Jimmy thought he heard a response, but the voice, if it was a voice, cracked up. And that's when Jimmy finally ran out of space. He felt the rubber strips pushing on his shoulders. They came with a surge in the noise and the heat. Jimmy frantically tried to work out some way of stopping the conveyor belt, or jumping off it without getting shot. But it was too late. Suddenly he was inside the machine, and everything happened at once.

A burst of high-pressure steam blasted towards Jimmy's head. He rocked backwards so quickly he didn't even know what he was reacting to until the steam roared past the end of his nose. It felt like the sweat on his face was so hot it was bubbling. At the same time two metal arms punched towards the kiosks from either side at the level of Jimmy's knees. He jumped up, ducking his head at the same time so he didn't knock himself out on the low ceiling.

The arms clamped on to the base of the kiosk in front of him, ripped off the casing, spun it round and slammed it down flat on the conveyor belt. Then, with despair, Jimmy saw the hard drive extracted by another metal arm and flung up into a slot overhead. *Where does that slot go?* Jimmy cried in his head. There was no time to find out. The conveyor belt moved on, with metal arms swinging out from every direction to continue the dismantling.

Jimmy swivelled and twisted to dodge the mechanical blows and spray bursts of some kind of coolant. All he could feel was heat and the swirling movement of his own limbs, swishing and leaping so quickly that his head spun. His coat wafted around him like the wings of a bat. At first it protected him from the heat, but soon he wanted to rip it off and abandon it. He knew he couldn't. He could feel the weight in the pockets of objects that could save his life.

Eventually the attack paused and Jimmy found himself lying flat on his front, on top of two sheets of metal from the casing of one of the kiosks. The clanking and crunching of the mechanical arms was left behind. Jimmy looked up, searching for the hard drives. Was there any chance they hadn't all already been wiped or destroyed? That moment, a few metres ahead, a huge iron press slammed down like the fist of a giant squashing a beetle. It was crushing the kiosk casing into totally flat sheets of blue metal, and Jimmy was next.

He threw himself forward and pulled his legs up into his chest just as he hit the conveyor belt. The iron press thumped into the rubber behind him. The conveyor belt took him past the first stage of machinery, but there was another tunnel coming up and another rubber curtain. He snatched one of the flat sheets of blue metal just before it was sucked through the rubber curtain. Then he jumped down off the conveyor belt and ran.

It was a couple of seconds before the guards realised what was happening. They hadn't expected Jimmy to emerge from the decommissioning tunnel in one piece. When they finally spotted him, all they saw was the flash of metal. Jimmy blazed through the darkness, holding the metal sheet ahead of him with one hand while with the other he hauled himself up the outside of the decommissioning machine he'd just been through. Despite the bullets, the heat and the strain on his muscles, he was totally focused on leaving Chisley Hall with the hard drive from one of the kiosks.

At the top of the machine were dozens of chutes where the inner components of the kiosks were sorted and zipped away to the next stage in the process. The hard drives were small black boxes being spat out of the machine so fast they may as well have been giant bullets. So that's what Jimmy used them for.

He heaved his whole body up and swung round, landing a double-footed kick against the chutes on top of the machine. The force of one blow was enough to dislodge the chutes. The mechanism screeched and clanked, but the kiosk components kept firing, a shower of metal blocks, circuit boards and electrical tubing.

The guards were bombarded by the parts being spat out across the hall. They ran for cover, while Jimmy jumped down, shielding himself with his metal sheet. Before the guards could start shooting again, Jimmy reached into his coat. He gripped a cardboard tube strapped by elastic bands to a mobile phone: one explosive device that Jimmy had kept with him instead of sending on the rubbish truck for Saffron to distribute around the grounds.

Immediately Jimmy lobbed the device over his head

like a grenade. The arc of his arm was perfectly steady despite the speed he was running. The explosive device soared through the falling debris, over the heads of more guards who'd appeared on the viewing platform. It dropped perfectly – right down the hatch that led back to the control room.

Jimmy's fist was already clenched round his mobile phone, his thumb pressing the call button so hard the handset was about to crack. *Where's the explosion?* Jimmy thought, frantically. The delay seemed to last forever. Had his phone lost reception? He had to keep moving, sprinting between the machinery from shadow to shadow, dodging the bullets or shielding himself with his metal sheet, all the time running towards the platform where the guards loomed over him, towards the guns, but also towards his only possible escape.

Finally the floor rocked. A massive white flash blasted round the hall. Then came the noise – a thunderous crack that echoed off the machinery and resounded in Jimmy's skull. A shaft of black smoke rushed up from the hatch, pouring into the hall. Jimmy powered through it, skipping over the guards, who'd been blown off their feet or fallen from the platform. On his way he snatched a stray hard drive from the floor and stuffed it into his pocket.

In seconds, he was through the hatch. He was choking on the black smoke as he locked the hatch behind him, but he was buzzing with new focus. *Get what you came for*, he told himself. Getting in and out of Chisley Hall was useless unless he could somehow salvage all the data he needed. Unfortunately, the blast hadn't just allowed Jimmy to evade the security force. It had also ripped apart the network of computers in the control room.

Jimmy peered through the smoke, covering his mouth and spluttering with every other breath. The monitors were smashed. The keyboards were nothing but melted plastic. How could he have been so stupid? He'd assumed that Saffron hadn't been in the room, but he hadn't thought about the damage to the computers. Desperately trying to keep himself calm, he wafted the smoke away from the work station to get a better look at the equipment. Had any of it survived?

A noise pricked his senses. Boots pounding up the hall. There was no time to analyse the computer system. Jimmy reached to the very back of the desk and snatched the one metal box that looked more intact than any of the others. He ripped it out of the tangle of half-melted leads, tucked it under his arm, then barged out into the corridor to meet the guards.

13 CHECKING OUT

Jimmy raced through the grounds of Chisley Hall, constantly scanning the surroundings to judge the timing of his explosions. He set off two in quick succession, distracting and dispersing the security force. One of the earlier blasts had sparked a small fire. The flames were just visible, threatening to leap over from outside the wall into the gardens. *Chaos*, thought Jimmy. *Perfect.*

He twisted through a walled rose garden, crunching the gravel with confidence and strength. His pre-planned escape route was waiting, and there was nothing to get in his way. If only he could be as certain that Saffron had escaped ahead of him. Where was she?

For Jimmy, getting out of the house had been a relatively simple matter of using the narrow corridors to his advantage. One attacker at a time, he'd fought his way out with a minimum of fuss and a maximum of efficiency. Chisley Hall may have been a fortress, but it wasn't designed to defend against attackers who were already inside.

He emerged from the rose garden by the perimeter wall, but his pace never relented. He ran through the flowerbeds along the line of the wall, flicking his eyes ahead, searching for his marker. Less than an hour before, he'd found the only corner of the estate that met woodland, not open field, and he'd expertly cut the branches of the trees outside the wall. He'd created a blind tunnel – a passage away from the perimeter wall that was completely masked from the security cameras. As long as he found that spot again, he'd be invisible.

There it was: the white streak down the wall that told him where to climb. Slipped between curls of barbed wire at the top of the wall was the upturned cone of the third Cornetto, the ice-cream filling melted into a clear marker-line down the brickwork.

In seconds Jimmy scaled the wall, one-handed: the box of the computer was held firm under his left arm. The fingers of his right hand dug into the bricks like tunnelling worms, sending tiny cascades of red dust to the ground and gradually accumulating a sticky covering of vanilla ice cream.

At the top, he perched precariously and laid his coat over the barbed wire. He pulled himself over the wall without hesitation, leaving behind the shouts of panic and the sirens. His only obstacle was a fat wood pigeon trying to get to the Cornetto cone. The swivelling security cameras held no threat for him. His preparation with the handsaw had been perfect.

As he scrambled over the bracken, Jimmy pulled his coat back on and awkwardly snatched his phone from the pocket, still careful to keep hold of the computer, and checking that the kiosk hard drive was still in his pocket. The responsibility of carrying people's votes seemed to make all the equipment heavier.

"Where are you?" he barked as soon as Saffron picked up. He hadn't expected her to answer. If she was able to answer her phone it meant she wasn't in danger, and if she wasn't in danger, why hadn't she been there to help him?

"I made it out, Jimmy," she announced, "I'm OK."

For a second Jimmy was angry that she'd assumed he would be OK. He swallowed the emotion and ran on, batting away branches from his face.

"You need to come back here and pick me up." Jimmy glanced around him. Something in his body had kept track of his precise position. "I'm halfway across the field a kilometre to the south of Chisley Hall. I can see a road up ahead. What happened to you? Did you get the data?"

"I'm sorry, Jimmy," said Saffron. "There were too many of them. They dragged me out of the control room and up to a holding cell. But they couldn't hold me." Now Jimmy could hear the smile in her voice. "It sounded like there was an explosion in the basement, and they panicked."

"I'm glad I could help," Jimmy muttered. "Did it cross your mind that I could have been in trouble?"

"Why would anybody but you be blowing things up in the basement?" Saffron asked with a soft laugh. When Jimmy heard her voice again, it wasn't through the phone. "And if you're blowing things up I know you're OK," she called out from the window of the Bentley, pulling up on the other side of the road. Jimmy's face melted into a grin.

"So stop moaning and get in," said Saffron.

Christopher Viggo listened to his own heartbeat, consciously willing it to slow down. He breathed deeply, counting the rhythm of his pulse. He didn't know exactly what the Capita had injected into his spine, but whatever it was he had to delay its course through his body. He had to stay focused, stay functioning, and reveal nothing about the H Code. His life depended on it, and so did the lives of Jimmy and all the others. If he revealed his secret, they would be killed as soon as they turned up at the rendezvous.

Viggo couldn't see anything because of the black linen

bag tied over his head, so he focused on his other senses. He knew his wrists were bound together behind his back and his ankles were tied to the chair legs. But what had the Capita used for ties? If he could work that out he'd know whether it was worth trying to free himself – and what he would need to do.

Just as he started rubbing his wrists together to test the bindings, he heard the door open.

"Ready for more?" It was the small Capita woman called Miranda by her colleagues. "You should find it very easy to talk to me now. You can't fight what's in your bloodstream." Viggo didn't respond. Instead he listened. Every piece of information was a vital weapon in his war to stay conscious, to keep his secrets and ultimately, to escape.

"Where is the H Code?" Miranda asked, with a sigh. When there was no reply, she muttered, "You're a fool."

"What does that make you?" Viggo rasped. His throat was so dry, but he couldn't let his weakness show.

Miranda said nothing. Instead, she slammed her fist into Viggo's stomach. Viggo gasped for air and strained to double over, but the wrist and ankle restraints held him in place. *Pain is good*, he told himself. *Pain will keep you focused.*

"How does your precious democracy feel now?" Miranda snorted. "Come on, you had your chance to change the world. You failed. You must be hungry, thirsty... in pain. Give it up," she insisted. "Give us the H Code and you can go home."

Viggo heard the clink of glass.

"Tell me now and we can share a lemonade," said Miranda. Viggo heard her scrape the bottle against the wall to remove the cap. The cool fizz of the drink seemed to rush through Viggo's blood, spreading pain, desperation. *No*, he told himself. *The others will come. Hold on. Just a little longer.* But the noises tormented him: Miranda glugging the liquid down her neck, her satisfied sigh, the metal bottle cap still tinkling on the concrete floor.

"A toast," Miranda announced. "To democracy!"

Without even waiting for Viggo to respond, she thumped the base of the lemonade bottle into his cheek so hard that he reeled backwards and toppled to the floor, still attached to the chair.

Rope, Viggo realised at last, crashing on to the concrete. *They've used rope.*

"How long until the meeting with the Capita?" Jimmy asked, as the countryside rushed past at Saffron's usual sharp pace.

"Long enough," said Saffron. "We need to get this stuff straight to the UN Inspector first."

"What if we have... nothing." He drummed his fingers on the black computer box in his lap, while the smaller hard drive nestled in his coat pocket.

"We have no choice," Saffron said, not sounding certain. From her face, she was obviously still working things out in her head.

"But what if we give it to the UN guy," said Jimmy softly, gathering his composure, "tell him everything we know to convince him to have a look at it, then when he does it turns out to be full of, I dunno, the laundry receipts. We'll be going in to face the Capita with nothing!"

"There must be *something* on there," Saffron muttered, sounding like she was trying to convince herself.

Jimmy smoothed his hands across the metal casing, brushing off the dust and debris from his escape from Chisley Hall. They had to take the risk of presenting what they had to the UN Inspector while they could still get to him. If they had nothing, at least they might convince the man to investigate further. *We'll be persuasive*, Jimmy thought, in a voice that wasn't his own. It felt vicious, determined. But it felt so right.

"I'll text Mum," he announced suddenly, trying to distract himself from the violence lurking inside. "I'll tell her we got it." He pulled out his phone and started texting. "They'll need to keep the UN guy at the hotel until we get there. How long?"

"Am I driving too slowly for you?" Saffron slammed her foot down and the Bentley smoothly surged forward. It was like sitting in a rocket – a rocket with heated seats and full leather interior.

Another plane ripped through the clouds overhead and Georgie couldn't help following it with her binoculars.

"This one's going to Spain," she muttered, not expecting her mother to hear. Georgie's binoculars were pressed up against the window, which she could feel vibrating with the drone of the plane even though it was the thickest pane of glass she'd ever seen. Helen Coates was sitting on the bed behind her, checking her phone.

"Keep your eyes on the limos," she said firmly.

They were on the fifth floor of the hotel opposite the Langley Georgian, in the cheapest room available that overlooked the Langley's forecourt. Georgie swivelled the binoculars back to where they were meant to be aimed.

"They're on their way," Helen announced, a slight tremor in her voice.

"Did they get it?" Georgie asked.

Helen took a deep breath. "Jimmy said they did," she sighed, not at all convinced.

"That's great!" Georgie turned from the window and was surprised by the serious expression on her mum's face. "Isn't it?"

"We'll see," said Helen calmly. "It's only half the job, isn't it? It's going to take them a while to get here. An hour or two at least. According to Eva, Dr Longville's meant to leave on a plane in forty minutes." She let the numbers hang in the air for a moment, then nodded towards the window. "Keep watching the drivers. They'll tell us when our target's on his way down."

Georgie didn't need to keep watching much longer.

"I think it's happening," she said less than a minute later. "They both just got a phone call within a few seconds of each other."

"Now what are they doing?" Helen jumped up and joined her daughter at the window.

"The one that's been asleep for ages is putting his tie back on. The other one's checking himself in the rear-view mirror."

"Signal Felix," Helen ordered. "Time to move."

Felix wandered through the corridors of the Langley Georgian Hotel, which stretched out for what seemed like miles. He had never seen a hotel so big, nor one with a fountain and a grand piano in the lobby. But now he felt like the carpeted quiet was closing in around him, stifling his breathing. He knew that at every step he was being tracked by cameras. How much longer did he have to pretend to be making his way to his parents' room? If any hotel staff happened to notice him on surveillance, his casual air wouldn't help him. He'd be challenged. Politely at first, but then he'd quickly be in trouble.

He could feel the sweat crawling down his neck. From somewhere the drone of a Hoover started up. Felix had already passed two cleaners, one of whom had eyed him suspiciously. He hoped his smile had been enough to stop her enquiring about him. Now that noise drilled into his head. *How does Jimmy live like this all the time?* he asked himself. Suddenly he jumped and let out a silent gasp. It was a moment before he realised that what had shocked him was the vibration of his mobile phone in his pocket.

It buzzed once, then stopped. That was the only signal he needed. It was time to move. He picked up his pace and strode towards the lobby. He got there just in time to see Dr Newton Longville, Chief UN Inspector, exiting the lifts with an entourage of three other men. *Security*, Felix realised with a jolt of panic. But he couldn't change his plan now. Dr Longville was already marching past the fountain towards the door. In another second he'd be gone, and any chance of exposing the corruption of the election would go with him.

"Dr Longville," Felix panted, scampering after him. Two of the security agents swivelled to face him. Longville just glanced over his shoulder, while the third security guard stood in the doorway. All around them hotel staff looked on. The receptionists obviously weren't sure whether to intervene. If anybody else had tried to intercept such an important American guest, the security guards and the hotel staff would instantly have swooped into action to put a stop to it. But this was a child. And that had made them hesitate. That's why Helen had sent Felix to do the job. He could still hear her instructions in his mind: *you have to delay him. Do whatever you can to keep him at the hotel.* It had sounded to simple, but now Felix could feel everybody's eyes on him. *Time for a show*, he thought.

"Dr Longville," he said again, "I've been waiting just to see you. I want to be a politician when I grow up." Felix put on his goofiest grin, but the security guards didn't relax a muscle. "What do you think I—" Suddenly he grasped his throat. A violent cough lurched out of his chest, jerking his whole body. He spun a half turn and collapsed on the floor, gasping for breath. "Help!" he wheezed between desperate heaves. He writhed on the floor, spluttering, "Help me, doctor!" and clawed at his own chest as if he was trying to massage his heart.

"I'm not a medical doctor," Longville explained calmly. "I have a PhD in Political Philosophy. I can't help you." He turned to reception. "Call an ambulance!"

Felix stopped squirming. "Wait," he gasped. "I think I'm OK."

"What a miracle," said the American in a flat tone. "Thank you for the entertainment, but now I have to go. My plane is leaving."

Felix jumped to his feet and watched Dr Longville gliding through the hotel doors towards a waiting limousine. *I'm so stupid!* Felix screamed inside his head. *Why didn't I realise he wasn't a real doctor!?* He ran for the door and stepped outside just as Dr Longville was sliding himself into the back of the limo. Felix's first instinct was to pull him back, but one of the security guards was holding the car door. At last, Felix blurted out,

"The election was fixed!"

The limo door slammed shut.

14 *YOU'RE RIGHT, BUT YOU'RE WRONG*

"What's happening?" Georgie asked, her face pressed up against the window. Helen had taken the binoculars so now the figures below were too small for her to work out what was going on. She could just make out Felix's performance in the lobby of the Langley Georgian, but the reflection in the glass frontage of the hotel made everything unclear. Then she saw Dr Longville rushing outside with his security guards to get into the limo.

"He didn't do it," Helen said, fear in her voice. "Felix didn't stop him."

That's when Felix burst into the street.

"What's he saying?" Georgie asked.

"Wait – Longville's getting out of the car." Helen leaned forward in her excitement, knocking the binoculars against the window.

"I can see that!" Georgie cried, exasperated. "Why? What are they saying?"

When the limo door opened again and Dr Longville stepped out, Felix had to catch his breath. The man brushed his security guard out of the way and stepped right up to Felix. Suddenly pretending to be suffering some kind of fatal attack seemed easy. This was the real performance, thought Felix.

"It's true," he said quietly. "I can give you proof, but my friend has it. He's on his way. He'll be here any minute. You have to wait for him." All his words tumbled over each other as Dr Longville's huge grey eyes looked him up and down. "Seriously," Felix continued, "he'll be here. He's bringing the evidence. The whole election. It was, like, rigged. What have you got to lose? Miss your flight. Get the next one. It's all paid for by some government anyway, right?"

Dr Longville drew himself up to his full height and raised his eyebrows. When he spoke it was slow and quiet.

"Some government?" he repeated. "You mean the United Nations?"

"Er, yeah. Same thing."

"Same thing?" Longville ran his hands over his head. "It is most definitely not the same thing. I thought you wanted to be a politician."

"I lied."

"Well that's a good start." A smile creased Longville's already lined face.

"But I'm not lying about this," said Felix emphatically. "Even if I am, you'll find out for sure in a few minutes, and what's the worst that can happen? You'll miss checking in for your flight. So what? And if I'm telling the truth, you'll have evidence that the whole election was fixed."

Longville looked all around him and seemed to give some sign to the security guards. Felix braced himself, flooded with the wish that he could find the powers inside him that Jimmy could call on. He closed his eyes and waited for the grip of the guards. After a few seconds he opened them again to see that two guards were unloading the back of the car and the third was inside talking to the receptionist. Dr Longville was still standing over him.

"I don't need to check in for my flight, young man," said the Inspector with a slight smile. "My car takes me straight on to the runway and the plane waits." He leaned down to come face to face with Felix. "So it can wait a little longer, can't it?" Before he stood upright again he glanced round and dropped his voice to a whisper. "My assistant is clearing things with the hotel." His words were almost lost in the wind, but there was a gleam of excitement in his eyes. "So we can find a place to talk."

*

Jimmy and Saffron were silent for a long time. Even the noise of the road rushing under them was muffled by the plush insulation of the Bentley. In the near silence, Jimmy couldn't stop his mind circling through all his fears. He stared out of the window, letting the world fall into a blur. Everything he saw reminded him of the danger facing the entire country, but if he closed his eyes, the danger inside him was so much worse.

"It was the right decision, you know," Saffron said out of the blue. Jimmy was startled. She obviously thought he was still sulking about her leaving him behind to fight his way out of Chisley Hall alone.

"Yeah, I know," Jimmy said, sincerely.

"And it's exactly why I said your mum had to stay in London." It sounded like Saffron was trying to justify things to herself, not to Jimmy. "She would have gone back for you. It would have put you both in more trouble and threatened the whole mission."

"Forget it," Jimmy insisted. "I know." He desperately tried to think of some way of changing the subject. "We did the best we could, right? Now we have to get Chris back." Then he added, with a dry laugh, "Somehow."

"You're right," Saffron said quickly, even smiling a little.

"And then make him Prime Minister." Jimmy was surprised at his own words. He didn't know what had made him say that. Perhaps the doubts at the back of his mind were stronger than he realised – was he testing Saffron? Immediately he saw those doubts flash across her face.

"Jimmy..." she began, tentatively. "Do you think..." She trailed off with a sigh.

"What?" Jimmy asked gently.

"It's nothing. It's just that, you know, we're doing all this for Chris, but lately he's been a bit, well..."

"I know." Jimmy was relieved to hear that Saffron hadn't been ignoring Viggo's erratic behaviour. Jimmy suspected they were all doubting whether he was still the man to rescue Britain from Neo-democracy – the system that had abolished voting entirely until this election. Could they rely on Viggo to lead the nation? If he was like this when he was campaigning for the election, what would he be like in power?

"But we still have to rescue him. Even if he can't save the country..." Jimmy's thoughts were hazy, as if he was trying to work out how he felt at the same time as the words were leaving his mouth. "...we still have to save him, right?"

"Of course." Saffron jerked round a sharp bend in the road. "But if he's no good for the country, and if he and I don't..." She turned away, pretending to check her mirror, but Jimmy had already seen the battle raging in her eyes.

"It's OK," Jimmy whispered. "We're going to save him."

Saffron's reply came quickly in the strong voice that she usually saved for combat situations:

"We'll save him," she confirmed. "But then what will we do with him?"

The steam room in the hotel spa was the perfect place to talk. The air was so thick with steam that Felix could hardly see his own knees, let alone get caught on any cameras. He was sweating more than he had ever done in his life and every breath pulled the intense, damp heat into his lungs. He was starting to question his decision to keep his clothes on. Nonetheless, the important thing was that nobody could watch them or listen in on the conversation.

"How long?" Dr Longville asked, panting. He wafted the steam away from his face. In the momentary clearing, Felix caught a glimpse of the man's greying chest and the small pot belly that hung over the top of his towel, gleaming with sweat. The sight made Felix queasy and he wished he could un-see it.

"I don't know," Felix admitted, "but he's on his way." He slipped his phone from his pocket to check for messages, hoping the steam would hide his anxiety. With frustration, he saw there was no phone reception. He'd sent a text to Helen Coates just before coming into the steam room to tell her what was going on. He had faith that she'd pass the message on to Jimmy and Saffron, but the wait for news was becoming agony.

Two of the security guards were in the steam room with them, on either side of Dr Longville, while the third waited outside the door. Like Felix they were also fully dressed. Felix searched through the steam to try to get a look at one of their faces. At least their discomfort would distract from his own.

Suddenly there was a loud clunk from outside. Through the frosted glass door, Felix saw the smudged shadow of the security guard keel to one side, then slump to the floor. The door burst open with a rush of cold air. Felix sucked in a deep breath, glad for the cool relief. As the steam twisted and danced, Felix's face melted into a huge grin. In the doorway was the familiar silhouette of his best friend.

"He wouldn't let me in," Jimmy announced, nodding to the unconscious mound of the guard at his feet. He stepped over it and let the door shut behind him.

"He's just cautious I guess," Dr Longville replied, his American twang making it sound like the first line of a song.

"Do you have it?" Felix panted, jumping towards Jimmy. He reached out for the black metal box under Jimmy's arm. "Is this it?"

Jimmy hesitated. Only Felix was close enough to see the uncertainty in his friend's face.

"Dr Longville," Jimmy declared in a commanding voice, all the time exchanging doubtful glances with Felix. "I've brought something that you have to see." He held out the metal box and pulled the kiosk hard drive from his pocket. "Do you have a laptop?"

Within seconds they all reassembled in the men's changing room.

"Where's Saffron?" Felix whispered.

"The men's and women's saunas are separate," Jimmy replied. "She couldn't come in with me."

"We'll be able to talk in here," Longville cut in. "There are no surveillance cameras in a locker room." He perched on the edge of a bench, still dressed only in his towel, and took the two hard drives from Jimmy, nodding to one of his security team at the same time. The guard knelt down and brought out a laptop case from one of the lockers. "Where did these hard drives come from?" Longville asked, examining it. "How did you get them, and what exactly do you claim is on them?"

Jimmy took a deep breath. He wasn't sure how much information to reveal.

"They're part of the Government's voting system," he explained at last.

Longville's face fell. He closed his eyes for a moment.

"I really thought you were going to give me something," he muttered. "Something that could bring down this..." His voice grew in anger, but he cut himself off before it could bubble over. "You're wasting my time," he announced softly, putting the computer equipment to one side and standing up to start putting his clothes back on. "I helped design that system. It's securely and secretly housed..."

"At Chisley Hall," Jimmy cut in. "I know. That's where I got these."

Longville's cheeks, which had been flushed red from the sauna, drained to paper white. His lips twitched as if he wanted to say something but his brain wasn't providing the words.

"This is from one of the kiosks," Jimmy went on, "and this is part of the main computer system." He picked up the hard drives he'd carried from Milton Keynes and shoved them roughly back into Dr Longville's hands. "Look at them." The heat rose up in Jimmy's veins, and it wasn't from having been in the sauna. "The election was fixed!" He started pulling leads and wires from the laptop bag.

"HERMES..." Longville muttered. He dropped his eyes to look at the computer boxes in his hands. "You...?" He slowly lowered himself back to the bench, suddenly looking a hundred years older. "HERMES is..."

"HERMES is in need of a bit of repair, I'm afraid," said Jimmy awkwardly. He glanced at Felix, who gave him a firm nod of solidarity.

"I bet you blew it up," Felix whispered, far too loud. "Did you? Did you blow it up?"

Jimmy's gave a sheepish smile and shrugged.

"Yes!" Felix hissed, clenching a fist. "That's so cool."

That moment, the door of the changing room creaked open and the bodyguard that Jimmy had knocked out staggered in. His appearance seemed to bring Dr Longville out of a trance.

"Stay outside," he ordered, full of excitement again. "Guard the door and do a better job this time."

The security man shrunk away again. Longville and Jimmy set about the leads. At first Jimmy was baffled by the different connections and exposed wires, especially on the hard drive from the voting kiosk. There was no obvious way of connecting it to the other machines. But his hands moved confidently, guided by the unseen technical knowledge locked in his brain.

Dr Longville clearly knew what he was doing as well. "We'll connect everything up," he said, breathlessly. "If you took these by force then we don't have much time. NJ7 will find out my flight hasn't left the ground and if they're good they'll link it to what you've done." He looked up for a moment, his eyes expanding to stare into Jimmy's. "And they're very, very good."

Jimmy felt Dr Longville's fear. The man had no way

of knowing that Jimmy lived every day with first-hand experience of exactly how good NJ7 were. There was never a break. No relief. They were in Jimmy's thoughts every second. Every moment of his life he was running from their weapons.

"This could bring them down," Jimmy whispered, his voice hoarse.

"If there's anything to find, I'll find it." Dr Longville powered up the laptop, which now had six separate cables running between it and the backs of the two hard drives from Chisley Hall.

Jimmy and Felix instinctively moved closer to look at the screen over Dr Longville's shoulders. The Inspector's hands floated over the laptop keyboard. His fingers were as long and bony as his nose. They danced across the keys like snow-covered twigs shaking in the wind.

Jimmy watched the screen intently. The software felt unfamiliar to him but as each new grid or number chain flashed up he could feel the shadows of his mind sucking up the figures, manipulating them like children's toys. The pace was relentless. More and more numbers flew through his brain, crashing against the insides of his skull. *Enough*, he screamed to himself. He forced himself to close his eyes and staggered back to sit on one of the benches. His head was suddenly searing with pain and he thought another nosebleed might be coming on.

"You OK?" Felix asked. Jimmy nodded, but couldn't make eye contact.

"I'm past the encryption," Dr Longville announced without any triumph.

"That was quick," said Felix.

The doctor smiled. "I wrote the codes."

"So what have you found?"

"This might take a few minutes." Dr Longville hit the return key with a flourish and leaned back to button his shirt. "It has to search both hard drives in their entirety and compare them to the outline back-up systems that I have on my laptop. That will tell us whether they're operating correctly, but then my laptop will compare the two sets of data on the hard drives to each other. That will tell us whether the numbers of votes tally."

"Then we'll know." Jimmy could feel himself growing more and more agitated. His programming was telling him to move. It went against every one of his assassin instincts to stay trapped in this small room for any length of time without being able to see whether anybody was coming up the corridor, or even entering the hotel. He wiped his face and ordered himself to calm down. Saffron was watching the front of the hotel. If anything was wrong she would deal with it. Meanwhile, the three computers whirred and clicked, the search continuing.

Longville impatiently drummed his fingers on the

black box of the larger hard drive. "I've been waiting for the chance to bring them down," he whispered, half to himself. "I couldn't stand them parading me across the media just to show the world how fair their election was. I knew they weren't playing fair." He leaned his face so close to the laptop that Jimmy could see the coloured flashes of the search reflecting off his skin.

At last, the laptop emitted a high-pitched 'ping'. Felix and Jimmy rushed forward, but all they could see on the screen was a black graph with green bars of different sizes. Longville's eyes darted all over the data.

"What does it mean?" Felix asked, gripping his hair in his fists.

"It means…" Longville rocked backwards. He stared at the laptop, his cheeks quivering as if they were directly connected to the computers in front of him. "It means that you're right…."

Felix let out a yelp of triumph and punched the air.

"But you're also wrong." Longville's voice was shaking.

Jimmy felt like his head had been knocked sideways.

"What?" he said. "That makes no sense."

"You're right, but you're wrong," Longville repeated, holding his head in his hands.

"We're right, but we're wrong?" Jimmy looked at Felix, who stared back, blankly.

"What are you trying to say?" Felix demanded.

"It means you're right," Dr Longville exclaimed suddenly. "Somebody did try to rig the election. But they tried to fix it *the other way*."

There was silence. Jimmy and Felix looked at each other, then at Dr Longville.

"Wait," said Felix, "I don't understand. What do you mean, *the other way?*"

"I mean that whoever tried to fix the result of the election," explained Dr Newton Longville, "was trying to fix it so that the winner would be Christopher Viggo."

15 ALPHABETICAL ADVANTAGE

"But he lost!" Felix cried. "How could someone have fixed the election for Chris if he lost? Jimmy?" He turned to his friend and spun the laptop to face him. "It's a mistake, isn't it?"

Jimmy could hardly think for all the horror and confusion swirling around in his head. Felix's face had faded into even more of a fuzzy mess than usual and the laptop screen was a brightly coloured blur.

"I don't..." he began. "I can't..." He didn't finish his sentence. He wanted to say that he was as much in the dark as Felix. For all he knew Dr Longville could be making a mistake – or even lying. But Jimmy felt something more in the back of his mind, forcing its way to the front. He looked from Felix's wide eyes back to the laptop, and suddenly the colours seemed even brighter, the shapes more distinct. Each digit carried new meaning, the connections obvious.

"It's true," Jimmy croaked. His head was clearing, but at the same time, despair crept up in his throat. "I can understand all this." He waved his hand at the laptop. "Sort of. I think. It's my..." He rubbed his eyes with his palms. "The numbers aren't right. They're different on each hard drive." He looked again at the screen. "And there's a new string of programming in the hard drive from the main computer that isn't in the laptop's outline of what the system *should* be."

"That's right," Dr Longville gasped. "How can you...?"

"The new code is simple," Jimmy continued, ignoring the UN Inspector. "It changes the numbers as they come in from the voting kiosk. It's an instruction to duplicate votes for any candidate representing a party whose leader has a name that comes in the second half of the alphabet." Jimmy dropped his head into his hands.

"But 'Chris' begins with..." Felix stopped himself. "Oh. Viggo. I get it." He slumped against the lockers.

"The only serious candidates," explained Dr Longville, "were representing Ian Coates or Christopher Viggo. Two choices. Different halves of the alphabet. And the system was hacked to give one of them an advantage."

Jimmy couldn't hold his anger in any more. When he heard his father's name he felt like he was back in the sauna, his skin simmering with the heat. He jumped up and landed a kick against the bottom row of lockers.

"Coates!" he grunted as the wood split. "Viggo!" He slammed his other foot through the door of the next locker. "Coates! Viggo! Coates! Viggo!" With alternate feet he reduced a whole row of lockers to splinters.

"Jimmy!" Felix yelled to bring his friend back. Jimmy froze, breathing hard, and realised his nose was bleeding again. He wiped it with the back of his sleeve. Just then, the door of the locker room burst open.

"There's a woman here," said the guard posted outside. "She says—"

"We have to go." It was Saffron. She forced her way past the guard. "Now." Her eyes caught the chaos that Jimmy had made of the lockers. "What happened?"

"I lost my locker key," said Felix. He leapt to his feet, thrust the laptop into Dr Longville's hands and grabbed the two black boxes from Chisley Hall. "Let's go!" He swept to the door, bringing Jimmy and Longville with him.

Jimmy moved automatically, almost in a trance. He felt calmer now, but everything seemed edged with blackness.

"What's happening?" he asked, his voice low and stern. They filed out of the locker room and ran up the corridor, the security guards at the front and rear of the column.

"I got a call from Jimmy's mum," Saffron explained, jogging just ahead of Jimmy and Felix, half-turning to talk over her shoulder. "From where she and Georgie are posted, they can see the traffic heading for this hotel in both directions."

"They're coming?" Jimmy said. He was so certain that it hardly sounded like a question.

"But only from one direction," Saffron confirmed. "We've got a chance if we leave now. Before air support arrives to cover the other exit route."

"NJ7?" gasped Dr Longville. "Already?" He was second in line, just behind his own guard, but now he stumbled and looked back.

"Come on," Saffron insisted, catching the old man and pushing past him to keep up the pace. They charged through the hotel, heading for the lobby.

"You knew this would happen," Jimmy called out to Dr Longville, who was just ahead of him now. "You warned us."

"But that was before we found out..." Longville panted.

"What did you find out?" Saffron asked over her shoulder. Jimmy and Felix exchanged a glance. Before they could say anything, Dr Longville stopped, reached past Jimmy and snatched the larger computer hard drive from Felix. Immediately he started clawing at the screws that held the casing together.

"Give me a screwdriver!" he ordered the guard who's been leading the way. The huge lump of a man was swinging Longville's laptop case as he ran. He'd continued a short way up the corridor, either not realising the others behind him had stopped, or not wanting to wait for them. He turned back now and reached into the laptop case. Instead of producing a screwdriver, he pulled out a gun.

"What are you doing?" Longville gasped. The other two guards reached for their weapons, but found their holsters empty. In shock, they stared at their colleague, whose face expanded into a wide smile, a dozen rounded, yellow teeth clearly visible. He advanced cautiously, sweeping the barrel of the gun from side to side to keep all of them in his sights.

"If you're armed..." he began, addressing Saffron. The guard was edging closer all the time, but Jimmy and the others were backing away.

"Stay put!" ordered the guard. His voice was as solid as his shoulders, with a thick South London accent. *I took him down outside the steam room*, Jimmy thought. *Twice is easy.*

"He can't shoot," Jimmy announced, ice-cool in his tone. "If he does, he might have time to hit one of us, but it'll give the rest of us the chance to get away – or fight back."

The guard didn't react, but kept approaching, one step at a time. He slid his back against the wall of the corridor, trying to get a better angle so he could cover all of his targets at once.

"Jimmy," whispered Dr Longville, still twisting frantically at the screws of the hard-drive casing. "That's your name, right?" Jimmy nodded, flicking his eyes between Longville and the barrel of the guard's revolver.

"This has to be destroyed," Longville went on. His fingers were raw from the metal. Blood spread over the screws, but he kept on trying to loosen them. It wasn't working. Jimmy's programming was keeping his attention fixed on the immediate danger – the gun. But his senses were pricked by Longville's desperation. What did he want?

"Viggo is the only opposition this Government has," Dr Longville explained, his voice quaking. "If the evidence on this gets out, he's finished. NJ7 mustn't get it. Nobody must ever see it. I never saw it! Do you understand? Help me destroy this!"

"But..." Jimmy wanted to protest, but he instantly knew the old man was right. Whatever Viggo had done wrong to lead to this situation, whatever he was involved with – all that was still a mystery that Jimmy had to uncover. But he had to uncover it himself, and not allow NJ7 any chance to prove that Chris had cheated.

"Give me that box," grunted the guard, taking an extra step closer. "And the other one." He pointed at Felix.

"You want this?" said Felix, waving the smaller hard drive. He held it out, then immediately pulled it back.

"Oh, sorry, just a twitch in my shoulder. Try again." Once more, he slowly extended his arm, but the guard knew he couldn't grab it without losing his position on the others.

While Felix was infuriating the guard, Longville slowly leaned down to whisper straight into Jimmy's ear. "I don't know who you are," he said, "but if you can break into Chisley Hall, you can obviously do amazing things." He thrust the larger box into Jimmy's arms. "Destroy this. Then keep fighting. Fight until Britain is free."

Suddenly he twisted his wiry limbs and leaped towards the guard, a bloodcurdling scream exploding from his lips. The crack of the gun exploded up and down the corridor. Dr Longville crumpled in two and staggered forward, reaching out for the guard's gun. At the same moment, Saffron launched her own attack. Longville tried to fill the space in the corridor to shield the others, but the guard ducked to one side and aimed through the space under Longville's lurching body.

Saffron darted forward to strike, but the guard had a clear shot. Jimmy felt his muscles firing up like the engine of a fighter jet. In a split second, his brain buzzed with a million calculations – the angle of the guard's body, the calibre of the gun, the trajectory of the bullet. Before he was aware of his own movement, he realised he was diving for Saffron. He bulldozed her out of the way. The guard's bullet tore towards the centre of Jimmy's chest. The hard drive made the perfect shield.

The bullet struck the metal casing. Jimmy felt the black box rattle against his ribs, but the bullet didn't penetrate. He tumbled to the floor on top of Saffron. He got up straight away, ready to fight. All he could hear was the blood in his ears and the rapid breath in his throat. It took a second before he realised the guard was face down on the carpet. Longville's body was slumped over him like a snake across a mole hill. The doctor was wheezing for breath, blood frothing through the wound in his chest. Meanwhile, the guard's neck was oozing a black pool into the carpet, a liquid shadow that spread around him like the soul escaping his body.

"What...?" Felix choked, barely able to speak.

"The bullet," Jimmy gasped, still unable to even hear his own voice. "It..." He held up the hard drive. There was a huge dent in the casing, but no hole and no bullet. It had ricocheted back in the direction it had come from. And at such short range, it still had enough power to lodge in the neck of the man who'd shot it. Jimmy stared down at the two bodies that formed an 'X' across the corridor. *I didn't want this*, thought Jimmy. *I didn't mean for this...* But how could he have stopped it? Everything had happened too quickly.

He clasped his skull as if he could wrench the horror

from his brain. Saffron pulled him towards her and forced him to turn away.

"We have to go," she commanded. The two other guards pushed their way to the bodies. One of them grabbed the gun from their attacker's hand while the other rolled Dr Newton Longville on to his back. Jimmy didn't need to look. He already knew it was too late. Both men were dead.

Jimmy lifted the dented black box above his head, then hurled it crashing to the carpet. The impact did little to damage the hard drive, but Jimmy's fists pounded down on it. Then he took the smaller hard drive from Felix and knelt down, crunching the metal of both boxes like it was nothing but mashed potato. In no time he'd ruptured the casing. He tore out the guts of the two computers, ripped every wire and snapped every circuit board.

"Jimmy!" Saffron shouted. "Jimmy, that's enough!"

All Jimmy could see was fury. He slumped forward on the carpet, one hand squelching in the expanding black circle of the guard's blood. He closed his eyes, half wishing the blackness would wrap him up entirely and take him away forever.

"Come on," said Felix, grabbing Jimmy by the shoulder. There was a quiver in his voice, but his grip was firm. "We have to get out of here."

Together they pelted to the hotel lobby. *Out of here,*

thought Jimmy, over and over. *Out of the hotel, out of danger…* But now escaping from NJ7 didn't seem enough any more. Because as Jimmy's feet hammered into the marble floor of the lobby, the truth began to sink in: every vote for Viggo had been doubled. But he'd still lost the election. That meant he'd lost by a huge margin. Almost everybody in the country must have voted for Ian Coates. *The madness is everywhere*, Jimmy thought. He heard his own desperate plea: *out of here… out of London… out of Britain!* The more he yearned for relief, the more his pain grew, and then he realised why: how could he ever escape his own mind?

16 CATCHING A PLANE

They hurtled through the lobby and on to the forecourt. The motor of the Bentley was already growling. The driver's door opened and out stepped Helen Coates.

"Go!" she shouted, pointing Saffron towards the wheel. "Get to the rendezvous! Get Chris! We'll take care of *them*."

"Who?" Felix asked. Helen grabbed him and sprinted with him across the forecourt to one of the limousines.

"Them," she said, nodding up the street. Jimmy turned to see a fleet of long black cars racing towards them, spread out across the whole width of the road. "Go with Saffron!" Helen called to Jimmy. She flashed him a huge smile. It felt like the warmest relief he'd ever had. "You make a good team!"

"But, Mum..." Jimmy cried out. He wanted to tell her everything that had happened: the explosion at Chisley Hall, the data they'd found on the computer, the fight, the bullets... the blood. He felt tears sting the backs of his eyes and his throat went dry. He wanted to pour everything out, but before another breath could reach his lungs, Saffron grabbed him and guided him into the back of the Bentley. They blasted off, and Jimmy pressed his face to the window in time to see his mum giving instructions to the two bemused security guards. They hurried to the second limo, while Helen Coates took off in the first with Felix and Georgie in the back.

NJ7 had obviously cut off the traffic, so with no other cars in the way, there was nothing to hold Saffron back. She thrust the Bentley forward so hard that Jimmy was thrown back in his seat. Finally the full power of the machine was unleashed. It streaked across the tarmac like a comet across the night sky. Jimmy twisted and watched out the back of the car.

The two limos tore after them, but spread out across both carriageways. One of them flashed its headlights.

"Did you see...?" Jimmy started, but Saffron was already responding. She nudged the wheel to send the Bentley screaming across the lanes, past the opening to a slip road.

"It's your mum," she said. "Telling me to go down here." Suddenly she yanked the wheel to the side. The Bentley careered sideways, swinging and screeching back round to power on to the slip road. Jimmy was flung across the back seat, crashing against the door.

"How about warning me?" Jimmy spluttered.

"Aren't you strapped in?" Saffron called out, with a laugh.

Jimmy scrambled back to his seat in time to see what was happening behind them. One of the limos followed them up the slip road but then, at the narrowest point of the carriageway, swung itself round sideways. It was blocking the road so NJ7 had no way of following the Bentley.

"They've blocked the..." gasped Jimmy, his heart thrilling to every moment.

"I know," replied Saffron, gritting her teeth and tearing the Bentley round a curve in the road.

"But how will they get away?" Jimmy asked.

"It doesn't look like they will."

The Bentley roared round the bend, but just before his view of the limo behind them disappeared, Jimmy caught sight of the two beefy bodyguards stepping out, their hands raised, and three NJ7 cars screeching towards them. He was relieved to see that it wasn't the limo carrying his mum, his sister and his friend, but at the same time he wondered what NJ7 might do to two innocent security guards.

"They'll be fine," said Saffron, reading Jimmy's thoughts. "They'll cooperate with NJ7 the way that other guard did."

She smiled and slammed her foot down even harder.

Jimmy hadn't realised any more acceleration was possible, but they surged forward again, cutting every corner, winding their way towards Central London. "Fortunately," Saffron went on, "those guards know nothing about us that will help NJ7."

Jimmy was suddenly brought back to the bigger problem – the rigged election. He realised he hadn't told Saffron the truth about what they'd found on the Chisley Hall hard drive. But the guards had been in the room. They knew someone had tried to fix the election for Viggo. What if they told NJ7? Jimmy's mind turned over rapidly. *There's no evidence*, he told himself. *Without the hard drive it's just a story.* Jimmy was reassured for a split second before rage blew up in his mind again. Was Viggo behind this?

"Move!" Saffron hissed, swooping past a truck that had been taking up the road, slowing them down.

"Wait," said Jimmy, rocked out of his thoughts by the speed of the car. "Pull up under the next bridge."

Saffron glanced round at him with a flash of confusion.

"They're tracking us," she insisted. "Even if there aren't any cars behind us, they're watching us on satellite and they'll send a chopper, or they'll just wait to see where we stop and close the net. We have to get underground. I'm heading for the nearest tunnel."

"No." Jimmy was firm. "That wouldn't help us anyway, we—"

"It gives us the best chance..."

"Listen!" Jimmy surprised himself with his forcefulness, but he knew he had information that Saffron didn't. "They don't have satellite surveillance."

"What?"

"Eva told us they were having problems with it. We can pull up under the next bridge, wait for the search helicopters to scan the area and move on, then keep driving."

"Eva told you?"

"Yes." Jimmy was trying to sound his most confident, even though he could feel his doubts squirming in his stomach. It seemed like a long time since Eva had told them about NJ7's satellite problems. What if the system had been fixed since then? "It's our best chance," Jimmy urged, more to reassure himself than to convince Saffron.

Without another word, Saffron slowed to a more normal speed and in under a minute they were parked on the hard shoulder under a road bridge. Jimmy clicked his door open a crack so they'd hear the choppers above the traffic noise, and waited.

Felix craned his neck to see the two guards surrendering

to NJ7 as Helen zoomed onwards past the slip road. She was testing the limo's engine to its limit.

"Jimmy and Saffron got away, I think," said Felix, with no certainty. "But what about the guards? What if...?"

"I gave them very specific instructions," Helen Coates explained with a soft smile.

"But wait..." Felix slumped down on the leather, his mind racing. "Basically, we've just given them over to NJ7. Won't they get, you know..."

"You're actually *worried* about them?" Georgie was shocked. "What, are they your mates all of a sudden?"

"Well, they weren't the ones that tried to shoot us, were they?" Felix's face was pale and he couldn't help his lip trembling. It hadn't sunk in yet that he'd just seen two men shot dead right in front of him. He could feel the shock inside him like a block of ice, waiting to melt through the rest of his body.

"Don't worry," said Helen. "They'll say they're the victims – and it's true. They had no choice but to help us, and NJ7 have no reason to do anything to them except give them a cup of tea and ask them a few questions about us."

"I can't imagine anybody at NJ7 serving tea," Georgie muttered.

"I can't imagine them serving anything else," said Felix with a hint of anger. "Tea in English china with English biscuits, sitting on their hard English sofas talking about English things like, I dunno... fruitcake."

"How does a sofa talk about fruitcake?" Georgie pretended to be confused until Felix dug his elbow into her ribs. He knew she was just trying to distract them from the horror of what they were going through. *That's my specialty*, he thought to himself.

"Put your seat belts on!" Helen ordered, slamming her foot on to the accelerator and swerving to dodge traffic. "We're not the ones who got away."

"They're still after us?" Felix sat bolt upright and craned his neck to see out of the back window. "Go faster! They're catching up!"

Helen stayed calm. She was already weaving in and out of spaces in the lines of cars that were barely big enough for the limo. Twice the back bumper caught on the front of the car they were overtaking. They ripped up the road in front of them, careering across the lanes, sending the vehicles behind them into spins, spreading chaos in their path. But the NJ7 cars weren't far behind. They were faster and more manoeuvrable than the limo. They darted between the other vehicles like charging dogs, their grilles seeming to snarl and spit.

"We have to get off this road," said Georgie, through gritted teeth. She was braced in her seat. "If they get people ahead of us they can block us in!"

"Captain Obvious strikes again," said Felix.

"Any suggestions?" Helen flicked her eyes to the rear-view mirror.

"The airport!" Felix exclaimed suddenly.

"There's more security there than anywhere else in the—"

"No, we can," Felix cut in. "The UN guy, he said he didn't need to check in or anything like that. He just gets driven straight on to the runway and his plane's waiting for him."

"He said that?" Georgie asked, disbelieving.

"He just drives straight in!" Felix repeated. "In *this* car!"

"Then what, genius?" Georgie asked. "Even if we can get on to the runway, we'll—"

Suddenly Helen jammed the steering wheel fully to the right. The limo spun full circle in a squeal of rubber. The cars charging up behind them couldn't stop in time – including the NJ7 unit. They swerved and twisted, but the limo split them down the middle and sped back towards the airport.

"What are you doing?!" Georgie shouted. "We'll get trapped on the runway!"

"Sometimes you have to choose your trap," Helen explained. "Our choice: a blocked road or a runway full of planes."

"We're going to hijack a plane?" Felix beamed.

"No," said Helen. Felix slumped back, disappointed. "We're going to improvise. We have more options on an airport runway."

Helen circled the main terminal buildings, following the airport signage. Police cars and armed trucks poured on to the roads around them, but in no time they were charging along a narrow strip of concrete with high walls on either side – the VIP vehicle route to the aircraft gates behind Terminal 3.

The limo bounced over the speed bumps so hard that Felix and Georgie hit their heads on the roof. But Helen didn't slow down.

"You're sure he said he just drove on to the runway?" Helen called out, suddenly sounding less sure of herself.

"Yes!" Felix yelled. "Why?"

Helen didn't answer. Looking out of the front window, Felix and Georgie saw the problem. The end of the passageway was blocked by raised steel bollards, behind a line of jagged metal in the ground.

"Stop!" Felix shouted, digging his nails into the leather.

"Did you say faster?" Helen replied. She'd spotted the laser scanner beside the security measures. At the last second, it read the limo's number plate. The jagged metal retracted into the ground just as the limo passed over. The steel bollards sunk agonisingly slowly. The bottom of the car scraped their tops, then screeched away on to the huge expanse of concrete ahead of them.

"Which one of these do you think is the right plane?" Felix asked, his voice shaking.

"The right plane?" Helen asked. "Since when were you so fussy?"

They charged towards a line of huge jumbo jets, all of them waiting at their gates. Security vehicles and sirens swarmed towards them from every direction. Baggage cars and airport workers scurried to get out of the way. The limo snaked between the planes, swooping under the wings like a gnat buzzing round sleeping seals. At last Helen saw what they needed – a smaller plane that was still empty of passengers. It was being refuelled while luggage was loaded up the conveyor belt ramps on either side.

"Get ready to run," Helen ordered, sending the limo rushing across the tarmac in a race with the police and the NJ7 cars. "When I give the word, get out my side of the car and sprint."

"Sprint where?" Georgie asked, managing to keep her voice surprisingly calm.

"Into the plane. And keep your heads down." Helen twisted the wheel to send the limo into another giant skid. The screech pierced through the noise of the sirens and the whole vehicle tipped up until Felix was sure they were going to topple over. They careered into the side of the refuelling buggy and bounced back on to four wheels.

"GO!" Helen shouted. They exploded from the limo and sprinted the few metres to the plane, keeping their heads ducked down below the level of the limo's roof. Helen jumped up on to the plane's loading ramp while the baggage handlers rushed away in panic. Georgie and Felix were right behind her. Together, they leapt over the bags, straight into the belly of the plane – but they didn't stop. Helen led them straight out of the other side of the plane, down the other baggage ramp. This ramp was moving upwards, requiring a burst of even greater effort. Felix nearly stumbled, but righted himself to take in the new surroundings.

It was chaos. While the police and NJ7 descended on the plane, the baggage handlers were tearing in the opposite direction. Helen, Georgie and Felix joined them. They dashed on to the nearest abandoned baggage cart. Helen snatched a handful of fluorescent vests from the back, threw one over her head and thrust the others at Felix and Georgie.

"Get right down!" she shouted, bundling her hair up into a cap that had been left on the front seat. She started up the cart, which whined and heaved itself along the tarmac at a steady crawl.

To Felix's amazement, the security forces blasted straight past them, ignoring the terrified herd of airport staff that was fleeing the scene. Instead, they encircled the plane. The flashing blue lights of the police vans reflected off the spreading black pool of aviation fuel in a haze of fumes. The smell burned into Felix's nostrils. The pool of fuel had spread out under the whole plane, with parallel trails leading all the way back along the route of the baggage car's wheels.

"Felix," said Helen firmly. "I'm about to ask you to do something which you must promise never to tell your parents about."

"What is it?"

"I want you to blow up that plane."

Felix's mouth dropped open.

"Look through those bags behind you and find a lighter," Helen went on.

"I will absolutely do that for you!" Felix exclaimed, his eyes wide. He frantically heaved on the suitcases one at a time and ripped them open, searching through the contents. "There must be a lighter here," he muttered. "Doesn't anybody pack a lighter? Come on! This might be the only chance in my life I get to make something massive blow up!"

"I can't believe you're letting him do this..." said Georgie, with a small smile.

"It'll take them a few seconds to search the plane and see we're not there," her mum explained. "But if they had to search a wreckage for our bodies..."

"Yes!" Felix punched the air, a pink plastic lighter in his fist.

"Wait until all the fuel is off our wheels," said Helen, glancing back. "I don't want you setting light to us at the same time." The trail from one of their wheels had run out, leaving just a single, thin line connecting them to the highly inflammable reservoir.

Felix clambered over the baggage towards the back and leaned over the side. He ignited the trail of fuel just as Helen surged the cart forward, out of the danger. The flames licked the ground behind them, almost invisible, until a sudden streak of fire ripped towards the plane.

BOOM!

A huge black and orange fist seemed to burst out of the ground and squeeze the whole plane. Vehicles toppled over and the security forces were knocked off their feet.

"This is the greatest moment of my life," Felix whispered.

17 A LEASH LOOSENED

The constant buzz of the helicopters overhead went on longer than Jimmy or Saffron expected. NJ7 weren't giving up the search easily.

"Looks like you were right about their satellites," Saffron said. They'd left the car now and were sitting near it on the muddy verge under the bridge. "They might keep the choppers up until it gets dark."

She peered out, trying to get a glimpse of the helicopters' flight patterns. The light was already fading. Next to her, Jimmy wasn't interested in looking out at the world. He was staring down at what he held in his hands: the small rectangle of card that the Capita had shot through the window after they abducted Viggo. The corners were dog-eared and some of the print had rubbed off a little from all the wear and tear it had suffered in Jimmy's back pocket, but the type was still bold and clear: LOCO.

"Once it's dark we'll have to move quickly," Jimmy said.

"The Capita said twenty-four hours and I doubt they admit latecomers." He stuffed the flier back into his pocket. That black mist was already building up inside him: his programming swirling into action. Was it formulating a plan? Jimmy had no idea how his own body was preparing for the night ahead, and he realised he probably wouldn't find out until he was executing the will of his assassin instinct. How was he going to get Viggo back? He searched inside himself, longing for some clue about how he could handle the battles to come.

"We have nothing to negotiate with," he sighed, almost to himself. "Nothing. We don't have the money Chris owed them, we don't have the H Code, and the computers from Chisley Hall were useless. We're going up against the Capita with nothing."

For at least an hour they'd been sitting under the bridge watching the shadows lengthening and listening to the helicopters. Jimmy's hunger had grown and he'd felt his energy fading. The crack of gunshots haunted his imagination. He was sure they wouldn't be the last he'd hear. He couldn't stop himself picturing Dr Longville and his guard slumped over each other. One enemy, one man who had turned out to be a friend. Both dispatched in an instant with no second chances.

"We'll find a way," said Saffron gently. "We have to. We owe it to Chris. However he's acted lately, we have to get him back."

Jimmy let her soothing voice wash through him. He was hardly listening. She didn't understand what was on his mind, or the torment he felt twisting his guts.

"I've been thinking about it a lot," Saffron went on. "Even if things between us all are different afterwards – even if Chris isn't…" She paused, searching for the right word. "We owe it to everybody in Britain to save him. This country deserves the leader it voted for."

Jimmy felt a shiver rip through him. He hadn't been able to tell her. *She still thinks NJ7 fixed the election for the Government.* Jimmy held himself still, not wanting to give away that he was hiding this secret. He wanted to give Viggo the chance to defend himself first, if he could. Had Viggo been behind the corruption, or was it all down to the Capita? Jimmy wanted to believe his friend was innocent, but the more he thought about it, the more unlikely that felt.

The darkness in Jimmy's mind was growing. Why had so many people voted against Viggo? Enough people for it not to matter that the HERMES system was crooked. Jimmy looked up to watch the cars whizzing past. All these people – did they really believe in Ian Coates? Jimmy hated even thinking about the man, but he had to. He had to work out why so many people seemed to want him to stay in charge of Britain. He noticed that a few of the cars even had bumper stickers with the Government's election slogan: *Efficiency. Stability. Security.* Maybe they'd been fooled, Jimmy thought. Maybe Miss Bennett had organised such a brilliant campaign, and been able to manipulate the TV, the press, the radio... and ultimately the voters.

Or maybe they were right. Maybe people had voted for Ian Coates because it was the right decision. Even though he had promised to abolish voting again – once and for all, this time. Maybe that's what people really wanted. Maybe it was the best way to run the country... *Efficiency. Stability. Security.* Christopher Viggo couldn't have offered any of those things.

Jimmy held his head in his hands. Where were these thoughts coming from? Was this his NJ7 programming throwing up a belief in Neo-democracy? But it didn't feel like his programming. It felt like him.

"Listen," said Saffron, gripping Jimmy's arm and startling him out of his thoughts. "I think they're..." She looked up, craning to see the sky. Jimmy suddenly noticed how much darker it had become. And at last the sound of the helicopters was gradually receding, swallowed by the drone of the traffic.

"Let's go." Saffron pushed herself to her feet and held out a hand for Jimmy. They both hurried back into the Bentley.

"LOCO," said Jimmy, reading the card. He took a deep breath, steeling himself for the fight ahead.

The fleet of black cars split up and swept through London to over a dozen different locations. Each of them was unmarked but for small, vertical green stripes by the front grilles and by the rear lights. They were an army of shadows, gliding into every street, hiding themselves in the night.

Only one had been dispatched from NJ7 HQ, and that one pulled up now on the lowest level of an underground car park on Great College Street in Westminster, Central London. An anonymous-looking white door opened in the darkest corner of the car park. Only a discreet green stripe by the hinge gave away where it led.

Miss Bennett and Eva were waiting for the agents – was it to welcome them, Eva wondered, or to interrogate them about what went wrong? Miss Bennett certainly wasn't here to congratulate them – they had completely failed in their mission to eliminate Jimmy and the others. Eva was still getting used to the way her boss's moods could shift. Sometimes even if she was happy she would pretend to be furious, or vice versa, just to make a certain point.

Eva watched the driver and two other men get out of the car. All were the standard template of NJ7 agents: tall, broad, with fiercely cropped hair, plain black suits and thin black ties. A couple of them wore small green stripes on their lapels. Eva guessed the others weren't yet senior enough. Then, bringing up the rear, came a fourth person, and when she saw him Eva realised why Miss Bennett had made the effort to come and greet this team.

This was Miss Bennett's second protégé, but unlike Eva, this one was a genuine devotee of NJ7. In fact, he was a remarkable one. Like the other agents, he was dressed in a plain black suit, but his tie was hanging loose with the knot swinging over his heart. His shirt was untucked. At first glance he looked like a messier and slightly shorter version of the others, but his face was much younger. And although he had the broad shoulders of a man, they were hunched over and his hands were shoved roughly into his pockets. His cheeks were fresh and smooth, but they bore a scowl. Eva knew this boy could look quite good when he smiled, but she rarely saw that.

"Good evening, Mitchell," said Miss Bennett. Mitchell Glenthorne grunted an indistinct response while the other agents filed past. They all avoided catching Miss Bennett's eye, Eva noticed, and for a second she thought she heard Miss Bennett softly tutting.

"Looks like you missed again," said Miss Bennett to Mitchell, once the others had gone. Mitchell stopped dead and his face flushed red.

"It wasn't me this time," he said through gritted teeth.
"I saw him. He was running about like a... like a..." His
intense frustration was obvious. "Then I saw him squirming
about in the back of one of the limos. He's a little boy."

Eva sunk back into the shadows. She felt so awkward –
like she had stumbled into an argument between a mother
and a son. It was so strange that they were arguing over
matters of life and death.

"You should have sent me on my own," Mitchell insisted,
breathing heavily to control his emotions.

"We've tried that before, haven't we?" Miss Bennett
spun on her high heels and marched away up the corridor,
back towards the hub of NJ7. Mitchell was visibly stung.
Eva was shocked to feel a pang of sympathy for him.
He lived to destroy Jimmy Coates, yet every time they'd
been up against each other, Jimmy had escaped him by
a whisker.

"But if you send in a whole squad..." Mitchell called
out, hurrying after Miss Bennett. Eva followed them at a
distance, "it's... clumsy. We all go crashing in and Jimmy
knows we're coming." Mitchell was running his hands
over his head frantically, tearing at the tiny spikes of blond
hair. "The only way to take him out will be to surprise him.
A single assassin. From out of nowhere." He slammed his
palm against the wall to emphasise his point. "Me." Eva

felt the emotional force of it, even several metres back.

"Do you trust me?" Miss Bennett asked, gently.

Eva shuddered at the question, but knew Mitchell would be a fool not to answer straightaway. He did.

"Of course." From Mitchell's voice, Eva considered that he might actually mean it.

"Do you believe that I care for you?" Miss Bennett asked, again in that silky tone, as if she was coaxing a baby to sleep. Mitchell was slower this time, more suspicious. He dropped his gaze and nodded.

"If you care for me," he mumbled, "you'll let me do my job."

Miss Bennett let out a deep sigh. It hissed round the NJ7 tunnels.

"You might be right," she said. "We have to analyse what happened this afternoon and put right the mistakes for next time. Maybe that will mean sending you alone. Or maybe you'll need a different kind of support." As they walked through the labyrinth of grey concrete, she placed a hand on Mitchell's shoulder. Her bright-green nail polish flashed in the fluorescent strip lights. "Remember," she went on, "you're not fully... developed yet. You will be soon. I don't want you getting hurt before then. I have your best interests at heart."

They stopped at an intersection of tunnels. More NJ7 staff hurried round them, grey people in a grey world.

"You do believe that, don't you, Mitchell?" Miss Bennett turned him towards her and looked at him hard until he nodded. "Good. Now go and get debriefed. Eva," she called behind her. Eva jumped to attention. "I'll need thorough notes from the debrief. Go with Mitchell."

Before Eva could respond, Miss Bennett strode away towards her office.

"I can almost feel the leash!" Mitchell snarled when he was alone with Eva. He tore his tie from his neck and threw it to the ground. "Why won't she let me...?" He tailed off with a grunt of frustration. Eva stared at him, trying to understand. What was it like inside his head? One minute she'd find him clumsy and a bit of a lout, the next she might look in his eyes and see a cruel and efficient assassin.

"Why do you even want to...?" Eva began, but stopped herself. How could she challenge what he did when it was part of his blood? His DNA was designed to make him a killer. How could Eva possibly question it?

Mitchell leaned against the wall and bent forward, resting his elbows on his knees. He stayed like that for a long time, his head down. Eva shifted from foot to foot. She didn't know whether to comfort him or creep away. *Or run for my life*, she thought, then immediately hated herself for thinking it.

"I have nothing else," Mitchell whispered at last.

Eva struggled to catch the words. She'd never known Mitchell's voice to be so soft and vulnerable. "I have nothing else," he whispered again, looking up at her. He wasn't crying, but every muscle in his face was clenched to prevent it.

"You have nothing but..." Eva spread her arms and looked round at the bare concrete walls. "Nothing but this?"

"I was born for this," Mitchell said, breathing heavily. "Made for this. There's nothing for me except NJ7. Nothing *in* me except—"

"I don't believe that." Eva was surprised at the force in her own voice. Why did she care how Mitchell's life went? Why was she even standing there talking to him? "Your life is a lot more than NJ7. Or it could be, even if it isn't now."

"How do you know?" Mitchell snapped back. "Your life isn't much different. When was the last time you even left this place? Why don't your parents know—"

"They don't need to know," Eva insisted. She forced back the lump rising in her throat. Her parents didn't deserve to know anything. They'd betrayed Jimmy and tried to force her to be loyal to an evil government. "You don't know anything about it."

She stared into Mitchell's eyes and refused to let herself flinch. In that moment she wanted to hit him as hard as she could, but at the same time she wished she could tell him everything. She longed to spill out her secrets, to explain every detail of the double life she'd been leading. *Then he'd understand*, she thought, trying to stop herself shaking. Maybe then he'd see that there was more to the world than Miss Bennett and NJ7 – and that Eva was prepared to risk everything for that cause. If he knew that, she thought, how would he look at her then?

Eva pressed her lips together. *Don't say a word*, she ordered herself. *Don't even breathe.* She squeezed her hands into fists, physically restraining herself from trying to win Mitchell round. *He'd attack before he understood.* More than ever, she was aware of the thick muscles in the boy's neck and shoulders. The harsh light overhead cast deep shadows in his skin, making him look older than he was.

"Why are you looking at me?" he asked, shifting uncomfortably.

"Nothing," Eva said, quickly. "I..." She tried to force out of her mind the thought of Mitchell's blood and what it made him capable of – what it compelled him to do. Could the boy in front of her ever realise the good that he could achieve? "I need to show you something," Eva added suddenly. "Follow me."

She didn't wait for a response, but hurried away

through the murky tunnels. After a second she heard Mitchell's steps behind her.

"Where are we going?" he asked. Eva didn't reply. "I've been everywhere in this whole underground maze. There's nothing you can show me I don't know about."

Eva just kept walking, taking quicker and longer strides. She was scared that if she slowed down, or distracted herself by replying to Mitchell's questions, she'd lose the courage to lead him where she wanted him to go.

Eventually they were away from the busier areas of the network and into the tech department. Once again Eva noticed how much murkier it was here.

"Stupid energy-saving light bulbs," Mitchell muttered, just half a pace behind her. "I reckon the science lot must all be vampires or something." He choked up a nervous laugh.

Eva led him through the labs. To her relief, they were largely deserted, with only a couple of cleaners and a lone technician totally absorbed in his work. Eva shuddered at the thought that she might encounter William Lee again. Her heart eased in the next lab when she saw that Lee's blue chair was empty. However, it was swivelling. Was the man still lurking somewhere? Perhaps this was where he liked to hide from Miss Bennett, thought Eva. Or perhaps he was working on something. *Still fixing the satellite surveillance system?* she wondered. No – surely he would have called in an entire tech team to help him by now.

Eva hurried past, and in the tunnel that led them away, they came at last to the slim gap in the concrete wall. Eva couldn't help smiling. A small part of her had wondered whether she'd imagined the whole thing and that the gap would have disappeared. She paused on the threshold and took a deep breath.

"What's in there?" Mitchell asked, confused. "I've never seen..."

"Mind the steps," Eva whispered, without turning to look at him. Was she doing the right thing? Was this what Mitchell needed to see? It was too late to doubt herself now. She stepped into the darkness and led Mitchell down the narrow flight of stairs, towards the strip of bright light at the bottom. Mitchell had to squeeze his shoulders in to fit, but he was following keenly. Eva could feel his breath on the back of her neck.

At the bottom Eva paused again, listening. There were no voices from inside the lab this time. She peered out at the brightly lit chamber to double-check, then finally stepped out.

"What does...?" Mitchell wandered in, gazing around and blinking hard.

"I saw this the other day," Eva explained, nervously. "When I realised what it was... I mean, *who* it was..."

"What do you mean?"

Eva marched right up to the metal table in the centre of the room. A black plastic sheet covered the human-shaped mound that lay on top of it, but the green laser was still firing, and still in place. When Eva got closer, she saw there was a tiny hole in the black sheet around the eye. The laser was still at work. Eva could hardly breathe at the horror of seeing it in detail, and the faint smell of bleach made her feel sick, but she couldn't stop now. Mitchell had to see. He had to know what NJ7 was doing. He had to realise that there was something more he could do, another way he could live.

"Show me, then!" Mitchell huffed. "You've led me all round this stupid..."

Eva whipped the sheet away. She did it in one smooth, swift movement, so she wouldn't have the chance to back out. Suddenly the temperature of the room seemed to drop several degrees. Eva stepped back and looked away, wincing. Mitchell staggered forward. A noise escaped his mouth that Eva had never heard before – the whistle of breath from a parched throat, a silent scream. He seemed to buckle at the knees and had to plant his hands on the edge of the metal slab to support himself.

Eva backed away and watched Mitchell's back arch forward over the ragged, but still breathing, body of his only brother, Lenny Glenthorne. And that's how she left him.

18 *LOCO*

The ornate red letters of LOCO hung from the awning over the pavement like four twisted devils trying to snatch the people below. There was already a crowd outside the venue so Jimmy and Saffron drove past without dropping their speed and pulled up round the corner. The Bentley would have drawn too much attention. He saw it for only a second, but the image of the scene froze in Jimmy's mind. The first thing he remembered were the two huge bouncers. A man and a woman. Both armed. Why weren't they hurrying everybody inside? And why hadn't the police come to disperse the crowd — or arrest everybody?

"I thought crowds like that were illegal without a licence," Jimmy muttered, almost to himself.

"They are," Saffron replied. "Looks like the Capita pays off the local police."

Jimmy nodded, already shifting his focus to the other features of LOCO. He found himself mentally deconstructing the building: a huge place, detached from the houses around it. A converted cinema, Jimmy quickly realised from the crumbling art deco façade and the fact that it was all brick, no windows. His brain filtered the information, rubbing every detail together, testing connections to see what became significant. The size of the crowd outside, for example. Jimmy found he was comfortable assuming that the place was similarly packed inside. And from the size of the building, that meant a lot of people.

A lot of places to conceal a hostage, he thought, picturing Viggo strapped down somewhere, possibly unconscious.

"We'll need to get the vehicle close," he said, scared for a moment at the unfamiliarity of his own voice. It sounded flat, almost mechanical. "The subject might be immobile." These words were coming from somewhere else, a deep inner sense that operated more clinically, more automatically. A place where people were 'subjects' or 'targets' and life was just a mission to be executed. No doubts. No hesitation. No feelings.

"Can we be sure he's definitely in there?" Saffron asked. It had crossed Jimmy's mind too. What if the Capita were really keeping Viggo somewhere else? *What if he's dead?* Jimmy thought suddenly. He shook off the question, not wanting to acknowledge that his programming was right to ask it. Without evidence that Viggo was still alive, and that he was at LOCO, was it too risky to go in trying to find him? *No*, Jimmy told himself, struggling to keep control of his thoughts, like they were wild dogs. *The risk is* not *going in. If Viggo is there and we leave him, he will be dead.*

"We have to assume he's in there," Jimmy announced. "And the Capita has to assume we have the H Code."

"The H Code," Saffron repeated, blankly. She stared into the middle distance, terror gradually creeping across her face. "What are we going to do?"

Jimmy leaned over and ran his fingers up either side of the centre panel of the dashboard.

"We don't need the H Code," Jimmy said, his voice growing stronger every second as the dark energy of an assassin flooded his body, blotting out the human vulnerability. "We just need a few extra seconds." There was a click, and the dashboard panel came away. Jimmy carefully lifted it out of position and reached into the secret compartment behind.

The Bentley was full of hiding places like this. It had first belonged to the French Ambassador, and he'd used it to smuggle documents, among other things, from Britain to France. Then NJ7 had seized the car and been in the process of searching it when Viggo had used it as his escape from Secret Service life. Ever since then it had been disguised many times, reconstructed, repainted and considerably battered by Viggo and Saffron's muscular driving. With every fix-it job on the bodywork, Viggo had discovered more and more hidden compartments. This one was the most obvious. Jimmy and Saffron had been using it to store the laptop.

"This will give us time," he said.

"It won't work, Jimmy. They won't let us out with Chris in return for a laptop. We'll have to prove that the H Code is on that computer."

Jimmy shrugged. "That's just something we'll have to deal with." He searched his mind for a strategy, but all he found was darkness, like a swarm of wasps cutting out the light. It was time to act. Jimmy took a deep breath and steadied his shoulders.

"We have to plan this," Saffron said urgently. "And we should wait for the others. Helen will be able to help, at least."

Jimmy glanced at the clock behind the steering wheel. He didn't need to say anything. The rendezvous was scheduled for eight minutes' time. The Capita wouldn't wait.

"OK, Rambo," said Saffron, showing her anger now. "You're just going to blast through the front doors? Through the crowd? The bouncers?"

Jimmy thought for a few seconds, but no more. His

mind was heavy with strength, but serene at the same time, as if a thick black ink had injected itself and was infusing every thought.

"Who's Rambo?" he said, thrusting the car door open and stepping into the night. Saffron had no choice but to follow. She kept her head down and jogged to catch up with him. Jimmy kept the laptop tight under his arm.

Every step swept leaves into a swirl that picked up with the wind and curled round their feet. They were two thunderstorms picking up momentum.

"They'll see us," Saffron whispered. "They have cameras."

The position and angles of the security cameras were already fixed in Jimmy's head. It seemed so natural to him that he hadn't even thought to comment on it.

"We walk straight past," he said under his breath. "Head down. To the row of houses."

Jimmy's mind zoomed from the image of the security cameras back to something else, another detail so small he hadn't even realised his eyes had registered it. When they drove past, the leaves and litter in the gutter had been dancing. Not drifting in the wind, not resting in the shelter of the curb, but trembling. *Rhythmically*, thought Jimmy.

"The bass is coming up from the underground level of the club," he announced, picking up his pace. "Strong enough to feel it on the pavement. We go in through the basement flat of the house next door."

"And the people who live in that flat?" Saffron asked.

"I..." Jimmy trailed off. He could only guess how he would instinctively react in order to take control of the flat. All he could predict was efficiency, speed... violence.

"Leave it to me," Saffron ordered. She diverted into the crowd outside LOCO. Jimmy slowed his pace so as not to lose her, but she disappeared from view for a moment. Jimmy felt his eyes flicking from side to side, always searching, spotting every detail. They locked on to the faces of the people in the crowd. The assassin in him was analysing everything about them, picking up on body language. Was it hostile? Wary? Had these people been warned about Jimmy? Would they offer any resistance? Would they be easy opponents if they did?

All the time, Jimmy felt like he was watching through frosted windows, seeing the same faces with his other self — his purely human side. He wanted to wonder how old these people were, whether they had families who knew where they were and that they were breaking the law to be there... whether he would ever be able to come to a club to relax, instead of to attack.

He felt himself wanting to consider those questions, but he couldn't. His brain and body were locked. He was like a missile, primed for launch. He let his frail thoughts fall away, driven out by the tremors coming up from the pavement that confirmed the presence of the underground club.

There was a shout. Jimmy tensed, but held back. One corner of the crowd was bustling, and Jimmy could hear the female bouncer taking control. A second later Saffron was spat back out of the throng of people. They marched on together, keeping their heads low.

Saffron rang the bell of the basement flat just past the club. It was the first in a line of old-fashioned houses that had been converted into flats years ago. Saffron and Jimmy lurked in the shadows at the bottom of the steps, hidden from more of LOCO's customers hurrying past on the pavement.

A middle-aged woman answered the door with a napkin hanging from her trousers. She was still chewing.

"Sorry to disturb you, madam," Saffron began straight away. She sounded firm, but friendly. "We're from the electricity board." She thrust an ID card towards the woman's face. Jimmy smiled as the woman peered forward, squinting.

"I don't have my glasses," she shrugged. "What's the matter?" In the shadows it would have been impossible to read the ID card anyway. Jimmy glanced back towards the street, wondering whether the female bouncer was going to have any trouble controlling the crowd without her security pass.

"This is an emergency call out, madam," Saffron explained. "We've got a surge in the network that we think is being caused by a fault in your wiring. If you don't mind, we're going to have to come in and do a quick scan."

The woman looked bemused, but Saffron's patter was fluent.

"This is my nephew," Saffron added when the woman looked suspiciously at Jimmy. "He's on work placement with me. Bit of a computer whiz." She leaned forward to conspire with the woman. "I couldn't do this job without him, if I'm honest."

The woman shrugged, still chewing on the same mouthful and stepped out of the way.

"We won't be a moment, madam," said Saffron. "You just enjoy your dinner."

Jimmy unfolded the laptop, switched it on, then held it up against the walls, pretending to be scanning for something. Saffron went ahead of him, tapping and pressing her ear against the paintwork, gradually working her way through the flat.

"James!" the woman called out. "It's the electricity!" She pushed open the door to the kitchen and Jimmy caught sight of the woman's husband tucking into some delicious-looking food – from both plates. "I'll bet it's because of that hellhole next door," the woman added, to Jimmy and Saffron. "Can't hear myself think most nights."

Meanwhile, Jimmy had made his way into the room at the side of the building. It turned out to be a small bathroom: their portal into the club.

"I'm afraid we have to strip the tiling on that wall," he called out, re-emerging into the hallway.

"Strip the tiling?" The woman was aghast. "That doesn't sound..." She looked Saffron and Jimmy up and down. "Let me just make a phone call..."

"Wait," Saffron urged as the woman reached for the phone.

"What's going on?" It was the man, hurrying from the kitchen.

"OK," said Saffron with a deep breath. "Here's the truth: Christopher Viggo is in the building next door."

"What?!" gasped the woman.

"And if we don't—"

"Yes," Jimmy cut in. His eyes flicked to the pot of pencils by the phone. "If we don't get in there to arrest him, we'll never stop what he's planning."

"What's he planning?" asked the man.

"I'm afraid we can't tell you that, sir," Jimmy replied. "We're from a government agency called NJ7. This is top secret and vital to the security of our nation. Can we rely on your loyalty?"

The couple looked at each other.

"Of course," whispered the man.

"I knew you weren't from the electricity company," said the woman with an excited smile.

"Your government will reward you for this," said Jimmy. "You!" He turned to Saffron. "Come with me and take notes." He grabbed a pencil from the pot by the telephone and thrust it at her. Printed along it were three words: *Efficiency. Stability. Security.*

"He's the technical expert," Saffron explained, following Jimmy into the bathroom. "But we might need some tools..."

Within a minute, the bathroom tiles were clattering round Jimmy's knees as he knelt in the bath with all the necessary tools. "You sure we won't be disturbed?" He nodded towards the door.

Saffron shrugged. "They seem pretty excited. I told them a back-up team was on the way."

"Back-up team?" Jimmy's confusion melted into a smile when he saw Saffron texting. "Tell Felix to bring me something to eat," he said. "The smell of that dinner is driving me nuts."

Jimmy worked on a small, clearly defined square, not wasting any effort making the hole bigger than it needed to be. Once the tiles were off, he quickly went through the plaster, then the brick. A layer of stone slowed his progress before he hit clay, but by now the tunnel was almost long enough.

Jimmy drilled into key stress points in the earth, then chipped away at the rest, while Saffron worked behind him to remove what he dug out. His right arm slammed down with the regularity of the heavy beat pounding through from next door. Every bit of force Jimmy hammered through the chisel was magnified by the vibrations of the club. It was as if LOCO was drawing them in, willing them to break down the last barriers between them and Viggo. Them and the Capita.

"Wait," Jimmy shouted over the noise of the drill. He dropped the chisel into the bath and rested a finger on his lips. When the drill stopped, the noise from the club was obvious. Now it wasn't just a bass line or a drumbeat they could hear, it was the full blast of the music. Jimmy closed his eyes for a moment. He could even pick out voices. He scraped at the end of their tunnel. A flurry of red dust came away – brick dust. They'd reached the wall of the club.

"Get the laptop," Jimmy ordered.

Saffron crawled backwards and reached for the laptop they'd left in the bath. "What's the plan now?" she whispered, lying on her front and clutching the computer to her chest.

"You circle to the left, I'll go right. Cover the whole floor looking for exits, staircases, lifts, security personnel..."

"I know what to look for," Saffron cut in. The light from the bathroom caught the outline of her face, glinting off her cheekbones. Jimmy felt the force of her determination. For a second it cracked the stone inside Jimmy's skin and he felt his human emotions seeping through the assassin.

"Are you still going to be his girlfriend?" Jimmy whispered, before he could stop himself. Saffron tensed up.

"What do you...?"

"You don't look scared," said Jimmy, studying her face. "You used to be scared for Chris, but now you..."

"Get through that wall," Saffron ordered. "Let's do one job at a time."

19 EXTRACTION

Jimmy emerged from the hole in the wall at knee level. He immediately rolled to one side then bounced to his feet, his eyes darting in all directions. Had he been spotted? Was the Capita's security force coming for him? Jimmy saw the throng of people heaving in all directions, barely in time with the music. They pushed him back against the wall. Above the pounding, his ears picked out the swivel of the security camera on the ceiling. With the place so packed and the darkness only broken by coloured flashing lights, there was no way he could have been spotted by security. Not yet.

Saffron rolled out of their tunnel straight after him. Jimmy saw her disappear into the shadows of the club. Even the black hole in the wall was invisible from more than a step away. Jimmy moved around the edge of the room, knowing Saffron was doing the same in the opposite direction. The ceiling was low and the whole room was packed. The smell of sweat and stale nuts infused the air.

Jimmy quickly picked out the only exits: a spiral staircase leading up to the rest of the club, manned by a security guard, and the doors to the bathrooms. There was also a bar on Saffron's side of the room, and Jimmy guessed there'd be a ladder up to the street somewhere back there. But he didn't need Saffron to confirm it. His body had already chosen his strategy. It was simple, direct and lethal.

Jimmy circled back to the security guard at the bottom of the stairwell. He was a huge man, dressed all in black, but his size was already working against him. From the bulges in the man's clothing, Jimmy could see the location of the man's weapon as clearly as if it had been lit up by a spotlight. He knew that was what the man would go to first to defend himself, and a predictable opponent may as well already be on the ground.

Jimmy twisted and ducked, swivelling into the guard with his head bowed and his shoulders low to the floor. He swept his heel into the guard's knee and his hand beneath the man's jacket. The guard let out a gasp of pain as his knee crunched in the wrong direction. He reached for his gun, but Jimmy simply grabbed his wrist and used the man's own momentum to bring him to the floor.

"Take me to Viggo," said Jimmy, bending to speak directly into the guard's ear as the man writhed face down in a puddle of something fizzy. "I have an invitation." Jimmy flicked the guard's gun to the ground, where it spun directly in front of the man's face. Stuffed down the barrel was the LOCO flier, rolled into a thin tube.

Just then Saffron appeared at Jimmy's back. They smiled at each other and lifted the guard by the shoulders. Without another word, the man stumbled up the stairs, leading Jimmy and Saffron towards their appointment with the Capita. Saffron pocketed the gun to keep it out of sight and clutched the laptop under her arm.

When they reached the ground floor the true size of the club became clearer. The floors above had been replaced with balconies to create one huge, dark, circular hall with a massive dance floor in the middle and bars around the edges of the room. Large balconies ran round the whole hall at eight or nine levels overhead, all of them packed with people.

The guard led Jimmy and Saffron up to the very top floor, to the back corner of one of the balconies. He ushered them behind a bar, watched suspiciously by paying customers and servers alike. The barman aggressively sliced through a lemon when he saw the strangers slipping past him. They marched through a more brightly lit storeroom, stacked high with crates of bottled drinks, until the guard paused at the door of a back office.

"Don't stop," Jimmy ordered, shouting over the music.

He gestured for the guard to open the door and get out of the way.

The guard scowled at him. "I'm only doing this because they're expecting you," he grumbled.

"Yes," said Jimmy with a sarcastic grin. "It's so very kind of you." He burst forward and slammed his foot into the door, just below the handle, missing the guard's hand by a millimetre. The door crashed open, but Jimmy held back. His instincts kept his feet locked to the floor, not letting him plunge straight into danger, and not wanting any startled Capita security agents to launch an unwise counterattack.

"You could have knocked," shouted a woman in the middle of the room. Jimmy instantly recognised her: the short woman who had come to Viggo's headquarters. The dim light caught her cheeks, which almost glowed from behind the black curtain of her hair. She was still wearing that thick white coat that swamped her tiny frame. For a second she looked like a baby polar bear looming out of an Arctic night.

"We've come for Viggo," Jimmy announced, stepping into the office. His senses were tingling. He could feel every movement reverberating in the stale air and every shift vibrating in the floor. There were Capita guards posted in every corner of the room and Jimmy saw them draw their weapons.

The light from the bar came through the door and cast Jimmy's own shadow across the floor. Caught at the edge of the brighter rectangle was a man's bare foot. There was dried blood on the nail of the big toe. Jimmy knew he had found Christopher Viggo. He was strapped to a chair in the middle of the room, his hands tied behind his back, a bag covering his head. Was he even still alive? *Yes*, Jimmy told himself. *He has to be.*

"The H Code?" announced the woman in the white coat. Jimmy felt his muscles creeping with tension and knew Saffron must be feeling the same. But was she also rapidly constructing a plan to extract Viggo and escape?

The door had swung closed, cutting out most of the noise of the club, but there was still a pounding thud. It reinforced the power of Jimmy's thoughts. They wouldn't stop. They piled over each other, swamping his consciousness until he didn't know whether the music was hammering the inside of his skull or the walls of the room.

"It's here," Saffron responded. She pointed to the laptop. "But we need guarantees first."

"Guarantees?" snorted the Capita woman. "I'm not selling you a washing machine."

"Show us his face," Saffron ordered, ignoring the other woman's jibes. "You promised us he'd be alive."

"He's alive." The Capita woman whipped the bag off

Viggo's head. Jimmy felt ice trickle down his throat. Viggo's eyes and mouth were open and from what Jimmy could see in this darkness, there weren't any serious cuts or bruises on his face. But though he was still breathing, he looked totally unaware of anything that was happening around him. His zombie-like expression seemed to loom at Jimmy, who couldn't bear to look away.

Jimmy's gut churned. How was he going to get this man out alive when he was bargaining with nothing?

"I know you rigged the election," Jimmy announced to the Capita woman. *Put them off guard*, he told himself. *Let them know their secrets are coming out.* He felt Saffron shift uncomfortably at his side and he realised he'd caught her off guard as well – she didn't know what Dr Longville had really found on the Chisley Hall computer.

"Just protecting our investment," the Capita woman barked after a long time. Then she added in a grumble, "Trying to, anyway."

"It's a hard system to hack," said Jimmy, all the time assessing the surroundings, looking for escape. His eyes flashed imperceptibly, taking in the positions of the guards, the dimensions of the room, the single bare bulb that illuminated it in the centre of the ceiling...

"Sometimes humans are more effective than systems," the Capita woman replied. "We had a man working on the HERMES project from the beginning. Deep cover, I suppose you might call it."

"You had a Capita man working on HERMES?" Jimmy said sharply. *Unsettle her,* he thought. *Provoke her. Anger creates mistakes.* "And you still lost the election? Your man didn't do a very good job, did he?"

"He's been processed," replied the Capita woman automatically.

"Processed?!" Jimmy couldn't hide his disgust. His effort to unsettle the Capita had backfired. "Bring him into the bar," he said firmly, waving a hand at Viggo with a lurch of revulsion.

The Capita woman snorted. "You know you're too young to buy him a drink?

"Just do it." Jimmy's voice was flat and strong, while his eyes watched every movement of the guards that surrounded him. "We need to know you're going to let us out alive once you have the H Code. We need to be where people can see us."

The woman let out another snort. "Give me the laptop first," she insisted, then looked to Saffron. "And the gun." Saffron glanced across at the guard, whose weapon she had taken. His embarrassment was as obvious as the bulge in Saffron's pocket. Saffron tried to protest, but Jimmy raised a hand to stop her. There was no point with so many armed guards surrounding them.

The Capita woman stuffed the gun into her coat and

thrust the laptop to the guard next to her.

"Plug this in," she ordered. "Or do whatever you need to do to tell me we have the H Code."

"Do you know what you could do with that?" Jimmy asked, trying to sound like he knew what he was talking about. In truth, he just needed to slow down the Capita. It wouldn't take long once the laptop was powered up for them to realise that Jimmy and Saffron were bluffing.

"Sorry, Jimmy," said the woman. "Enough conversation."

"But you know what you've..."

"Be quiet." The woman folded her arms and watched her assistant as he cradled the laptop in his arms and powered it up, still standing at the back of the room. *Stop him*, Jimmy heard himself thinking. *Destroy him.* He squeezed his fists, forcing the blackness of the club out of his head.

"Do we have it?" asked the woman. There was no response. "Do we have it?" she shouted. Jimmy knew his time was running out. He could hear the whirring of the laptop's fan as the hard drive started up. All the time, the pounding of the club's music was relentless. It seemed to surround him. But there was another noise too – a faint tapping. Viggo's big toe was bobbing up and down in a slow but regular rhythm and Jimmy was the only one in the room able to hear it.

Jimmy glanced up at Viggo's face. For a split second

the zombie was gone and the man's spirit was back. Jimmy felt a flood of exhilaration. Had Viggo's body and mind been strong enough to withstand whatever the Capita had done to him? The next instant, Jimmy was sure. Viggo jerked a single eyebrow and flashed his eyes to one side. He was signalling. Immediately his expression switched back to the zombie, but Jimmy knew what to do.

"There's a password," he announced. "On the laptop."

"No, there isn't," said the guard, looking at the screen.

"It's an encrypted operating system," Jimmy lied, stepping forward slowly.

"Stay there," said the woman, positioning herself between him and the laptop. "What's the password? Where does he enter it?" Jimmy was almost eye to eye with her. He could feel his limbs preparing for combat, throbbing with controlled power. But the assassin in him disguised his strength perfectly. He couldn't afford to give away that he was ready to strike at any moment.

"You have to search for a file," Jimmy explained, speaking slowly and clearly. "Open a search box."

"What next?" asked the guard, urgently. "What do I type in?"

"Type in 'now'," Jimmy replied.

"Now?" the guard repeated, confused.

"N, O, W," said Jimmy, then he shouted: "NOW!"

Suddenly Jimmy and Viggo burst into action. Jimmy

leapt up and slapped at the light bulb in the centre of the ceiling like a basketball player delivering a slam dunk. In one movement he ripped the bulb free and threw it straight at the Capita woman. She just put her hand up in time to shield her face and the glass smashed against her elbow, but Jimmy followed it up with a kick while he was still in midair. The ball of his foot struck the woman's temple with pinpoint accuracy and she staggered backwards, her eyes rolling in her head until she was able to support herself against the wall.

At the same time, Viggo swung his arms round in front of him. Somehow, he'd cut through the bindings at his wrists. In the chaos, nobody noticed the lemonade bottle cap falling from his fist. He ducked and swivelled, still sitting on the chair, and landed the base of his palm in the gut of the guard next to him.

At the door, the other guards tried to raise their weapons, but Saffron was quicker to react. She chopped both guards' arms at the same time, slamming their wrists against the wall. As they struggled to hold on to their guns, Saffron delivered a knee to one man's groin, then twisted to land a fist in the other man's nose. Immediately she grabbed Viggo by the collar. He was still attached to his chair at the ankles, so she dragged him out into the storeroom.

Once Jimmy shattered the light bulb, the guard with

the laptop spun it round to illuminate Jimmy and fight back. But he was too slow. Jimmy's heel shot into the centre of the computer's screen. Not only did the screen crack, but the force of the blow sent the laptop into the guard's chest like a battering ram. Jimmy didn't wait for his enemies to catch their breath. He dashed out, skidding into the storeroom after Saffron and Viggo. They were nowhere to be seen, but on the floor was the barman's knife, a lemon and Viggo's severed ankle ties.

Jimmy vaulted over the bar and landed among the crowd. He ignored the shouts, barged through to the edge of the balcony and looked out into the blackness. His eyes scanned the huge dance floor below, then the circles of the balconies below him. In a second, his mind highlighted what he needed to see – Saffron and Viggo had already made it to the next level down. They were charging round the balcony, ploughing people out of the way, heading for the stairs.

We're going to do it, Jimmy thought. *We've escaped the Capita.*

BANG!

The shot ripped through the pounding music, straight to the centre of Jimmy's senses. He automatically dropped low, but kept moving. His eyes were wide, every muscle tingling. Nobody round him had reacted. They didn't know what they'd heard. Jimmy doubled his efforts, sprinting on, but then, abruptly, the music stopped. The lights came on. Everywhere, people blinked and staggered about, shouting and complaining.

Jimmy shoved his way through to the edge of the balcony again. He had to see what was happening. His mind raced to reconstruct the sound of the shot and isolate its source. From that he could work out the position of shooter and the identity of the target. Were they aiming at Viggo? Saffron? Jimmy himself? Before Jimmy could take two more steps, a second gunshot ripped through the calm confusion of the club – and it sparked chaos.

20 *THIS ISN'T GENETICS*

Jimmy was pressed up against the balcony railing by the surging mass of people, all screaming, all rushing for the exits. In the centre of the hysteria, Jimmy was focused. He had to decipher what was going on. He crawled to a solid pillar to shield himself, in case the shooting was aimed at him, bracing himself against the buffeting around him.

Another shot blasted through the screams. Something inside Jimmy was primed to pinpoint the noise. He turned just in time to see the black tip of a rifle on the balcony directly opposite him, on the same level. It withdrew immediately and disappeared into the crowd, but Jimmy knew that the angle of the shot had been levelled downwards. His eyes darted across the hall, tracking where his brain calculated the bullet must have been aimed.

It was pandemonium, but amid the surging sea of bodies on the level below, Jimmy spotted Saffron, lurching from side to side, with Viggo draped over her shoulders like a lion's fleece. He was hit! Jimmy peered closer, but as soon as he looked, the heads of his two friends disappeared again into the mass. *They'll be OK*, Jimmy told himself. *It's probably just a graze. No marksman could hit a single head in this crowd.* But the crowd was gradually dispersing, especially on the top level, where Jimmy was. He was becoming more and more exposed.

He spun round, searching for the assassin. Then, through the crowd, he saw the white coat of the Capita woman. Was she the shooter? Jimmy instantly knew she wasn't – she climbed on to the bar to look over the heads of the crowd. Her hands were empty and there was fear on her face.

"Don't shoot!" she cried out. Her voice was completely lost in the clamour, but Jimmy's eyes locked on to her lips and the words were obvious. "We need him alive!" She cried out. "Don't shoot!" As the top-level balcony cleared and the constant screams travelled down the building, her voice finally broke through for Jimmy to hear: "We don't have the H Code!"

Of course – Jimmy knew the Capita would be fools to try to kill Viggo now. They had taken him hostage for the H Code and that's still what they were after. Viggo was the only one who could tell them where it was. Jimmy didn't even know *what* it was, and the Capita must have realised by now that he'd been trying to bluff.

The Capita woman marshalled her guards, who gathered in a force around her. She issued orders in a forceful stream: "Stop them! Bring Viggo back alive!" Then her eyes fell on Jimmy. The woman dismissed her guards and called out to him.

"Stop them!" she shouted. *Does she mean me?* Jimmy thought, frozen in her gaze. He wanted to run, but his programming was keeping him locked in place. A would-be assassin was up here somewhere trying to kill Viggo, so that's where Jimmy had to be.

"Why are your people shooting at Viggo?" the woman screamed, marching right up to him. "Tell them to stop!"

"It's not..." Jimmy said, stumbling over his words. The confusion on his face was reflected by the Capita woman. They stared at each other, almost nose to nose. They realised together that the situation had drastically changed. Somebody was trying to kill Viggo, and neither of them knew who it was.

Another shot made Jimmy shudder. His programming seemed to slap him from the inside, forcing his senses to focus again. But then came the blackness.

William Lee's fingers trembled on his keyboard. He hunched over the computer as if people were constantly trying to watch what he was doing over his shoulder. But in reality, the large NJ7 tech lab was empty apart from him. He hammered each key like he was trying to kill an ant. This was his weapon. So far in his career he'd never been good at direct confrontation with an enemy. Guns made him nervous. All he could do with a knife was chop an onion. But at a computer keyboard, there was so much more that could be done, more cleanly, more efficiently, and more secretly.

With the tap of one final key, he sent out his carefully worded security alert to all NJ7 operatives in the area and every member of staff currently at NJ7 HQ. He had left out Miss Bennett, of course. He wanted her there. He had plans for her. But he double-checked that the recipients included the Prime Minister's personal bodyguards.

A nervous smile wobbled his lips. He jumped up from the computer and ran through the corridors of NJ7. With delight, he watched agent after agent receiving the alert. Some of them consulted with each other, some were content to be confused on their own, but they all knew about the recent problems with the NJ7 satellite surveillance system. A security alert was to be taken seriously – especially a warning that they should all leave NJ7 HQ, and even clear the surrounding streets.

Lee was panting by the time he reached the distant corner of the NJ7 complex where there was an exit into the Great College Street car park. He supported himself against the wall, trying to breathe deeply. His heart was pounding with excitement, terror and a thousand other emotions. He couldn't force from his head the idea that he was about to bring down a government. Where a democratic election had failed, where a genetically-programmed boy assassin had fallen short, William Lee was certain that he was about to triumph. In minutes, Ian Coates would be dead.

What's more, if the coordinated attack on Christopher Viggo was going according to plan, then that man wouldn't be around to take over. *And I'll deal with Miss Bennett myself*, Lee thought. There would be only one person left to take over. It didn't matter to Lee that the plan had come from his new masters, and that he was simply helping to put it into operation. *They might think they have control*, he thought, *but I'll be in power*. William Lee would be Prime Minister, and once he achieved that, the people who thought they were controlling him would find things a little more difficult.

Lee took a deep breath and glanced up the corridor to check once again that it was empty. He didn't have to worry about the CCTV cameras. He'd dealt with that already. He waited as long as he dared, to give the NJ7 agents time to clear the corridors, then pushed open the small white door that led out into the car park. His guest arrived as if the entrance had been timed down to the second. It was a woman, tall and elegant in a long grey coat. A single silver stud shone out from her ear, behind a curtain of long black hair.

The assassin didn't acknowledge William Lee's presence. She simply glided past him, her steps silent, and floated towards Number 10 Downing Street.

Eva hurried through the NJ7 corridors. She had to get to her appointment with her boss on time. If she was even half a minute late, Miss Bennett would be suspicious. There might not be any comment made, but she would still suspect something. And Miss Bennett's slightest suspicion could be enough to prevent Eva from finding the information that would help Jimmy.

Eva was finally becoming comfortable with the strange and secretive systems used in the NJ7 archives. She was sure that eventually she would find what Jimmy needed. She couldn't put that at risk with something as stupid as being late for Miss Bennett.

Suddenly she felt a fist on her arm. She was spun round and pressed up against the wall before she could even take a breath to scream. The whole corridor seemed to whirl round in a haze of blackness.

"What are they doing to him?" came a sharp whisper, barely a millimetre from her face. Mitchell pressed her against the wall and stared. Eva felt a thrill of relief and terror. She couldn't look away from his huge, slate-grey eyes.

"You better let me go," she insisted quietly, surprised that she sounded so calm when inside her there was so much confusion.

"You can't just take me to see my brother lying unconscious on a slab with a laser in his eye and not tell me what's happening. I knew they had him somewhere, alive, but what have they been doing to him? How long have they...?" Mitchell broke off, unable to finish, and looked down.

Eva took a moment before replying. She didn't know how much to tell him. If she was honest, she wasn't even sure how much of what she had found out could possibly be true.

"I think it's..." She caught her breath as Mitchell's eyes jumped to hers again. "I found something about it in Dr Higgins' old files."

"Dr Higgins?"

Eva immediately scolded herself for revealing that she'd been searching that man's files. Dr Higgins had started the programme to create organic assassins through genetic manipulation, but he'd escaped from NJ7 and was possibly even dead. What reason could Eva have for snooping through his papers?

"I didn't understand it all," she went on, hoping to distract Mitchell by playing the ignorant little girl. "It all looked so complicated." She let her lips bloom into a pout and sensed Mitchell's grip weaken.

"What did it say?" he asked, a break in his voice.

"I'm sorry, Mitchell. I think Dr Higgins was trying to work out a way to give your brother new... abilities."

"You mean, like... like me?" Mitchell stammered slightly over his words.

"You have them genetically, but your brother doesn't. I think Dr Higgins revived an older experiment. Before he could create assassins genetically, he tried to do it through..."

"Through what? Tell me!"

"Mind control," said Eva quickly, unable to believe she was even saying it. She didn't understand it completely, but that was what she'd understood from the dusty, faded government reports on Dr Higgins' old experimental programmes. From what she'd seen, over the years, the NJ7 tech team had been forced to explain their science to the non-scientific people in the Government – especially when they were asking for more money. Those documents had been Eva's only hope of understanding why Lenny Glenthorne was being kept alive in the lab with a laser constantly trained on his eye.

"I think," she went on, gently, "I think they're still trying to work out a way to change a person's personality and intentions... through their brain."

"Can they change their genetics?" Mitchell asked. Eva was startled. That wasn't the question she'd been expecting. Why was that the first thing Mitchell wanted to know? And why was there such a strange expression on his face now?

He released Eva and backed away, suddenly looking more vulnerable than Eva had ever seen. "Can they...?" he whispered, looking everywhere but at Eva. "What if they can reprogramme..."

"I don't know anything about that," Eva replied, frowning. "This isn't genetics. This is brainwashing! They're keeping him alive to continue the old experiments into changing a person's brain when it's already fully grown."

For a few seconds the two of them stared at each other, slumped against the walls on opposite sides of the corridor. The positions of their bodies perfectly mirrored each other.

"They're changing who he is," Eva explained, though she was far from certain that was the truth. Really, she had no idea what was being zapped into Lenny Glenthorne's mind. "If they bring him round," she went on, "he might not be the same person."

To Eva's surprise, Mitchell let out a rough grunt of a laugh.

"The same person?" he spat. "You mean a miserable, mean..."

"He might not remember you," Eva cut in, desperate to bring back the softness she'd seen in Mitchell only moments before. But the more he thought about his brother, the more hardened he seemed to become, in body and mind. "He might not be *him* any more!" Eva exclaimed.

Mitchell just stared at her. Eva wished she knew what he was thinking. For the first time she felt like Mitchell couldn't even see her, and she realised that she hated it. At last he was pulled back to reality by his phone vibrating in his pocket. Startled, he pulled it out and checked the message.

"Security alert," he muttered. "We've got to get out of here."

"But Miss Bennett..." That second, Eva received the same message on her phone. At least this would mean she wouldn't have to explain her lateness to her boss. "Come on," she said. "Let's go."

"You go," Mitchell replied after a second. "I'm staying." He looked up the corridor in the wrong direction – away from the nearest exit. Eva realised straight away he was looking back towards the tech labs where his brother was.

"You can't..." Eva tried to protest, but her words were

lost as a line of NJ7 agents rushed past her. "What about…?"

"If he won't be him," Mitchell said softly, "maybe he'll be worth saving." He gave her one final glance before he disappeared into the gloom of the NJ7 labyrinth. "Thank you, Eva."

"If you're staying, I'm staying!" Eva whispered after him. As soon as the words left her mouth, she asked herself why she'd said them. Had Mitchell heard her? Eva settled her nerves and rushed back up the corridor towards Miss Bennett's office.

21 BLACKOUT, WHITEOUT

Jimmy's eyes adjusted to the dark after just a moment. He was buzzing now with the full force of his programming fizzing through him. He fought to keep his human mind active, desperate to control his instincts, but also to use what he knew to puzzle out what could be happening.

He was on the top-level balcony of the club, and he knew the last shot had been fired from the same level. Meanwhile, Saffron and Viggo were fighting their way through the crowd on the level below. Somewhere out there in the blue haze, there were answers that he had to find.

Then, just as he thought he was winning control of his mind and bringing together the courage to act, his world was blown apart again. This time it wasn't by a bullet, a crossbow dart or even a fist, but a sudden burst of light. Everything flashed white, then disappeared immediately. Then again, the whole room exploded into brightness before plunging back to total black. Strobe lighting – the would-be assassin had activated the club's strobe system and it made Jimmy's night vision useless. There wasn't enough time for his eyes to respond to the constant shifts between extremes of light and dark. Effectively, Jimmy was as blind as any normal human in the room, seeing events only in momentary slices. The moments in between were blank – and blank moments, Jimmy knew, were deadly.

Before he even had the chance to panic, Jimmy climbed over the balcony railing. It was the only way to keep moving. The club was still packed with people, and although the top level had begun to clear, the staircases were blocked. Jimmy pictured his path down the outside of the balconies. *Protect Viggo*, he told himself, pushing away his fear. *Find the shooter.*

He gritted his teeth and quickly lowered himself, the confidence in his movements spreading to his consciousness. For once, he was grateful that he couldn't see how far he might fall. His programming screamed at him. *Get down! Protect Viggo! Find the shooter!* From the bottom edge of the balcony, he swung himself on to the next level down, crashing into a group of screaming clubbers. As soon as he clambered to his feet, he rushed to look out again over the balcony at this new level.

He felt a burning drive inside him to keep moving, but forced it away for long enough to piece together the flashes of what he saw. Saffron had made it another two levels down. Jimmy picked her out among the crowd, on the side of the club to his far right. But she wasn't with Viggo. Under fire, she'd had to let him go. In the next flash, Jimmy saw that he was struggling behind her. *He's moving*, Jimmy realised with relief. *He can't be hurt that badly.*

Jimmy pushed himself up over the balcony railing, ready to vault two more floors to reach them, but the next flash showed him that the crowd around Viggo was clearing. Saffron was too far from him – she'd been swept forward in the people's panic to get down the next staircase. Then, out of the shadows swooped the Capita's team of guards. They swamped Viggo. Jimmy watched the man struggling and tried to work out where he'd been shot. How badly would it hamper his combat skills? In seconds, Jimmy saw the answer: the Capita guards easily overpowered him and bundled him away.

"NO!" Jimmy cried, leaping over the balcony. He caught the balcony below and pulled himself over the railing, landing with a roll, but he was still one level too high. He peered out across the void, but Viggo and the Capita guards had disappeared.

BANG!

Another gunshot, a new wave of screams from the clubbers fighting to get out. *The Capita wants Viggo alive,*

Jimmy thought to himself. *They'll shield him from the bullets.* And that's when he glimpsed his friend again, in the thick of the crowd, being frogmarched on either side by Capita operatives. They were forcing their way through the crowd on the next level down, barging everybody out of their way. *They're using the crowd to shield him,* Jimmy realised. The assassin in Jimmy let out a ripple of appreciation – the Capita tactic was one that would probably work. But Jimmy pushed away the joy, horrified that a part of him was enjoying a strategy that could cost innocent lives. *Find the shooter,* he told himself, trying to order his thoughts, *then save Chris.*

Jimmy twisted to check the sightlines. Where would an assassin be hiding? Another gunshot, and everybody flinched except Jimmy. *The rifle!* Jimmy had seen it – without even realising what he saw. It was just a solid black line that appeared for an instant above the balcony railing on the level below to Jimmy's left, on the opposite side of the club to where Saffron and Viggo had been. At the next flash, the black line was gone and the shooter was on the move again, but Jimmy had seen enough. He climbed up on to the balcony railing to extract himself from the crowd and ran along to his left, not believing he could travel so fast on a strip of metal so thin.

He leaned into the curve, racing round the room, his toes beating the handrail, propelling him forward faster, into the darkness and the flashes of light. Jimmy cursed the strobe light. It meant he was always half a second behind the real world. He scanned the level below, checking for the movement of the shadows. A figure caught his eye. Saffron was climbing out over the balcony on the level below. Was she also trying to get out of the crowd? Was she trying to go back for Viggo? Jimmy kept running, streaking through the lighting, away from Saffron and closer with every step to where he'd seen the gun.

But he couldn't help looking back again. Something inside him, some instinct – human or not – fired him with concern. What he saw tore his hopes in two. A single strobe flash picked out the silhouette of a woman clinging to the railing of the balcony. In that same flash, the shooter must have seen the same thing. Another gunshot ripped through the club. Jimmy watched helplessly, still running, but unable to stop himself slowing down. Saffron's body shuddered. Her shoulder spat blood and she lost her grip.

"NO!" Jimmy screamed.

In the next flash, Saffron was hanging by one arm from the bottom edge of the balcony. Her other arm was swaying limply by her side, a trail of red snaking down from her shoulder. Jimmy stopped dead, barely able to keep his own balance, teetering on the handrail. On one side of him, Saffron was swinging in the air, her fingers slipping, losing her grip, with a huge drop beneath her. On the other side, somewhere in the darkness there was an assassin waiting to strike.

The mission, Jimmy heard in his head. *Find the shooter.* His thoughts seemed to be attacking him from the inside like rapid-fire bullets. His programming would accept no other answer – he had to run on, he had to ignore Saffron and find the shooter. For a split second, Jimmy remembered Chisley Hall. *Leave her! Complete the mission!*

But Jimmy refused to give in. He locked his muscles in place, risking losing his balance and falling from the balcony. All the time, he watched Saffron swinging in the void, each flash of light revealing her to be slipping further and further down. There was nobody to help her. The crowd had streamed away, fleeing from the latest shot, stampeding on to the lower levels.

The mission! The words screamed in Jimmy's head. *Save Chris! Find the shooter!* Jimmy's head throbbed and his chest felt like it would burst. *Let her drop! She's not important!*

"The mission is to get out alive!" he shouted, desperate to overpower his own instincts. "All of us!" He tore the soles of his feet from the handrail and sprinted – to his right, towards Saffron. The screams of the crowd had faded for him now. All he could hear was the pounding of his own blood through his head. His steps hammered into the balcony rail at twice the rate of the strobe light, as if the flashes were fuel to his engine.

He was only a few metres away when a final shot erupted through the hall. It echoed round the balconies and in Jimmy's head. His mind automatically analysed the sound of the shot, and the faint sounds that had come directly after it. The noise told him that this bullet had landed in flesh. *I could have stopped it*, Jimmy heard himself thinking. He knew that with as much certainty as he knew anything. That single shot was the one he could have prevented, if he'd followed his programming and run after the shooter, instead of going back for Saffron.

He pumped his limbs harder, straining for the extra speed that could save Saffron's life. He squinted into the flashes of white, the strobe mixing with bitter tears, smearing his vision to a blur. All he could see was the image in his head of the one bullet that should never have been fired. Who had it hit?

Mitchell hauled off the black sheet that covered his brother. He gazed at the unconscious body. A part of him felt like the first time he'd seen it might have been some kind of dream. But there was Lenny Glenthorne, staring blankly up, with a green laser burning into his right pupil.

It serves you right, Mitchell thought. He crept closer,

planting his hands on the slab right next to his brother's shoulder. He was disgusted with himself when he saw that his fingers were trembling.

"It serves you right!" he said aloud, confident that nobody would disturb him. On his way to the tech labs he'd passed line after line of NJ7 staff. By now, everybody had evacuated the underground complex. Mitchell was alone with the young man who had once been his only family. *And my worst enemy*, he thought. Through his mind flashed a thousand images of his brother's snarl, the sound of his mocking laugh, the feel of the back of his brother's hand across his cheek.

"Does it hurt?" Mitchell whispered, leaning down to his brother's ear. His words echoed back to him off the walls of the lab. Mitchell clenched his fists. What was happening? Why wasn't he happy at what he saw? When Eva had first shown him this sight, he hadn't felt the flood of joy he'd always expected to have when he finally got to see his brother suffering. *That was shock*, he'd told himself. Now, the second time, he wanted that rush of vengeful pleasure.

"You had it coming!" he shouted, trying to force his spirit to feel something. But still his hands trembled and his chest felt empty. He slammed his fist on the slab. "What are they doing to you?" he whispered. "Are you still in there? Are you still... human?" He swallowed the word, feeling his head swirl.

At last he pushed himself away from the slab, short of breath. He circled the slab, inspecting the machine that was firing the laser into Lenny Glenthorne's eye. There were tiny flickers in the green light. What did it mean? Was the laser doing something to Lenny's eye, or was it meant to go straight to the brain, carrying some kind of information? *Or training*, Mitchell thought.

There were no clues on the machinery, but Mitchell inspected it closely anyway, thankful for the details to distract him from the torment in his mind. Then a noise broke his concentration. A soft shuffle. Were there still NJ7 agents marching past the labs on their way out? No, this was a single person, and not somebody marching. This was the step of someone who didn't want to be heard.

Mitchell's defensive instincts surged into action. He didn't want to be seen. He wasn't meant to be here. He quickly replaced the black sheet over his brother and dashed silently back up the dark staircase that led to the main corridor. There, from the shadows, he saw a tall woman in a long grey coat gliding past. The light caught her earring. Mitchell held himself still in the darkness, analysing everything he could about the stranger. She wasn't NJ7 – she didn't move with the precision or strength of anybody with a military background. In fact,

Mitchell thought, she moved more like a zombie. Her gaze never wavered, her steady pace never changed.

For a second Mitchell considered whether he was watching a ghost. A shiver ran through him. *Don't be stupid*, he told himself. Then, at the end of the corridor the woman paused. From under her coat she produced a black balaclava and pulled it over her head. *Some ghost*, thought Mitchell.

22 HE DIDN'T STAND A CHANCE

Ian Coates let the music fill his head, wishing it could wash away his thoughts completely and take him to another world. He was alone for the first time in what seemed like a lifetime, relishing the cool air and the soothing orange glow of the desk lamp. He didn't know where his staff had gone, and he didn't care. Even his bodyguards had been called away on some emergency. He might be the Prime Minister, but he knew that Miss Bennett was the one in charge, and if she'd decided to use the entire Secret Service to mount some huge operation without telling him, he wasn't going to try to get in her way.

Maybe it's a training exercise, he thought to himself, *or someone's coming to kill me*. He dropped his head back in his chair and allowed himself a laugh, though there was no happiness in it.

He closed his eyes, trying once again to focus on the music. Every note of the baroque piano piece seemed to hammer away at another fear, another regret. But very quickly his brain started twisting the music into new sounds. Instead of relaxing his mind, the melody taunted him, as if it was singing, and every note was another word he hated to hear: *power, betrayal, death, family... Jimmy.*

"Enough!" he roared, jumping to his feet. He picked up each speaker in turn and slammed it to the carpet, stamping on it until the music was a tinny whimper, then it stopped completely.

When he looked up, a shock ran through him that nearly knocked him off his feet. His heart juddered in his chest: there was somebody else there. A figure was standing in the shadows in the corner of the room.

"Who are you?" Coates barked, trying to force some authority into his voice. "What are you doing in here?"

Suddenly the shadow leapt forward. All Ian Coates saw was the grey coat billowing out behind his attacker, and the flash of a blade. Ian Coates let out a yell, but his body didn't panic. He was NJ7-trained, and even though he hadn't seen active duty for years, he still had more strength and speed than any civilian. He instantly dropped his weight to one side, letting the attacker come at him, waiting for the perfect split second to dodge.

The blade lunged straight for his throat. Coates leaned back, swinging his neck away, every fighting instinct firing inside him. But the attacker's reach was long. Coates had to sway so far that he almost lost his balance and had to step backwards to steady himself. As he stepped, he tripped on the remains of the speakers at his feet. He fell on to his back with a clatter, shards of plastic digging into his spine, a metal blade propelled towards his Adam's apple by the hand of an assassin.

CRUNCH!

The attacker was thrown to one side and crashed into a filing cabinet. Ian Coates blinked several times, gasped and clutched his neck. It was still whole. When he was at last able to focus, he saw Mitchell standing over him, holding out a hand. It took several seconds for Coates to realise that the first sound he'd heard had been Mitchell's knee breaking the intruder's ribs.

"Where are your bodyguards?" Mitchell shouted.

"They... they..." Coates could barely get his voice out. He still clutched at his throat, as if he couldn't believe there wasn't a dagger sticking into it.

Next to them, the intruder was wrapped in the long grey coat. Only now did Coates see from the curves of his attacker's figure that it was a woman. *Miss Bennett!* The name flashed through his mind, but he dismissed it straight away. If she wanted him dead, he wouldn't even have seen the blade coming. *Then who...?*

Mitchell spotted the woman's muscles twitch. He

grabbed her collar and hauled her across the room. "Your security!" he shouted. "Where is it?"

"I don't know... I..." Coates was at last finding his voice, but he couldn't take his eyes off the balaclava that covered the head of the woman slumped against the wall.

"NJ7 was being evacuated," Mitchell said, thinking aloud. "Every agent left. We got a message..."

"From Miss Bennett?" Coates blurted out. "She let in an assassin to—"

"No." Mitchell was firm, dismissing Coates' idea completely. He too knew that if Miss Bennett wanted Ian Coates dead, there would have been no mistakes. But the suggestion set Mitchell's mind racing. If Miss Bennett hadn't sent this assassin, who had? Surely not Christopher Viggo. He would have sent Jimmy or done the job himself. Surely not the French, who would have used Zafi, their own child super-assassin. And whoever *was* behind this, what good would it have done to assassinate Ian Coates if Miss Bennett was still alive? It wouldn't change anything. Miss Bennett was the one who really ran the country. If somebody wanted to change things, they'd have to deal with her as well. They'd have to...

"Miss Bennett!" Mitchell gasped. "Where's Miss Bennett!?"

That moment, the door crashed open and Mitchell's question was answered. Miss Bennett stood silhouetted in the doorway, her hair unusually wild, like a black fire round her head. She had one hand on her hip, while the other was tensed at her side, gripping something. As she strode into the Prime Minister's study, the light caught the fury in her eyes. That's when Mitchell saw what was in her hand. Her fingers were locked into the thick bush of hair on top of William Lee's head. The man's bean-like body extended across the carpet in Miss Bennett's shadow.

"Look what I found," Miss Bennett announced, anger infusing every syllable. She thrust Lee's body forward and dumped it into the centre of the room. The only sign that he was still alive was the grunt when his chest hit the floor.

Ian Coates looked at her, aghast. "He tried to...?"

"Yes, Ian," sighed Miss Bennett, expertly tidying her hair, "this idiot tried to stab me. You want to tell me what's going on?"

"I thought you had him under control," said Coates.

Mitchell felt Miss Bennett's gaze skip across him. She took in everything around them in an instant.

"This woman came for you at the same time," she said. It wasn't a question. "I'm relieved to see that."

"Relieved?" gasped Coates.

"Yes," came the sharp reply. "If she hadn't, I would have assumed that you were working with *him*." She thrust a thumb in the direction of the crumpled pile of limbs that William Lee had been reduced to. The breath barely wheezed from his lips.

"Who put you up to this?!" Miss Bennett snapped, shoving a foot into William Lee's ribs. The man's head lolled backwards, his eyes rolling without any control. "Who sent you?!" Again there was no reaction.

"What did you do to him?" Coates whispered.

"It was self-defence," came a new voice from the door. Mitchell turned to see that Eva had slipped into the room behind her boss. "Miss Bennett was attacked," she said, her voice trembling. "And then... then..."

"Thank you, Eva," Miss Bennett cut in, calmly. "What she's trying to say is that he didn't stand a chance." She narrowed her eyes. "Try that one." She ordered Mitchell to go to the masked woman slumped against the wall. "Bring her round. Find out who sent her."

Mitchell grabbed the woman's shoulders and dragged her closer to the light. He could feel his programming thudding through his veins, setting his thoughts racing. This woman's shoulders weren't big. This was no soldier. He propped her up against the Prime Minister's desk and slowly peeled the balaclava from her face, keeping his guard up, ready for anything, in case the woman burst into life and attempted a counterattack.

She didn't. She had been knocked unconscious and

was just beginning to come round now as Mitchell's hands clasped her head. But when her face was revealed, the effect on the room was greater than any attack. Eva let out a gasp and seemed to lose her breath for a few seconds. The Prime Minister staggered backwards and supported himself against the filing cabinet.

"Where am I?" said the woman on the floor. "What's...?" She looked round, squinting in the dim light to see the faces of the people in the room. After a few seconds, she saw the Prime Minister. "Ian..." she said, half-smiling at first, as if she'd seen a friend. Then confusion attacked her again. She frowned and looked round, frantic. "How did I get here?" She stared at Eva. "You," she said intently. "I know you too."

Eva tried to speak, but there wasn't enough air in her lungs. At last, the Prime Minister broke the silence.

"Olivia," he said gently. "We need to know who sent you here."

The woman looked up at him, her eyes wide, fearful, and her lips trembling.

"But where is this?" she whispered. "And where's Felix? Where's my son?"

Jimmy threw himself over the balcony, keeping his hands on the rail. He clambered down like a spider, shifting his weight with precision and speed, then swung towards Saffron. Together, they bundled to the floor of the next level down and Jimmy propped her up against the balcony rail.

"I'm OK," Saffron said, obviously trying to sound stronger than she felt. "I've been shot worse than this before, remember? This one's just a graze." She clutched her shoulder, where red was blooming over her hands. It flashed in the strobe light, but so did the determination in her eyes. "Get to Chris," she whispered intently. "There's only one shooter and Chris is the target. I'll get to the basement. Your mum and the others will take me from there."

"They're here?"

Saffron nodded. "They sent a text. They'll patch me up."

"Yeah," said Jimmy. "Felix is obviously a genius at first aid." He forced himself to smile, and was flooded with relief when Saffron smiled back.

"Go!" Saffron ordered, and Jimmy's body responded. He circled the balcony, peering into the darkness, learning the rhythm of the strobe flashes – when to run, when to look.

He spotted Viggo on the level below, being carried on either side by Capita guards, unable to fight. Jimmy ducked his head and sprinted round to the point exactly above them. Then, without even hesitating, he launched himself over the side. He caught the bottom edge of the balcony behind his back, his legs extended in a pike position like an Olympic gymnast on monkey bars, then swung down. A surge of power in his hips directed Jimmy's fall. He was so fast neither guard saw him coming. It all happened in the single breath between flashes of the strobe light. The back of Jimmy's heels connected perfectly with the collar bone of one of the guards, who staggered, tripped and fell.

Jimmy twisted in the air and used the body of the guard as his own bouncy castle to get back on his feet. The spirit of *La Savate* combat was surging through him again. He took down the second man with a *coup de pied bas* – a low kick with the arch of his foot that swept his opponent away at the knee. The guard crumpled and fell on top of his partner.

Now that he was unsupported, Viggo swayed, tried to walk, and fell forward. Jimmy caught his friend on the back and heaved him away from the guards, dragging him round the curve of the balcony. He could feel the warmth of the blood from Viggo's gut spreading over his own back. When they were out of sight of the guards, Jimmy brought his friend to the floor to look at the wound. Straight away, he saw the man was more badly hurt than he'd realised. He'd been shot twice.

"Jimmy..." gasped Viggo.

Jimmy was busy trying to work out if there was anything he could do to stem the bleeding. *I should have gone for the shooter*, he thought. He couldn't help reliving that split second – his moment of hesitation. *This is where the extra bullet landed! I should have followed my instinct!* Would that indecision cost Viggo his life? He might have had the strength to recover from one bullet, but two...

"Jimmy..." Viggo whispered again, more insistent this time, forcing his voice out. There wasn't time to say any more. Without looking round, Jimmy felt the heavy steps of two huge guards sprinting towards them. He launched a back kick at head height – with perfect timing. Even through the sole of his shoe, he felt the connection with the guard's teeth. Then he threw back his other leg, planting his foot in the stomach of the second guard.

Viggo struggled to his feet, swaying and clutching the wound in his belly. But instead of joining the fight, he twisted like a leaf in the wind and slumped over the balcony railing. Jimmy grabbed him with both hands. He held him firmly in his grip to stop him from falling. That's when Jimmy saw it.

A flash lit up the hall as the last of the clubbers dashed out of the doors. Left alone on the dance floor was a single figure: a masked man in a long grey coat, with a rifle in his hand. One glimpse of Jimmy and Viggo was enough. He started to take aim, but Jimmy's reactions kicked in before the shooter could raise his rifle.

In one movement, Jimmy hauled Viggo down behind the protection of a pillar and threw himself over the side, into the air. It was a five-floor drop, but he had no option. He pulled his knees into a tuck position and spun over himself. For seven seconds it felt like he was just revolving in space. The black floor of the club loomed towards him, but Jimmy's inner power was deeper and darker. He locked his fists together and brought them down perfectly on the back of the shooter's neck. The landing knocked the breath from Jimmy's chest, but the man underneath him cushioned his fall.

Immediately Jimmy tossed the rifle away. He turned the shooter over on to his back, with no doubt that the precision blow to the nerves in the back of his enemy's neck had knocked him unconscious. Jimmy planted his knees on the man's shoulders and peeled the balaclava off his face.

The next strobe flash seemed to last forever. The image of the man's face struck Jimmy's eyes, but his brain refused to understand it. *I'm hallucinating*, Jimmy thought. *This can't be true.* But he kept looking and the face didn't change. The man was unconscious, his eyes open – big, brown discs that Jimmy was used to seeing full of kindness. The same silver stubble that Jimmy knew flecked the man's cheeks. His face was thinner than the last time Jimmy had seen it, but there was still the hint of bagginess around his jaw. Jimmy's brain screamed out with confusion: *why is Neil Muzbeke here? Why is Felix's father trying to kill Christopher Viggo?*

23 LEE MAKES SPARKS FLY

Eva brought in a tray of tea, the shake in her hands causing the mugs to rattle against each other. Miss Bennett was issuing orders down the phone, recalling an NJ7 force to HQ and deploying others to strategic locations around the country, just in case the battle wasn't yet over. Ian Coates was slumped behind his desk, holding his head, while Mitchell was helping Olivia Muzbeke to an armchair. The pain in her ribs was obvious, but so was her genuine confusion.

"Get some answers out of her," Miss Bennett said firmly to nobody in particular.

"What do you want us to do?" Ian Coates sighed. "She doesn't remember anything!"

"I'm not suggesting we beat it out of her," Miss Bennett muttered, slamming the phone down. "She obviously knows nothing – consciously."

"I don't... I d-don't..." Olivia Muzbeke's voice quivered

and her hands were so unsteady that when Eva gave her the mug of tea, some of the hot brown liquid splashed over the sides. "I remember flashes..." Olivia muttered. "Just images, really... an old man..."

"What's the last thing you *do* remember?" Miss Bennett asked.

Olivia's eyes lit up. "Felix," she announced. "I remember seeing Felix. We were in New York. Yes, that's right – I remember being in America."

"The Americans," growled Miss Bennett. "That much is obvious. I knew we couldn't trust them! They just couldn't let Britain run itself, could they?!"

"What about him?" asked Mitchell, nodding towards William Lee. "He hasn't been anywhere near America."

"The CIA has tentacles everywhere," Miss Bennett replied. "They must have reached him when they saw he had no more authority here. Or he went to them. Either way, it doesn't matter."

"The satellite surveillance," Eva gasped. "Mr Lee was meant to be fixing it, but..."

"But he was the one jamming it." Miss Bennett nodded with a grim expression on her face. "He needed to create the surveillance blackouts so the CIA could send in their assassin."

"Assassin?" gasped Olivia Muzbeke, obviously fighting back tears. "Did I...?"

"It's OK," said Eva gently. She crouched down at Olivia's side and held her hands, clasping them round the warmth of the mug. Eva looked up into the woman's eyes and nearly burst into tears herself. She desperately wanted to tell her everything she knew about Felix. *He's OK*, Eva shouted in her head. *He's OK! He's out there with Jimmy and they miss you and they're OK!*

"Try to bring him round again," said Miss Bennett to Mitchell, indicating William Lee. "We need to know what he's done to the surveillance system so we can fix it."

"And find out whether there's anybody else..." added Ian Coates. He jumped up and shifted from foot to foot, peeping through the curtains. "There could be any number of them lurking out there... stars and stripes on the brain..."

Mitchell knelt down by William Lee. Mitchell let his arms be guided by the force inside him. In the chaos of tonight's events, it was a relief to feel that control taking hold. His hands locked round William Lee's left ankle. Mitchell didn't question it. He felt his fingers digging into a point just above Lee's Achilles' tendon. *Pressure point*, he heard himself thinking.

Suddenly Lee gasped for air. His eyes shot open and his body bucked. In a flash, he was sitting up, looking around at Miss Bennett, Ian Coates and the others. He looked like a startled rat cornered by hounds but, thanks to Mitchell, at least he was fully alert.

"Right then," said Miss Bennett with a sigh. "Anything you want to tell us?" She perched on the edge of Ian Coates' desk and smiled. William Lee said nothing, he just looked around, his terror obvious. "We know about the Americans already," Miss Bennett added, watching Lee's reaction carefully.

"You know...?" Lee gasped.

Miss Bennett's lips stretched into a bright-red sneer. That moment, her mobile phone buzzed. She checked the message and turned to Mitchell.

"Get to the labs, Mitchell," she ordered. "Some of the technicians are back. They're working on the satellites. As soon as they have anything, track Christopher Viggo from his last known location. Find out where he's hiding out now. Go after him. After this attack we'll have even more public support."

"You'll blame Viggo for this?" asked Coates.

"Of course," Miss Bennett explained. "It gives us the perfect justification for taking him out. Mitchell, go to it."

Eva watched Mitchell's chest swell. He stood tall, his chin held high. She was amazed at how quickly his demeanour shifted from muddled boy to trained military expert. But then she saw him hesitate. Her heart leapt. Was he having second thoughts? His mouth opened and Eva felt a surge of anticipation. She was sure Mitchell was going to say something about his brother. Or maybe he was simply going to refuse to go. Or perhaps...

"Pass on anything you get out of him," Mitchell announced in a gruff tone. He stuck out his chin in the direction of William Lee, then hurried from the room. Eva felt like a part of her spirit had disintegrated. Her eyes remained on the door long after Mitchell had passed through it. Even while Miss Bennett continued questioning William Lee, Eva couldn't help trying to puzzle out what was happening inside Mitchell's head. Her thoughts were only broken when Ian Coates' voice cut into Miss Bennett's interrogation.

"How did they do it!?" he roared.

"Calm down, Ian," said Miss Bennett. "The question of the satellite surveillance is more urgent."

"No!" Coates barked, running his hands frantically through his hair and gesticulating at Olivia. "I need to know! She was a friend!"

"Friends mean nothing," said Miss Bennett, holding up a hand to try to stop him. She turned back to Lee. "Ignore him. Tell me exactly what the tech team needs to do to unlock the surveillance satellites, and precisely what data the Americans had access to."

Lee's breathing was hard and fast. He was still on his knees, but Eva could see the panic growing through his body just in the way he held himself. There was nothing he could do. Miss Bennett didn't even have to threaten him. The knowledge of what she was capable of and what she had done to NJ7's enemies in the past – that fear was enough to drive any man over the edge.

Terror seemed to creep through Lee's entire body. He erupted into a flurry of words. Miss Bennett leaned back, smiling. *Was she even listening,* Eva wondered, *or was she merely enjoying the satisfaction of having won again, and so easily?* After a couple of seconds, Miss Bennett tapped a couple of keys on her phone and held the handset out to catch every word of William Lee's explanation.

Most of it Eva didn't understand, but she recognised enough of the technical language to know that in minutes NJ7 would have their full satellite surveillance capability back online, and the Americans would be locked out of the system. While Lee rattled on, Eva watched Ian Coates. The man was standing just behind the armchair where Olivia Muzbeke still sat, shaking, lost in her own thoughts.

"How is it possible?" Coates whispered, to nobody in particular. "A normal, healthy, kind human being transformed into... into..."

"It's brainwashing," announced Miss Bennett suddenly. Lee had finished his explanation and Miss Bennett turned her attention to Olivia Muzbeke.

"Brainwashing?!" Coates shouted. "What do you mean?!"

"If I have to tell you to calm down one more time," Miss Bennett said firmly, "I'll send you outside to sort yourself out."

Eva shuddered, remembering that this woman had once been posted undercover as a school teacher.

"I'm calm," said Coates. "I just need to know how many brainwashed zombie killers might be out there." He gripped the curtain, pulling it in front of himself slightly, almost as if he could hide.

"It isn't a very advanced technique," Miss Bennett explained, dismissively. "In fact it's quite old-fashioned. People have been trying it for over a century."

"I know people have tried it," Coates echoed. "It looks like they've succeeded!"

"*We* succeeded," said Miss Bennett.

"What?"

"It's an NJ7 technique. A very old one. It was replaced by the genetically designed assassins. But before Dr Higgins developed that concept, he perfected the art of brainwashing civilians to become unknowing assassins."

"It was Dr Higgins?" Coates asked.

"Yes, and it sounds like the Americans have got him now." She turned to Olivia Muzbeke. "That old man you remember – that must have been him."

Ian Coates stared at Miss Bennett in disbelief. "But if Dr Higgins developed this... technique... why can't *we* do this?"

Miss Bennett shrugged. "We can do it, we have done it and..." She paused. "...we are doing it."

"We *are* doing it?!" Coates charged up to Miss Bennett and gripped her shoulders, pulling her towards him. Eva felt a chill tearing up her spine – a part of her knew what Miss Bennett was going to say – but she fought it back, refusing to acknowledge the idea. Then Miss Bennett confirmed it.

"Mitchell has a brother," she smiled. Eva lost her breath. Her mug of tea tipped over in her hands and flooded on to the carpet. Nobody noticed. "If I give the word," Miss Bennett went on, "we could have another assassin alongside Mitchell in five minutes. We just need to specify the target and beam it straight into Lenny Glenthorne's brain with a laser."

"Send him!" Ian Coates begged, suddenly invigorated. "I want Viggo out of the way for good. He mustn't have the chance to gather support again. Send a whole NJ7 division!"

"Where do you want me to get a division from?" Miss Bennett asked. "Every agent was sent to who-knows-where by that CIA mole!" She jerked a finger at Lee without looking at him. "Even the security for this building is missing! Mitchell is enough. He's a precision weapon."

"He's failed before."

"Every time he fails, he learns, but I agree he needs

support. I'll send—"

Suddenly William Lee dived across the room. Miss Bennett and Ian Coates had become too distracted to keep an eye on him. But he wasn't launching an attack. Instead, he made for the broken remains of the Prime Minister's stereo. Nobody was in a position to stop him. Before Eva could draw breath, there was a crackling sound, a flurry of sparks, and an explosion. Eva jumped up, screaming.

The smell of burning filled the room and when the smoke cleared, William Lee was lying on his back, bare wires sticking out of his mouth. His eyes were wide open and the skin around his lips was black. Miss Bennett and Ian Coates rushed to him. Miss Bennett yanked the power cord out of the wall and pulled the wires from Lee's mouth. The man's body jerked horribly.

Eva couldn't watch. She looked away, instinctively burying her head in Olivia Muzbeke's shoulder.

"It's OK," Felix's mum whispered.

How is it OK? Eva shouted in her head. She fought to hold back her tears, but she couldn't stop her horror. A man had just electrocuted himself in front of her. The smell attacked Eva's nostrils. And this was just after she'd discovered that her friend's brother was being brainwashed to become an assassin. *My friend?* Eva was shocked at her own thoughts. *Is Mitchell my friend now?*

He's an assassin! A killer!

She buried her head deeper into Olivia Muzbeke's coat and felt the woman's soothing hand on the back of her head. *It's no good,* Eva thought. *Once they've got everything they need from you they'll probably kill you too!* Suddenly she felt a realisation jolt through her. The security forces were missing, sent all over the place on false emergencies by William Lee. The satellite surveillance system was still down. It would only be down for a few more moments, but maybe that was enough.

"You have to get out of here," Eva whispered, straight into Olivia's ear. She felt the woman's body tense up, but held her in a hug so that it wasn't noticeable. "Get out!" Eva insisted. "There's no security. No surveillance. Get out as quickly as you can and get as far away as you can." And then she realised. "No, go to London Bridge. Be under the flyover in the morning."

She could feel Olivia's breath quickening. "But... but..."

Eva glanced over her shoulder quickly. Miss Bennett and Ian Coates were crouched beside William Lee, trying to bring him round while shouting into their phones at the same time, trying to get hold of a medical team.

"Get out now!" Eva whispered. She released Felix's mother and threw herself across the room to the foot of Ian Coates' desk. Under the desk, glinting in the shadows, was the knife Olivia Muzbeke had tried to embed in the

Prime Minister's throat. Eva seized it now and, without even thinking, slammed it into her upper arm.

"Aargh!" she screamed. Blood spurted everywhere and pain shot through her whole body. *What have I done?* she cried inside.

"Eva!" said Miss Bennett, rushing to her. "What happened?"

"She attacked!" Eva yelled. "She found her knife! She's a killer! Stop her!"

Miss Bennett and Ian Coates stood in the middle of the study, confounded. Olivia Muzbeke's armchair was empty. She had already left the building.

24 SHADOWS AND ECHOES

Jimmy couldn't take his eyes off Neil Muzbeke's face until he was startled out of his thoughts by his mum's voice.

"Jimmy!" she shouted. He looked round to see her lit up by a flash from the strobe light. She was crouched at the top of the stairs that led down to the basement of LOCO. "Find cover!"

Cover, thought Jimmy, desperately trying to piece himself back together. *Yes – protection. Survival.* His programming was humming inside him. It didn't care that his best friend's father was the would-be assassin in his grip. How was it possible!? *Enough!* Jimmy ordered himself. He quickly pulled the balaclava back over Neil Muzbeke's face. He couldn't let the others see who it was – not yet. Only the cool, unfeeling killer in Jimmy stopped his focus evaporating in a storm of confusion. It kept him moving.

"Get this man out alive!" he ordered, dragging him

across the floor. He saw his mum hesitating, confused. "Just do it!" he shouted.

"Where's Chris?" his mother asked.

Before Jimmy could answer, they heard Saffron's voice.

"He's up there," she said softly. She had struggled down from the higher levels, clutching the wound in her arm. "They took him again. The Capita. They have him up on one of the balconies."

"Which level?" Jimmy asked.

"I don't know," Saffron's voice was ragged.

Jimmy could already feeling a thousand strategies taking shape in his head. "I'll find him." He silenced his mother before she could protest. "You make sure she's OK." He nodded towards Saffron. "Then find the lighting controls. Stop this flashing. Put the place in darkness again."

"I've been trying," Helen replied. "But..."

Jimmy was already dashing up the stairs. At the first level balcony he paused. He had to move carefully now. The club was almost silent. The crowd had made it outside, and only the occasional sound was coming through the walls. *The crowd will attract attention*, Jimmy thought. *They'll have called the police.* That was all bad news for Jimmy. The police would either be in the pay of the Capita, or under the influence of NJ7.

Jimmy crept round the balcony, listening, looking up at

the levels that circled the hall above him. Still the strobe flicked on and off in numbing rhythm.

"Chris, can you hear me?" he called out, then immediately dashed on in the shadows to mask his position once more. "I need to know you're OK!" *I need to know where you are,* he thought. *Any noise will do. Answer me!* There was no response, just Jimmy's own voice echoing back.

Jimmy moved up and up, circling each balcony, making sure there was no way the Capita could slip past him. *Come on,* Jimmy thought. *Any noise! Where are you?* The flashes of the strobe hammered into Jimmy's mind. When would they stop?

"You need Chris alive," he shouted, addressing the Capita now. "If you want the H Code, you have to get him to a hospital, which means bringing him down – past me. You're trapped!"

Still nothing stirred above him except the wafts of dust in the air. *Is there another way out?* Jimmy wondered. *The roof maybe?* It was a strong possibility. Had the Capita called for a helicopter? Jimmy expected to hear the sounds of a chopper at any moment. *I have to keep going,* Jimmy told himself. *Corner them. Create panic. Create mistakes.*

He made it to the seventh floor. *They're close now,* he told himself. As soon as there was any noise from above,

Jimmy would pin down the Capita's location.

"I'm coming for you," Jimmy whispered, knowing his voice would carry and the echo was enough to mask his position. Then it finally came – the noise Jimmy had been waiting for. But it wasn't a voice, or even the sound of a step creaking on the floor. It was a whirring, a soft buzz. *An electric motor*, Jimmy realised. He'd heard that noise before. In another country, another lifetime almost, when he'd last come across the Capita. It was the noise of an electric wheelchair. That meant only one thing: the Head himself was here.

The Head was the man in charge of the whole Capita organisation, the founder of a global crime network that made him more powerful than any head of state, despite his extreme physical weakness. Jimmy had never seen the man except in shadow, but still he had built an image of him in his mind: a withered, useless body that only existed to keep its head alive. The Head. That was him. Sometimes when Jimmy pictured the man he was just a head in a glass jar attached to a wheelchair, and he couldn't dismiss the image no matter how hard he tried. Nonetheless, if the Head was here, he would want to be right next to Viggo to hear the information he wanted as it came out of the man's mouth.

Jimmy rushed up the stairs to the next balcony. He was only one level below them now, he was sure of it.

"You're close now, Jimmy," came a voice, cutting through the hall like the next strobe flash. It was a thin, old voice with a strong Italian accent, but every syllable was clear, hissing with authority – the voice of the Head. "Don't worry about the lights, Jimmy," he said. "We've made sure they can only be controlled from up here."

Was that a lie? Jimmy tried to find clues in the voice, but he knew the Head was the master of manipulation.

"You're trapped," Jimmy called out, pacing across the balcony, searching for the point he thought was precisely below his enemy. Then came the whir of the Head's wheelchair again.

"You're just as trapped, Jimmy," the Head called out. "You want Viggo alive, but you can't get him unless you come to us. We don't care if he dies as long as he gives us the H Code first."

They've moved, Jimmy realised, constantly measuring where the voice was coming from. But there'd been no noise from the motor... Jimmy paused, recalculating his position. *Keep them talking...*

"There is no H Code," Jimmy shouted, desperate to find something that would make the Capita agents and the Head give away where they were hiding.

"But you're living proof that there is!" came the response from the Head.

Jimmy stopped dead. "What?" he gasped.

"What do you think the H Code is, young man?" asked the Head.

Ignore him, Jimmy ordered himself. *Keep searching. He's up there, above you. Listen for the motor.* The whir came again, and Jimmy followed it. *Listen for the voices.*

"Viggo promised it to us, and we will find it eventually," explained the Head.

"He lied to you," Jimmy replied. "It doesn't exist."

"But you exist!"

Then there was a new sound – a grunt. *Chris!* Jimmy sprinted a few metres further round, to where he thought the noise had come from, but he quickly realised he was going round in circles. He'd covered this part of the balcony before. They were just above him, but where? How were they confusing their position?

"Jimmy!" It was Viggo this time, for sure. He sounded in great pain, but it was definitely him. "I'm sorry, Jimmy!"

Jimmy picked up his pace again, following the voice.

"I told them I had the H Code, Jimmy," Viggo cried out, the blood bubbling in his voice.

Jimmy couldn't hold back any more. "Where is it?" he shouted. *Enough lies,* he thought. *I have to know.* "What is it? What is the H Code!?"

He heard another wheelchair whir and shadowed it, dashing back to where he'd just been.

"In a way, Jimmy," said the Head, with a soft laugh, "it's

you!" Jimmy felt the words stab him in the throat. "The H Code is the technology that's in you! It's the guidebook, the template... it's everything we need to reprogramme an unborn human's DNA to make them... not human."

Jimmy's blood seemed to freeze in his veins. "Chris!" he called out. "That can't be true!"

The only noise from Viggo was a low groan, almost drowned out by the whine of the Head's wheelchair. Jimmy fought back the insanity rising in his head and ran towards the sound.

"He has it, Jimmy!" said the Head. "He hid it! And we paid him millions for it!"

Lies, Jimmy insisted in his head. *Chris would never sell that!*

"He smuggled it out of NJ7 when he left all those years ago," the Head went on, "and he's had it hidden ever since!"

Jimmy shut out the voice as it echoed round the hall, flooding every floor. He leapt up, grabbed a strut in the ceiling and, in the same movement, punched a hole in the floorboards. The wood shattered instantly and Jimmy burst up through the floor above. The Head's voice might have been distorted by the echo in the hall, but the whir of his wheelchair had given him away. Jimmy had found him. He surged to his feet, ready to strike, ready to seize Viggo and take down his enemies.

But then the strobe light flashed once more. Jimmy spun round on the spot. He was still alone. The only thing he'd found was an empty wheelchair. It spurted forward half a metre on its own, letting out one more whir that seemed to mock the lone boy standing in front of it, ready for a fight, but with no opponent.

"No!" Jimmy cried. He brought his hand sweeping down into the centre of the wheelchair, connecting with nothing but air. "No!" How had he let a simple decoy deceive him? Then he spotted them – away on the other side of the hall at the same level, across the empty space in the middle.

The Capita woman's white coat flashed like a firework. Ahead of her were the four Capita guards. Two of them were carrying what looked like a wooden wheelbarrow. In the split second that it was lit up by a strobe flash, Jimmy realised it must have been some kind of antique wheelchair. Inside it, peeking out from under a pile of blankets, Jimmy just caught a glimpse of the back of a man's head. His view was cut off immediately by the other two guards, and what they were carrying – the bleeding, dying figure of Christopher Viggo.

"Chris!" Jimmy called out, hurtling round the balcony as the Head and his Capita guards reached a short flight of steps that led up to a trapdoor. Jimmy had guessed right: they were heading for the roof. But before they were up the steps, a new figure swept out of the darkness.

Jimmy only saw it for an instant, lit up in the flash. It bundled into the Capita unit like a bull blasting away a flock of pigeons. In the next flash, the Capita agents were scattered, confused. Viggo was gone. And Jimmy was sure that somehow a new enemy had arrived. One that didn't need to keep Viggo alive: NJ7.

And apart from Jimmy, there was only one other person in Britain who could have blown the Capita unit apart in a single moment. Jimmy knew it immediately: Mitchell had arrived to kill Viggo. Then,

BAM!

Something slammed into the back of Jimmy's head.

25 FALLEN IDOL

Jimmy stumbled forward, but caught his balance and turned the momentum of his fall into a spin. His foot came round at head height and smacked the cheek of his attacker. Jimmy saw the impact in a single strobe flash and what he saw astounded him. The face he'd just kicked was covered by a black mask, but the eyes were Mitchell's. So was the build of the body. And on the breast of the figure's black, silken shirt was a green stripe. But if that was Mitchell, who had taken Viggo?

Jimmy ducked instinctively, driven by his programming to protect himself. *Keep moving,* he heard. *Keep striking.* And that's what he did – he landed an explosive jab in Mitchell's middle then sprinted away, searching the darkness for Viggo. After two steps he ran straight into someone running the other way. Jimmy was barrelled to the ground and heard the other person fall too. The light flashed again and Jimmy saw him: the same figure sitting up on the floor right opposite him. Mitchell's eyes. Mitchell's body. Black shirt with a green stripe on the chest. How was this possible? Mitchell was in two places at once.

Jimmy pushed himself up, fighting his own confusion and fear. This Mitchell had been carrying Viggo, but dropped him in the collision. Jimmy dived forward, desperate to protect his friend. He scooped up Viggo in his arms, straining under the man's weight, forcing all his strength into his back and legs. He had no time to steady himself. He spun as soon as the darkness came and ran.

He knew that in seconds Mitchell would be on his feet and catching up. *He's faster than ever*, Jimmy thought, terrified that at any moment his enemy would spring up from the shadows, transported across the floor in an instant. Jimmy wrenched his legs forward, one step after another. If he could just reach the stairs, he had a chance...

"Jimmy..." Viggo wheezed. Jimmy felt the man's breath heaving in irregular lurches. *There's blood in his lungs*, Jimmy heard himself thinking. He tried to ignore whatever Viggo was trying to say and ran on. He could hear Mitchell's steps behind them, pounding closer. All the time, a hot glow oozed from Viggo's wounds across Jimmy's neck and back.

"Jimmy..." Viggo whispered again. "I'm sorry."

The words gripped Jimmy's brain and tore a new seam of despair.

"So it's true," said Jimmy, more to himself than to the man in his arms. "You sold everything to the Capita for your own power? And you tried to fix the election?"

"It was just..." The words died on Viggo's tongue. His eyes were pleading.

"And what you sold..." Jimmy went on, spitting out the words, "...was me?"

"Not you..." Viggo protested, his strength slipping away. "Just... the technology... a computer chip... the H Code..."

"You wanted the Capita to..." Jimmy couldn't finish what he was thinking. It was too horrible to imagine, but he had to say it. He wanted to scream it, to use the words to stab Viggo's wounds even deeper. "You'd let them make more of me!"

"No, Jimmy!" Viggo protested, but Jimmy watched his eyes in the next strobe flash. They were stretched wide and completely bloodshot. Was there any truth left in them? "Jimmy, I never..." He choked up every word, buffeted with each step that Jimmy took. They were only metres from the stairs now.

"So where have you hidden it?" Jimmy insisted. "Where is the H Code?"

"I can't..."

Suddenly a figure burst up from the stairwell. It swung through the darkness and knocked Jimmy off his feet. He and Viggo sprawled across the floor. In the next flash of light he saw the back of this attacker, bent over Viggo, arm raised, ready to strike. Was that Mitchell? How was it possible? He had been behind them!

There was no time for indecision. Jimmy leapt up and threw himself on to the boy's back. He caught the raised right hand just as it swept down towards Viggo's neck. Jimmy twisted the fingers until they snapped and threw the boy to one side as if he was flicking a rag doll to the floor. All the time, Jimmy was measuring his opponent's physical presence, his technique, his speed. The body was just like Mitchell's – perhaps even bigger – but the muscles were nowhere near as strong, the combat skills not as advanced. *So who is it?* Jimmy screamed to himself, just as the boy charged, burying his head in Jimmy's solar plexus.

The breath burst from Jimmy's body. For a second he thought his stomach was going to explode out of his mouth. He staggered backwards, but his attacker kept on driving forward. Jimmy felt his senses slipping away. He couldn't draw breath. If the pressure persisted he knew he would pass out.

There was a flash of red. The boy attacking Jimmy was knocked to one side. *Viggo*, Jimmy realised as soon as he saw the trail of blood through the air lit up by the strobe. Jimmy gasped for breath, forced to watch the rest of the action as if every tiny movement took an eternity. Viggo was on his feet, his last remnant of strength pushing him forward, driving the boy away from Jimmy – towards the balcony railing.

"No!" Jimmy called out as soon as he had enough breath in his lungs. Something inside him had seen what was going to happen. Perhaps if Viggo had been at full strength he would have had the control to stop, but Jimmy knew that wasn't possible now. Not with the bullet wounds he'd received and the brute strength he'd used up saving Jimmy.

Together, the two bodies slammed straight into the balcony railing like warring tanks butting a garden fence. The metal buckled. Viggo rose up, still clutching the mystery attacker. They tipped over, their heels flying upwards, right off the balcony.

Jimmy rushed forward, reaching out, urging his fingertips to somehow stretch through the air and pull them back. But he was too far away. The strobe light picked them out in midair, freezing them in position as if they were suspended in ice. At the next flash they were halfway down the hall. Jimmy stared down. He was certain that Viggo was staring straight back up at him. Before he could react, it was dark again, and at the next flash the two bodies were sprawled alongside each other in the middle of the dance floor.

"NO!" came a scream from below. Saffron streaked across the floor, still clutching her own injury. "NO! CHRIS!"

Mixed with Saffron's scream, Jimmy could hear those steps across the floor again, racing towards him. But he couldn't move. *Attack me,* Jimmy thought. *Whoever you are – Mitchell or Mitchell's ghost. I won't fight. Not now.*

Below, Saffron crouched over Viggo. Helen Coates went to the other body. Straight away, she pulled off the black mask. The light burst on again to show Jimmy the face.

"Lenny!" he gasped. The memory of seeing Mitchell's brother laid out on a slab at NJ7 was burned into his mind. Now this image would join it – Leonard Glenthorne turned into a killer by NJ7 experiments, lying dead nine floors below him, alongside the body of Christopher Viggo.

It took several seconds before Jimmy realised the sound of the steps chasing him had stopped. He felt his skin prickle. The assassin in him wanted to run, all too aware that his greatest enemy was with him, barely a metre away. Jimmy turned, and saw confirmation of what he suspected.

In a single strobe flash, Mitchell's face was opposite his. He too was leaning over the balcony. He too had seen Lenny fall to his death. The two boys stared at each other, wide-eyed, both full of fear and confusion, neither of them knowing what the next step would be.

Then the world went dark again and the moment was lost. Jimmy felt himself trembling. But no fist came flying out of the shadows. No kick landed in his stomach. And when the next flash of light burst on, Mitchell was gone.

The only thing that jolted Jimmy out of his black confusion was the chop of a helicopter landing on the roof. *The Head*, Jimmy heard in his brain. *The Capita guards – they're escaping.* His thoughts sounded distant, muffled by a horror that refused to sink in. He knew a part of him was considering going after the Head and the other Capita operatives, but what was the point now? *Chris*, Jimmy shouted to himself. *He was our hope. He was the mission.*

He turned back to look over the balcony. Saffron and Helen were struggling to carry Viggo across the dance floor. But Jimmy knew the truth. He'd felt the man's life slipping away in his arms. He'd seen all the fight left in Viggo's heart evaporate. The man had confessed to Jimmy that he'd bought the Capita's help with the promise of the H Code, that he'd tried to buy power, buy the election. *That's when he died*, Jimmy thought, finally noticing that tears were stinging his eyes.

He wiped his mouth and eyes with the back of his sleeve, then watched Saffron collapse to her knees. Helen tried dragging Viggo a few metres further, but then she too dropped to the floor. The sound of their sobs stabbed into Jimmy's heart.

"Leave him!" Jimmy yelled through his tears. A part of him didn't want to stop looking, while the rest of him never wanted to see anything again. He closed his eyes, but he could only see Viggo's face falling through the air. Jimmy pulled in a deep breath and let out a cry that rattled every plank of wood in the floor, every brick in the walls. But still the assassin in him wouldn't stop. *Get out,* it told him. *Mitchell is still here. Police sirens.*

Jimmy knew that Mitchell was no threat to him tonight. The assassin in him wouldn't understand that. But Jimmy had seen something in Mitchell's eyes in that split second. They contained the perfect picture of his own sorrow. It felt like everything Mitchell had lost, Jimmy had lost too. They were mirror images of each other, and tonight, Jimmy realised, neither of them wanted to lose any more.

Then the police sirens connected with Jimmy's consciousness. The noise of the helicopter was fading, replaced by the whine of the squad cars that would be surrounding the building within minutes. *I have to go*, Jimmy told himself, trying to gather his strength. *We all have to get out of here.*

He flew down the stairs, barely touching the ground. He raced on to the dance floor, but Saffron and Helen still hadn't moved. They were like statues.

"We have to go!" Jimmy cried out. "Get everybody out!"

"NO!" Saffron shouted, through her sobs. "Chris!"

"Leave him!" Jimmy ordered. "Take that man!"

Helen and Saffron looked up at him, startled. Jimmy thrust out his arm and pointed to the masked attacker – the one who had shot Saffron and Viggo. The one that Jimmy knew was Neil Muzbeke. He was still unconscious, but alive.

"Get him out with you!" Jimmy ordered. "Whatever happens, keep that man alive. Get him to the car. Get everybody out through the tunnel and into the car!"

26 HALF A REUNION

Once he had made it down into the tunnel, Jimmy could hear Felix's voice. It was the only thing that kept him moving forward. He carefully pulled Felix's father with him, while Helen carried the man's feet. Saffron had gone on ahead of them and had already reached the small bathroom, where Felix and Georgie were waiting.

"What happened?" Jimmy heard Felix saying. He could also hear the clatter of the medicine cabinet – Saffron was looking for first-aid supplies. Jimmy didn't listen for any more conversation. He just kept on heading through the tunnel, as if he could leave everything that had happened behind him in a nightmare, a different world, a different part of his brain. He focused on the image of Felix's face when he would see his father again.

"Hey, Jimmy!" Felix exclaimed, as soon as Jimmy emerged out of the tunnel. Saffron was sitting on the floor while Felix and Georgie crouched at her arm, surrounded by all kinds of bandages, plasters and lotions. Saffron was telling them how to strap up her injury; the tears on her face were obvious.

"Did you get…" Felix started. He stopped when he saw the unconscious body that Jimmy and Helen were carefully lifting out of the tunnel, into the bath. "What happened?"

Jimmy hid his reaction by marching straight across the bathroom and opening the door.

"We've got to go," he announced. The sirens outside were clearer now, and Jimmy welcomed them. They lent authority to what he'd said and pressed everybody into action. He'd have an extra few seconds before he would have to relive the night's events. Perhaps if he never spoke about it, it wouldn't be true. Perhaps any second, Christopher Viggo would emerge from the tunnel behind them and…

"Jimmy!" whispered Georgie, breaking into his thoughts. "You coming?"

Everybody else was through the door already and halfway up the corridor. Jimmy's mother was carrying Neil Muzbeke over her shoulder, with a bit of help from Felix.

"What happened to Chris?" Felix asked, awkwardly lifting his father's feet.

"I'm coming," Jimmy said, forcing his way past them

and out into the street.

"Thanks for the food, Margaret!" Felix called out, closing the front door behind him. "Nice woman," he added. "Good chilli."

LOCO was surrounded by police. The lights from the squad cars flashed, illuminating the pale faces of the crowd, who were all penned in by police tape along the pavement. Helen left Neil Muzbeke with Jimmy and slipped past the chaos to bring the Bentley round, while the others waited in the shadows.

"What happened to Chris?" Felix asked again, sounding more and more desperate.

"Not now," said Jimmy. "Let's get out of here first."

Within seconds they were all in the car, speeding across London. Helen drove, with Saffron in the passenger seat. In the back, there was just enough room for Jimmy, Georgie, Felix, and the unconscious masked man propped up by the door.

"Seriously," Felix said, squirming awkwardly in the squash. "Will you tell me where Chris is now? And who is *this*? I mean, it would make things a lot more comfortable if we could just, like, push him out."

Felix tried to make more room for himself, squeezing against Georgie, who ended up so squashed against Jimmy that his face was mashed against the window.

"Sit still," Helen insisted from behind the wheel. She

twisted the Bentley through the streets. In the passenger seat, Saffron kept her face turned to the window.

"Take off his balaclava," said Jimmy, struggling to say anything coherently with the car window in his mouth and the door handle in his ribs.

"Really?" asked Felix.

Jimmy pushed his sister back across the seat to give himself more space. "Really," he said. He searched inside himself for the happiness that he knew was there somewhere. After a few seconds, he could feel it welling up in his throat, but it mixed with his despair and left a strange taste on his tongue. Jimmy took a deep breath, calming himself. This was one moment he'd longed for, but he'd never dared picture it clearly. And now it was happening there was no room for delight. Too much had gone wrong. Too much had been lost.

Felix gingerly hooked his fingers under the bottom edges of the man's balaclava and started to peel it off. In less than a second he let out a gasp. The atmosphere in the car seemed to change, lit up by some kind of electric spark. Felix had only revealed the man's chin, but that was enough.

"Dad!" he shouted, ripping off the rest of the balaclava. "Dad!" He wrapped his arms round his father, knocking him sideways. At the same time, Georgie let out a shocked laugh that pierced Jimmy's eardrums.

"What?!" Helen Coates looked round, astonished. Saffron did the same, wiping tears from her eyes. In a second, the Bentley screeched to a halt at the side of the road.

"It's Neil!" Helen shouted. "Did you knock him out?" she asked Jimmy. "Bring him round!"

Jimmy responded like he was on autopilot. He found himself reaching down, past his sister and Felix, to Neil Muzbeke's ankles. He was trying to feel some of the enjoyment of the moment, but all his sensations seemed dulled. He let his hands guide him, not knowing what he was feeling for, but confident that his body had the answer.

"What's happening?!" Felix's father gasped, pulling in a lungful of air. He sat bolt upright, his eyes wide, his face a picture of confusion. Then he saw his son. "Felix!" He squeezed the boy so hard Jimmy thought his friend might pop. "Where... what...?"

"It's OK," Jimmy said. "Relax. Tell me everything you remember."

It took most of the night to work out all of the details. Jimmy's mother found an all-night café and hid the Bentley nearby. Jimmy was grateful to feel the hot food sliding into his belly and the tea soothing his parched throat. He was also relieved that his mother and Neil Muzbeke were doing most of the talking. He explained what he knew about the H Code, which was very little, and blurted out a question now and then when he couldn't force his programming to stop, but for the rest of the time he just listened, letting the information take shape in his head.

"Do you think it was Dr Higgins?" Felix asked, when they heard Neil say he remembered the face of an old man.

"Definitely," said Jimmy. "Last we heard he was in America, and from this it sounds like the US Government has got him working for them."

"And the green light?" Neil asked, his deep voice as soothing to Jimmy's soul as it ever was. "What do you think that was?"

"A laser," Jimmy replied, as if it was the simplest thing in the world. He didn't say anything more. The image of Lenny Glenthorne lying on a slab at NJ7 loomed at him in his head. Jimmy had seen the green laser. Then the image changed, and Jimmy saw Lenny's face staring up at him from the floor of LOCO, totally white in the flash of the strobe light, beside the body of Christopher Viggo. It was a sight he would never forget.

Felix and his dad talked rapidly for a long time. Felix asked again and again about his mum, but Neil couldn't remember much that had happened since he'd been taken by the CIA in New York. Soon Neil was desperate to hear about everything Felix had been doing, and Felix was excellent at telling him. The exploding plane played a particularly large role.

When the second round of tea arrived at the table, the moment came that Jimmy had started to hope would never come.

"What about Chris?" Neil asked.

"Yeah," Felix chipped in. "Where is he?"

"After he lost the election..." Neil went on, "where did he go? You told me these people, the Capita, took him, but was he at the rendezvous like you thought he would be? Where is he now?"

Jimmy looked to his mother, who was staring at the plastic tabletop. She reached out and placed a hand on Saffron's good arm. She too was just staring downwards.

"There's something we have to tell you..." Helen Coates began. Jimmy let his mother's voice surround him. Hearing the news from her mouth made it that little bit more real for Jimmy. He saw Saffron crying, and his mother too, and that made it more painful, but at least pain was something he could deal with.

When it came to the part about how Viggo died, Helen simply said that he'd been pushed off the balcony by an NJ7 assassin. Jimmy didn't add anything. He told himself it was true – which it was, even if it was only half the truth. He didn't know whether he would ever be able to tell Felix about the bullet from Neil Muzbeke's rifle that had played its part in ending Viggo's life. Saffron instinctively checked the bandaging on her arm. She had also been shot by Neil and was lucky that the bullet had only grazed her shoulder. But it looked like she too was preparing to live with the secret.

Jimmy distantly heard his mother go on, explaining what they had done to try to save Viggo. He couldn't stop the torrent of his thoughts: *I hesitated. I chose to save Saffron. Maybe if I'd gone after the shooter...* He watched the faces of everybody else, especially Felix. How could Jimmy explain that his actions had cost Viggo's life and turned Felix's father into a killer?

Felix wiped his eyes and that moment, Jimmy found it easy to cry himself, as if his body had been waiting for a cue.

Eva was already sitting up in her hospital bed at sunrise. A laptop was open on her knees and that morning's copy of *The Times* was on her bedside table, folded over to the Sudoku puzzle. She was typing frantically, frustrated that she could only use one hand. Her left arm was strapped up in a sling.

"Are you ready for your visitor, Miss Doren?" asked a nurse, popping her head round the door.

"Of course she is," said Miss Bennett, charging in before Eva had time to answer. "This girl means the world to me, and look at what she's sacrificed for her country."

The nurse nodded sheepishly and left, while Miss Bennett strode over to the window and closed the blinds.

"Did they look after you OK, Eva?" she asked. "They told me you were lucky – the knife went through the muscle, but nowhere near the artery. Did they tell you that as well?" She didn't wait for an answer. "Apparently you'll be fit to come back to work this afternoon, but I'm happy for you to take some time off, if you'd like it. You'd have to stay here, of course, but..."

"No, no," Eva insisted. "That's OK. I feel fine."

Miss Bennett smiled, and for the first time Eva thought she saw some genuine warmth in it. It was Miss Bennett who had personally seen to it that Eva received the finest medical treatment, rushed to a private room at St Thomas' hospital. *Don't get comfortable*, Eva told herself. *She's a snake. She'd kill you just as quickly if she thought she had to...*

"Did they find Olivia Muzbeke?" Eva asked.

"I'm afraid not," said Miss Bennett, hesitantly. "Our security resources were... insufficient at the time."

"Will we try to...?" Eva didn't know how to ask the question on her mind, but Miss Bennett seemed to know what to say.

"There's no point sending anybody after her, Eva. I'm sorry. You see, in herself she wasn't a threat. It was only the power of the brainwashing... We have higher security priorities. But I don't want you to worry about her. She only stabbed you in panic, in her desperation to escape. She has no reason to come after you again. You understand that, don't you? Promise me you won't worry about her."

"I promise," replied Eva quickly.

"That's good," Miss Bennett said brightly. "You might find yourself with some kind of medal for this, Eva. I don't know which one... but don't worry. I'll invent one. I don't know... the Secretarial Services Medal for Bravery in an Office Environment... how's that? Or something like that..."

Eva forced herself to laugh.

"But don't get carried away," Miss Bennett added. "Plenty more work to be done now. I'll need you to go through Dr Higgins' old papers."

A chill struck Eva like a thunder bolt up her spine. Was this a trick? Did Miss Bennett know that Eva had already been searching through Dr Higgins' old papers, unauthorised, searching for something that would help Jimmy?

"I'll brief you fully when you're back in the office," Miss Bennett went on, "but Mitchell might have discovered a clue to the whereabouts of the H Code."

"The H Code?" Eva said in a flat tone, desperate to seem calm.

"Yes. A computer chip went missing many years ago. The French were meant to have stolen it, but Mitchell heard Viggo admit that he had it, and that he'd hidden it, so..." She waved a hand in the air. "You know – we'll have to find it."

"What is it?" Eva asked. *And what happened to Viggo*, she wanted to add. *What did Mitchell do?* She forced herself to relax, but it took a huge effort. The answers to those questions would have to wait.

"Don't worry about that," Miss Bennett replied. "I'll explain everything later. I'll send a car for you. Lots to clear up after the mess we were left in by that man-sized rat!"

"You mean William Lee?"

Miss Bennett performed an over-the-top shudder, then laughed a little. "I don't like hearing his name," she said with a wink. "But it's OK. He's dead." She said it with the lightness of a person announcing the egg and spoon race at a fair. And with that, she straightened her hair and swept to the door. "I'll see you later today, then!" she announced as she left.

Eva was left feeling like a black whirlwind had destroyed her hospital room. Her whole body was shaking, bringing back the pain from her stab wound that she thought the drugs had brought under control. Fragments of the conversation shot through her mind: *William Lee, Viggo, Mitchell... the H Code.*

What did any of it mean? What had really happened last night? What about Jimmy? She slipped her good hand under her laptop and pulled out the scan of the old photograph she'd hidden there. The NJ7 scientists were lined up, as ugly as ever. But now, all of them had black crosses over their faces, except two. Dr Higgins was already circled, with *'USA?'* written above him. There was only one face left. A woman.

Eva flattened the scan on the keyboard of her laptop and picked up a marker pen from her bedside table. For a few seconds she stared at the woman, as if her expression would reveal the secrets that could save Jimmy Coates. Finally Eva clicked the cap off the pen and carefully drew a bold circle round the woman's face.

"You," she whispered to herself. "You're the one."

27 EVERYBODY'S LISTENING

As soon as Jimmy saw that morning's Sudoku puzzle, he felt a shiver. They were all back in the same café for a breakfast of more toast and tea, after a few hours' sleep in the staff room of Finsbury Park tube station. Saffron hadn't found the break in difficult, even using only one arm. Jimmy checked what he'd seen in the paper one more time, then slammed his palm down on the table. "We've got to go."

"Go where?" Felix protested. "I haven't finished my toast."

"Bring it with you." Jimmy was already moving. Saffron threw some money down on the table and they all dashed out.

Ever since Jimmy had seen someone shooting at Viggo, he'd been searching for the reason. Now, some of the mysteries of the previous night were beginning to clear in his mind. At first he'd assumed it was NJ7 trying again to eliminate the Government's opposition, but then Mitchell and Lenny had turned up, which meant that the shooter had not been sent by the Government. Afterwards, Neil Muzbeke's hazy memories suggested that he'd been brainwashed and sent by the CIA – but why? Why did the CIA want Viggo dead?

"They wanted everybody out of the way," Jimmy explained, leaning forward in the car to whisper to his mother where to drive them. The Bentley powered them on through London's traffic.

"Everybody?" said Georgie. "You're making no sense!"

"Listen," said Jimmy, piecing together the CIA strategy as he spoke. His brain seemed to take on the characters of a thousand other operatives, working out their interests, their tactics, as if the CIA had a shadow network inside his head. "With this Government in place, the USA is getting nothing from Britain. No power, no trade, no money. But it's no good getting rid of a government if you don't know what's going to take its place."

"They weren't getting rid of the Government," Jimmy's mother protested. "They got rid of..." She couldn't finish her sentence. Viggo's death hung over them all like toxic ashes.

"I think they were," Jimmy said quickly. He pulled out the newspaper again, but folded it from the Sudoku back to the front page, where one of the lead stories declared that Christopher Viggo had been behind an attempted attack on the Prime Minister late last night, and that he had been 'neutralised' by Government security forces.

"We only saw half the operation," Jimmy explained. "I think it went like this: get rid of the Prime Minister, but make sure you remove the opposition at the same time, so the only person who can possibly take over is exactly the person the CIA decides."

"Who?" Felix was gripped. He bit down on his toast so hard he almost lost a tooth.

"It doesn't matter who!" Jimmy exclaimed. "The point is they needed two assassins! We found one." He jerked his thumb at Neil Muzbeke. "And the other one tried to assassinate the Prime Minister last night in Downing Street."

Neil Muzbeke shifted uncomfortably at the word 'assassin', but before any of them could respond, the Bentley pulled up under a flyover by London Bridge station. Helen had spotted something. Jimmy's face relaxed at last and he smiled, looking past his friends' confused faces out of the window. It was several seconds before Felix, Georgie, Neil and Saffron turned to see what he was looking at.

"Mum!" Felix screamed. He barged Georgie out of the way, leapt out of the car and into his mother's arms. Toast crumbs sprayed everywhere. "I'm never letting you go again!" His voice was muffled by his mum's coat. A second later they were both swamped by Felix's father.

"How did you...?" gasped Georgie, looking at Jimmy in disbelief.

"Eva left a message," he explained, indicating the back of the newspaper again. "Hold the Sudoku squares over the crossword and it just says: *found someone, London Bridge, flyover.* I put it together with the story on the front page, and just, sort of..."

"You know," Georgie beamed, "for an idiot, you're a genius!"

They didn't linger under the flyover. Helen quickly hid the car in one of the disused garages that ran along the side of the road, thick with graffiti, and they met up again on the next train out of London Bridge. They didn't even know where it was going.

"We can get away now," said Felix. "Together." He sat between his parents, smiling like Jimmy hadn't seen for months.

Jimmy nodded, but his own smile was forced. *Get away*, he thought, repeating the words to himself, trying to make them mean something. But he couldn't. Getting away wasn't the answer for him. His problems stayed with him. He could almost feel them within the prison of his skin. The battle inside his body was just getting started.

"We'll have to keep an eye on you," said Helen Coates to Felix's parents. "You'll need plenty of rest to get over the effects of the brainwashing."

"And some good food too, I expect," Saffron added, winking at Felix.

"They look OK to me," said Felix.

"They look pretty cool actually," Georgie agreed. "When did you get matching earrings?"

Simultaneously, Neil and Olivia Muzbeke reached up and felt the silver studs in their left ears. From their faces, they were obviously stunned to find them.

"I never..." Neil began, bemused.

"I don't think..." said Olivia.

They both dissolved, their surprise turning to laughter. Jimmy heard the laughs, but his body tensed and stopped him from joining in. His eyes locked on to the silver studs.

"Get them off," he whispered suddenly. "Get them off now!"

"What?" Neil gasped.

Jimmy reached over and with an expert tweak pulled the earrings away from Neil and Olivia's flesh. He dropped them on the table in front of them, took off his trainer and slammed the heel down on one of the studs. It cracked cleanly into two tiny hemispheres. Jimmy did the same to the second stud. Inside each of them were the broken remnants of a microchip. Jimmy examined one of them closely, letting his mind read the connections, searching for recognition.

"They've been listening," he announced.

"We lost the transmission a few minutes ago, Mr President," said the new head of the CIA, standing proudly in the Oval Office of the White House for the first time.

"You have the transcript?" replied President Keays, not looking up from the papers on his desk. The CIA chief offered a thin folder. Keays took it after a second, leaned back in his huge leather chair and flicked through the folder, repositioning the reading glasses on his nose at the end of every paragraph.

While the President read, the CIA man let his eyes take in the historic office. He longed to be invited to sit down on the pristine sofas, to discuss world affairs with the President. Then he subtly craned his neck, peering at the papers on the President's desk. What was the man planning? *Perhaps one day soon*, the CIA chief thought to himself, *he would be able to examine the President's documents close-up, to stand with him on the other side of the desk... or without him. Perhaps he could one day sit in his chair.*

"What's this?" the President growled suddenly, sitting forward. Then he shouted to his secretary, "Get

Dr Higgins in here!"

"Is there a problem, Mr President?" asked the CIA chief.

"No problem," came the reply. "But you might need to take notes on this." He looked up at the CIA man for the first time, a smile creasing the lower half of his face. "A very clever man is about to tell us everything we need to know about something called the H Code."

"Who's been listening?" Felix asked.

"The Americans!" said Jimmy. "The CIA, the President... who knows!? But they've heard everything!"

He held his head, running through every conversation that had taken place in the club last night. What had been said loud enough to be picked up by the listening device on Neil Muzbeke's ear? How much would have echoed down to him as he lay on the dance floor, unconscious? Jimmy forced himself to focus on every detail. All he saw were the flashes of the strobe light, and Christopher Viggo's face. He let out a grunt, pushing away that anguish, and looked to his friends. He was desperate for them to say something. Didn't they realise what this meant?

"The H Code!" Jimmy whispered. "The H Code contains all the information about my DNA, about my body and how it's made. Chris said it was the programme that...

that made me. It's the key to the assassin technology. That's why the Capita wanted it so badly!"

He looked around at the blank faces. The others knew this much already.

"So now they'll know the chip is out there!" Jimmy went on. "The Americans – they'll know Chris had it. They'll know he hid the chip somewhere and they'll know what they could do if they found it!"

"Let them find it!" Saffron said, trying to keep her voice level. "It's nothing to do with us now. Mitchell heard every word too, so NJ7 will be looking for the H Code as well. Let them fight the Americans for it. At least they'll leave us alone."

Jimmy felt his heart pounding. He wanted to tear up the train carriage, rage growling in his chest.

"*I* need it!" he let out, with a roar. He spread his fingers on the table. The blue in his fingertips hadn't crept any further, but it wasn't going away. If anything, it was deeper, darker. Only Jimmy knew that the nose bleeds, the headaches and the pain in his muscles were getting worse.

"I might not be dead yet," he whispered, "or even soon…" He stared straight ahead, trying to focus on something to keep himself calm. "But this is doing *something* to my body, and it's not good. Eva's trying to find me an old NJ7 doctor, but what will they be able to do without an NJ7 lab, or Dr Higgins' files? Unless they have the H Code..."

"So where is it?" asked Felix calmly. "It's a computer chip, right? Did Chris really have it?"

"I don't know," Jimmy muttered. "He didn't have the chance to tell me before he..."

"What about the Capita?" Georgie said softly. The horror in Jimmy's mind grew. Georgie was right: the Capita would still do anything to get hold of the H Code, especially if they felt like they'd already paid for it. In his head the CIA, NJ7 and the Capita all swirled together into one huge monster the colour of night.

"So are we still going into hiding?" asked Felix. "We could all leave the country... go to live somewhere hot... you know, with beaches and fruit trees and crazy-flavoured drinks and stuff..."

"I'll come with you wherever you're going and make sure you're safe," Jimmy whispered. "But then I have to find the H Code. It might be the only chance I have to survive. Now it looks like I'll be fighting the Americans and the Capita, as well as NJ7. Fine. I'll fight whoever gets in my way. I'm getting the H Code, then I'm getting cured, then I'm going to make sure nobody can ever make..." He paused, unable to speak through his fury. He took two deep breaths. "They'll never make another one of me again. It ends here. It ends with me."

The rattling of the train was the only sound. Jimmy

closed his eyes, desperate to settle the turmoil inside him. He felt his friends shifting around him. Then there was a hand on his, then another. Then came a soft touch on his knee, and on his shoulder. One by one, his sister, his mum and his friends held him, and they held him all the way to the end of the line.

About the author

Joe Craig is a novelist, screenwriter, songwriter and performer. His award-winning thrillers have earned him a place alongside Anthony Horowitz, Charlie Higson and Robert Muchamore as "one of the best spy kids authors... outstanding at both writing and plotting." (The Times) The first Jimmy Coates book was published by HarperCollins in 2005. Since then the series has won over fans across the world and converted thousands of previously reluctant readers with an electric mix of action, suspense and thrilling twists.

Packed houses at festivals, bookshops, libraries and schools all over the world have experienced The Joe Craig Show. His tall tales, improvised stories, and surprising theories about writing have enthralled and entertained audiences every bit as much as his books.

He studied Philosophy at Cambridge University then became a songwriter. His first solo album ('The Songman & Me') was released in 2011. The success of his books led to a new career writing movies. Now he splits his writing time between novels and film projects.

When he's not writing, (or even when he is) he's visiting schools, eating sushi, playing the piano, watching a movie, reading, drawing, playing snooker or cricket, inventing a new snack, cooking, doing martial arts training or sleeping.

He lives in London with his wife (broadcaster & adventurer Mary-Ann Ochota), his dog (Harpo the labradonkey) and his dwarf crocodile (Professor Sven). You can get in touch with him through his website (www.joecraig.co.uk) or facebook (www.facebook.com/joecraiguk).